BURNING HEAVEN

THE SMOKE AND ICE DUOLOGY
BOOK 1

HAYDN HUBBARD

For all the girls searching for a book girlfriend.
Natalia is expecting you.

PROLOGUE
UNKNOWN

I knew from the moment I saw her she had to be mine. Addie Collins has a way of making people feel known with one glance. She draws you in with those blue eyes, then traps you with the light that exudes from her every time she speaks. There is no one else in the world other than her, and she will be mine.

Mine.

Mine.

Mine.

Mine.

Addie Collins, wait for me. I'm coming for you.

CHAPTER 1
ADDIE

I've never had a panic attack over a bloody nose before, but today feels as good as any for my first.

"Fuck," I hiss between clenched teeth as blood continues to dribble down my chin.

I scrub at the offending splotch on my white blouse with obscene violence, yet the crimson stain refuses to budge. Swearing through my teeth, I undo the buttons with fumbling hands and toss the top to the ground. Today will simply have to be a black shirt day given the nosebleed that will not cease to flow down my face.

It's all Mads's fault, of course. She has a habit of leaving her shoes out, and I tripped on them this morning, as I always do, which resulted in me having an intimate acquaintance with the floor.

The blonde pops her head in, her warm, brown eyes

wide and mischievous even in the early hours of the day. She leans against the door frame, arms crossed over her black top that matches the one I just pulled over my head. "I thought I heard you stomping around out here. You almost ready?" Maddy, my roommate and best friend since I moved to the city, smiles—smiles as if she didn't just cause this disaster.

Perhaps she didn't, and my clumsy feet were the true culprit. Still, I turn my face to her and offer a matching smile, sickeningly sweet, and let her see the rust-colored blood coating my teeth.

She shrieks into the ungodly hour of the morning, and it's worth the metallic taste in my mouth and the ruined work shirt. "Oh my god, what happened?"

"*You* happened, you tornado of a woman," I laugh, the blood finally slowing. "You left your shoes out when you came back from Donovan's—*again*." My voice drips with sarcasm.

Maddy and I moved to the city at the same time a few years ago to chase our respective dreams. I fell in love with capturing life with a pen, while she prefers capturing it with a camera. She has had a few successful galleries now—none large enough to propel her career forward, but they're important to us both, nonetheless. It was at one of these galleries that she met Donovan.

I've never cared for him. He's greasy in more ways than one, his hair always slick against his narrow skull, his eyes darting around when Maddy isn't looking. The man comes from old money, and while that has never been something to bother me, the way that he likes to throw it around in other people's faces does—for example, insisting on high-end restaurants for their dates that he knows Maddy can't afford, demanding they split the bill, then sighing dramatically before brandishing his card when she can't. Makes my blood boil, but Maddy swears she loves him, so I support them. But the minute that prick steps out of line...

"There. That's better," she tuts under her breath as she smears away the last bits of blood. "Wash your mouth out and meet me by the door. Breakfast is on the counter." With a dramatic flip of her blonde hair, she's gone, disappearing to the front of our small apartment.

I inhale deeply through my nose before turning back to the mirror and smoothing out my new top.

The first elastic snaps as I try to tie my curls back into a ponytail. Then the second one. *Fine*, I think with a huff, *you win today, hair.* I allow my wild curls to fall loose around my shoulders and quickly dart out into the kitchen to meet Mads.

The woman smiles brightly as she hands me a muffin she no doubt nabbed yesterday from work. Tella's has the best pastries and coffees, but we're always running too late to sample the products before our shifts while they're still fresh, so Mads started snagging leftover goods at the end of our shifts.

We both starting working at Tella's around the same time. Maddy, the realistic one, started first, since she knew she needed to find a job to support herself while she chased her dreams. I came to the city with hardly a dollar to my name and a wild thought that I would get a six-figure book deal in the first week.

A month later, she handed me my apron and taught me how to work the espresso machine.

The bell above the painted glass doors chimes

merrily in greeting as Mads and I burst through the door with only a few moments to spare before opening. Daryl shoots us disapproving glares as he tosses our aprons our way. I tug mine over my shoulders and tie it tightly around my waist, my handwritten name tag sparkling.

"Why do I bother keeping you both on staff?"

"Because we're charming and the customers love us." I offer the older man with a wink.

"And Addie can whip up a killer French-vanilla latte," Maddy supplies.

"I could train a monkey to do both jobs," Daryl muses before ducking to the back.

As far as bosses go, Daryl is not the worst one I've had. Sure, he complains about mixing our names up, which is fair, but his complaints are only met with Maddy's chipper "you can't spell Maddy without Addie." He tried to argue with her once on the matter but gave up eventually, as most people do. He's only as strict as the job requires, but he lets us get away with far too much. Besides, the pay is good and he isn't a creep, and those are both wins in my book.

The doorbell chimes again as the first customers stream in. Maddy takes over the register immediately, beaming broadly at a middle-aged woman whose blank-eyed stare says she won't give either of us the time of day. Mads still smiles brightly before passing me the cup where she intentionally spelled the woman's name wrong. I stifle a snort and let myself go on autopilot. Brew and pour, mark and snag a lid. The milk froths easily and settles nicely in the roast, taking on the shape of a rose. The offered lid snaps over the top, hiding the art from the ungrateful woman who takes it and departs, her kitten heels clicking on the vintage tile.

As the orders pour in, I let Maddy handle the register and the customers. Her personality is far more pleasant than mine so early in the mornings. I wouldn't say I'm not a kind person, but I'm definitely aware that I can be more than disagreeable in the earlier hours of the morning. Not Mads. No, I swear the girl comes pre-caffeinated.

The hours drag on until our early morning rush has passed and my brain has woken up enough that I bear a greater semblance to the welcoming woman I try to be. I smile kindly at the customers, add extra whipped cream to a kid's hot chocolate when Daryl isn't looking, and can slowly feel the life seeping back into my body.

My phone buzzes in my back pocket. I sneak a glance at the crowd to make sure no one is making a beeline for the café, and Daryl is in his office. Quickly, I sneak it out to steal a glance at the screen and find a text from an unknown number.

Unknown number:

You look beautiful today.

Weird. Slightly creepy, but also sweet? I pocket the phone again as Mads approaches, chalking it up to an odd wrong number and think nothing of it.

"Hey, do you think you could take over the register for a second? I won't be long, I swear, but Donovan's been blowing up my phone the whole time and I really should call him back."

"How do you know it's him?"

"He made me set a different buzz tone for him so I know if it's important."

I bite back my retort on just how fucking weird that is and simply nod with a plastered-on smile. "Yeah, go take the call in the bathroom so Daryl doesn't see you. I've got this."

I've worked register before, so it shouldn't be an issue. Now that the morning fog of sleep and grump has dissipated, I might actually be enough of a functioning human to deal with social interaction. Mads offers a grateful smile before slinking off to take her slimeball of a boyfriend's phone call.

I adjust my name tag, my name carefully drawn in whorls of pink paint pen. Mads has better handwriting so I asked her to do mine as pretty as she did hers, if only so people can actually read my name.

A woman approaches the counter, biting her lip and twisting the ring on her wedding finger. She's middle-aged and I haven't seen her around here before.

I paint on my best customer-service smile. "Hi, I'm Addie! Welcome to Tella's. What can I get started for you?"

"Do you have a menu? My husband recommended this place but I've never been and..."

The rest drones out as I hum occasionally and read from my mental script of our menu items, daily specials, and personal recommendations. I'm distantly aware of the door bell chiming again but think nothing of it as the woman begins to fret still, even more so now that there's a person in line behind her.

In the end, she orders a single water bottle and takes a menu with her to the table to think it over some more. I pay no mind—I know exactly how she feels, what the pressure of everyone's stares feel like, and how the attention forms a weight on your chest until you're drowning.

I struggled with social anxiety all throughout my high school years, and even now, though I've learned to manage it better. I know how it feels when panic is clawing up your throat and all you can do is stammer like an idiot, like everyone else is judging you for not having your shit together.

Someone clears their throat.

I raise my gaze to find a woman, maybe a year or two older than me, staring down at me with what can only be described as feline amusement. Her black hair bobs as she raises an eyebrow, the motioning bringing my gaze straight to her dark eyes, which are so dark they might as well be black. She crosses her arms over her chest, taut muscle rippling under a canvas of tan skin. My eyes slip to the hint of a dark tattoo peeking out from under the collar of her shirt. Beautiful. She has to be the most beautiful woman I have ever seen, and god, she looks like sin.

I realize with no small amount of embarrassment that I've been staring, and clear my throat. "Can I get your name please?"

The woman's eyes trail down to my lips when I speak and a fire sparks low in my gut when I realize she's also drinking me in, appreciating me, even in this god-awful uniform. Then she hesitates, and her voice comes out a purr. "Natalia. Large coffee." Her words are clipped but her accent is raw, thick and sweet.

My knees tremble beneath the my. I've always had a soft spot for beautiful women, but a beautiful woman with an accent? And her name—*Natalia*. It should be a sin to ooze that much sexiness.

But I force my voice into cool professionalism at her clipped tone. Two can easily play that game if that's what she prefers. "What type of coffee?"

Natalia starts as if she is a woman not used to being spoken back to, not used to being questioned. "Just a coffee," she says with a hint of irritation.

It's not enough. She walked in here full of swagger and confidence, giving me the same treatment as any hunter stalking their prey. But I equally enjoy the chase, the thrill of the flirt and seeing something other than unflinching calm in her eyes.

"So do you want a black coffee? Or were you looking for a latte? A macchiato maybe?" I press on, asking with a tone that Daryl might claim is unprofessional, but I'm too far in to care.

She sighs, the sound caressing my skin before she reaches up to run a hand through her short hair. Victory. "A black coffee then. Large, or whatever you make it is fine," she offers finally with a wink, her gaze drifting somewhere other than the menu before me.

That traitorous blush climbs back up my cheeks as I ring her up. From anyone else, the words might have put me in a sour mood and I would drag Mads to the front the rant about their behavior, but from this woman, it feels like something more. It isn't in the words, but her tone, her gaze. The look that says she has no intention of losing whatever showdown just happened, and the challenge she's leaving to me. It's addicting.

She stands at the end of the bar while I set to making her drinks. I know she meant to only order a large black coffee—she's not the first to order their coffee that way, so obviously anyone would know that—but there's something so satisfying in seeing her stumble. She doesn't look like the type of woman who ever falters, and pride swells in my chest that I'm the one to make her stumble.

Like hell am I going to let her have the last word.

I make the large black coffee she meant to order, then grab a drink tray and some lavender simple syrup. I work quickly and methodically before placing the iced vanilla and lavender latte in the drink tray beside the black coffee. I make to slide it across the bar, but not before writing a simple note atop the sleeve.

"Order for Natalia."

I'm gone before she has a chance to respond.

A soft chuckle comes from the other end of the bar right as Maddy returns, her sight immediately locking on to the stranger. Her cheeks flush as if she notices something, but she takes the next customer's order first. Meanwhile, I let myself duck below the counter for a moment to collect my thoughts.

What the fuck was that?

A set of footsteps.

Mads idles closer, her eyes flickering with mischief. "Tattoos, check. Dark hair, check. Probably a bad idea?"

"Check," I groan into my hands. I'm at work. I do *not* have time to be flirting with random women, not even a sex goddess like her.

Maddy places a sympathetic hand on my shoulder,

knowing all about my weakness. Despite being possibly the straightest person I know, Mads has never been anything but supportive. When I first came out to her about a week after living together, she just winked at me and said at least she'd never have to worry about us fighting over a boy. Then she kept on cooking dinner as if my heart hadn't been thundering at the prospect of potentially having to find a new roommate. I knew she was going to be my best friend then. I never wanted a grand, emotional confrontation—in fact, the thought of one sent bile crawling up my throat. I have no doubt that if I wanted waterworks and a confession of undying friendship, regardless of my sexuality, then Maddy would have equally delivered. But I didn't, so she didn't. Just like she wouldn't make a big deal about me totally crushing on a customer. Probably.

"So what did Donovan want?"

"Oh right, sorry, I got distracted by that goddess making sex eyes at you."

"Mads!"

"Fine, fine. He got us VIP tickets to that new club that opened downtown. Said a buddy of his wants to meet there and owes him a favor. We're heading there after our shift, and before you protest, it's Friday night and over-the-counter flirting is the most action you've had in weeks. So yes, you're coming."

I sigh, knowing there's no use arguing with her when she's like this. When Maddy latches on to an idea, she won't let it go.

I nod. "Fine, but only if you think you can wrangle this." I laugh, pointing to my tangled curls.

She sticks her tongue out in mock concentration but nods regardless, as if saying she'll manage.

Out of excuses, I relent and return to my favorite milk frother—I named him Loui—when a latte is ordered.

God, maybe I do need to get out.

Another text pings in my pocket.

CHAPTER 2
NATALIA

Unknown: Wear your hair down tonight.

I'm going to kill Riven, absolutely murder him the minute I land back on American soil. I splash water on my face, watching the blood, dirt, and dark powder drift down the drain right as someone bangs on the door.

"If you're scheming about my cousin's murder, I have better plans for you, Nat."

I throw open the door to the jet's bathroom, freshly changed into dress pants and a blouse dark enough to cover any blood that might sleep through if I tear a stitch.

A young man, thick in the face and wiry in his frame, stands at the door, leaning against it with a cocky grin. Riven may have gotten all the good looks, but Marco has the same bastard's grin.

"Thirteen stitches say otherwise, but go ahead, humor me."

Whatever this is has to be good, considering my second-in-command just sent me into a trap. I was the one to walk away—as I always am—but all their bullets managed to do was piss me off.

I've grown used to the dirty games that all the members of the Mafia play, and I trust no one—no one except Riven, who is practically my brother at this point. That's the only thing stopping me from actually killing him when I get off this plane.

"Riven found the mole who sold our guns to the Russos. He used the funds to open this nightclub downtown while you were gone, thinking Riven wouldn't hold a tight leash. He's cocky, unguarded, and yours to make an example of."

I swirl my whiskey, letting the sound of ice on glass fill the air. It might be eleven in the morning on American soil, but I'm running on Italian time, and it's five o'clock over there. I clasp Marco on the shoulder as the landing gears shift into place on my jet. "Not half bad, Barone." I finish the rest of my drink in a single go, letting the alcohol sting the cut on my lip. "We move tonight."

Tonight, when they'll be expecting me to rest and play it easy on them. Whoever planned this doesn't know me very well, nor how I operate. No days off. No mistakes.

Unless you're Riven, apparently—cocky bastard. *Lucky* cocky bastard.

"There's more. Another body came in."

I groan into my hands as two files are slid across the table to me. A girl went missing about a month ago, found suffocated and naked in the dumpster of a bar. Usually cases like this don't fall under my jurisdiction, but the girl was tied to one of Riven's brothers, an ex of a few years back. It was enough to warrant me looking into it, but there seemed to be no connection. Hell, the poor girl didn't even know what a sociopath her boyfriend was, nor his involvement with the Mafia.

Riven doesn't speak to his brothers for a reason, but if any trouble is stirring with them that could get pinned on me, I want it thoroughly investigated.

I look over the first file. Young girl, early twenties, taken around 2:32 a.m. Anna Russo. Aside from dating a Barone, she has a clean record. No known enemies, nothing that makes her special.

The second girl is the same age, taken at the same time. Dillon Lars. Clean record, no ties to either me or the Barones.

Thank god for one small miracle.

"Tell Riven I'll meet him at the morgue." I tip my head back, inhaling deeply. I need coffee to survive the grueling hours ahead of me, especially combined with jet lag.

The plane lands with a thud, throttling my already-pounding head.

"After I go to Tella's."

The bell above the door to Tella's Coffee jingles merrily when I enter. It lends to the cozy atmosphere, the coffee shop itself bathed in a warm, fluorescent glow.

I sigh deeply through my nose, inhaling the rich scent of freshly brewed coffee and warm pastries. I've been drinking coffee since I was nine, always the same dark roast, never enjoying it. It's simply a tool to stay awake during the long, grueling hours of work, and to stay sharp enough to keep my head. Then I found this place and realized I've just been drinking shit coffee.

The café is remote, small enough to boast quiet hours but well known enough that there's always at least one or two people in line. There's only one person before me today and she'd already fingered through half the menu pages by the time I step into the line. I roll my eyes as she asks a million questions about one blueberry muffin. Clearly not a regular.

My gaze flits to one of the baristas. Speaking of regulars, I've never seen her before. She must have arrived or switched to morning shift while I was overseas dealing with Riven and his bullshit. She smiles politely and answers all the woman's questions before the lady leaves with just a bottle of water.

I roll my shoulders out as I approach, already preparing my usual lines. I'm a regular here, and while the baristas are usually pretty and used to my flirting, this girl is new. Her reactions are some untouched thrill that I want to discover.

She's scribbling something down on a sheet of paper, the pen marking vicious strokes against what looks like the woman's receipt. I raise an eyebrow and clear my throat.

The barista looks up. Big blue eyes, chestnut curls, and freckles.

Fuck.

Anyone with eyes can tell she's the most beautiful woman in the room—hell, the most beautiful woman I've ever seen. A low pit forms in my stomach when I realize everyone else can tell, and that many are sharing less than friendly, appreciative glances her way—specifically when she bends over to pick up a loose napkin or leans over a table to clear it.

She smiles, and my breath hitches. It's a beautiful smile, but it stops right before her eyes. It's the same smile she gives everyone else in this line, and molten lava settles in my gut at the thought. I need to see that smile reach those big blue eyes, need her to smile like that at me—and only me.

I needed to see those curls sprawled across my pillow.

I drag my tongue over my bottom lip. She would look so damn good draped over my silk sheets, preferably with nothing else on. She's magnetic—a dangerous obsession when I can't afford one.

"Can I get your name please?"

Her voice is sweet, fitting for her round, innocent face. I spot her name tag. *Addie.*

I almost reach out to her, kiss her hand, anything, before I notice the dried blood beneath my fingernails—a reminder that I can't afford distractions, even if they come in the shape of a beautiful brunette. Besides, the possessiveness crawling up my spine is a ridiculous urge for someone who I've only just met—hell, haven't even had a proper conversation with yet.

"Natalia. Large coffee."

Addie huffs, her cheeks puffing. "What type of coffee?"

"Just a coffee."

"So do you want a black coffee? Or were you looking for a latte? A macchiato, maybe?"

I grit my teeth. I know exactly who this woman is— vexing, and she downright knows it too.

"A black coffee, then. Large, or whatever size you make it is fine," I drawl with equal sweetness, the words catching on my accent.

She blushes.

She fucking blushes.

My phone buzzes in my pocket as I watch her make the coffee. Her motions are fluid, like she's been doing this her whole life, but her gaze is faraway. Not in a sad way, but almost as if she's in a different world completely.

I pull out my phone, nearly cursing at the string of texts from Riven. Things are not looking good at the morgue and the last thing I need is the police or the Barones to get involved with this mess.

"Order for Natalia."

Addie is gone by the time I look up, ducked behind some door or office by now, but I breathe out a laugh. She scribbled across the top a note that reads: to your "just a coffee."

I pocket my phone and bring both drinks to the car waiting for me. Addie's specialty is pure sugar, and I promptly throw it out the window, but not before pocketing the lid.

Riven is waiting with his hands in the pockets of his dark jeans. Between his glare and the dark ensemble he wears, an outsider might easily mistake him for an angel of death. That is, if reapers chose to wear jeans and slim-fit T-shirts.

The man's face morphs into a cunning grin when his gaze finds mine. "Natalia," he croons.

"You'd better have good news for me or I swear to god I'll wear your ribs as a corset."

Riven only laughs, but his face darkens a fraction. Wordlessly, he leads me inside to where our coroner has already prepped the body for display.

Dillon Lars looks like she could be sleeping. She has long, dark hair, similar to mine if I chose to grow it out, and she looks peaceful in death. Rage coils an iron fist around my gut. She should have had a long, happy life.

"Anything physical linking her to the first girl?"

Riven shakes his head. "Aside from age and circumstance, we haven't been able to find anything yet."

"Cause of death?" I ask, even though the mottled necklace of bruises gives away the answer.

"Strangulation. There are no prints, but the coroner found latex residue."

God. For once, could the villain just be an idiot?

"So he knows to use gloves. Good for him." I pinch the bridge of my nose before fixing my second with a sideways glance. "Marco tells me you have news on our rat that's worth sparing your skin."

Riven's gaze drifts to my side that I've been favoring and winces. So Marco did fill him in. "Jon Michels. He's a lower-level hitman who generally guards our shipments when things are quiet. He thought I wouldn't notice him siphoning off some of the stock while you were gone."

I grit my teeth. Greed has killed more men than bullets have.

Riven settles on a chair at the far end of the room,

keeping his gaze trained on mine. His muscles strain beneath his tee as he braces his elbows against his thighs. "So," he murmurs, "what's your plan?"

I mimic his pose, a devilish grin lighting my face. "I think we should go pay Mr. Michels a visit."

CHAPTER 3
ADDIE

*Unknown: I've been wondering how those curls would feel
wrapped around my fist.*

I stare at my phone. Fourteen missed texts in the past hour, each growing more specific and volatile.

Unknown number:

> Wear red tonight.

> I know you're home from work.

> Is your roommate home?

> I'm growing impatient.

> Answer your phone, you bitch.

No form of identification. No effort to reveal who they are or why I should care.

Goosebumps prickle my flesh as I pocket my phone. I'll drive down to the police station tomorrow morning and see if they can trace the number. Tonight is about Maddy. She's been dying to go to this club for days now and the last thing I want to do is stress her out and ruin her night because some creep found my number. Besides, there's no indication that they even know who they're texting. Any of these could be lucky guesses or wild generalizations—that's what I tell myself, anyway, as I sling my purse over my shoulder.

I tug at a loose curl framing my face. Maddy piled my hair atop my head in a curly updo upon my request and left me to sort out my makeup by myself. I took my time with the look, enjoying each brush stroke as if I were painting my face. I drew on a sultry red lip, darker and bold in contrast to the nude eyeshadow and cat eye I drew on. The look is simple and classic, and complements the black silk dress I slipped on. Perhaps it's not wise to ignore the mysterious figure on my phone, but I haven't told anyone where I'm going tonight so it should be safe. Places like this are easy to blend into a crowd, melt away from the world, if only temporarily.

Mads appears at my door, a pale-blue mini dress hugging her every curve to the point where I wonder if the dress was custom-made. She paired it with simple strappy heels that I know she'll be carrying home at the end of the night. Her smile is infectious as she links her arm through mine and pulls me out the door. At the last minute, I silence my phone.

The mood is electric when we walk through the VIP entrance into the dimly lit nightclub. A dense layer of fog covers the floor, hiding everything below the mid-calf from view.

Maddy practically squeals as she sees an excuse to shirk her heels for barefooted dancing. "To feel the music better," she explains, as she does every time, tossing her head back to laugh. Her hair flickers golden in the light as it cascades down her back.

Donovan looks less than pleased standing in the corner but soon slinks off to meet whoever this friend of his is.

The strobe lights flicker across the crowd, all dancing to some early 2000s song I know the words to but not the name. Maddy reaches out to grab my hips, forcing me to sway to the song whenever I get too stiff or nervous. The trick always works, even if it's ridiculous. I let my head loll back, feeling the steady beat in my bones.

Throughout the night, various hands find their way to my arms, my waist, and hips. Maddy bats at them before they can go lower, as I assured her I do not intend to go home with anyone tonight. I don't tell her it's because I'm secretly inspecting every face, waiting for one of them to be the person who has been blowing up my phone.

No one comes forward and admits to it, of course, but my nerves are so bad that at one point, I nearly punch a man for sneaking up too close behind me. Before he can get the wrong idea, I flee to the bar, not wanting to deal with the whole "You just haven't had the right dick yet" talk. I need to be at least blackout drunk to deal with that.

I settle on a stool and call for a vodka cranberry, letting my head fall into my hands. Mads was right—it has been a while since I went out, and it's evident in the pounding headache that throttles my skull. It's enough that I debate whether or not she'd kill me if I went home, but the other side of that coin would be leaving her alone in a club with Donovan and his friend. I'm that bad of a friend, so I pick my head up and down my drink before glancing at the dance floor. So many bodies writhe together in the pit of EDM, strobe lights, and alcohol. In the middle, it felt nearly erotic, but out here, it just looks like a nightmare.

"I didn't think I'd be seeing you again so soon, Addie." A smooth voice pulls me from my thoughts.

My heart hitches in my throat as my chair is spun around to find Natalia's face a mere breath away from mine. Her eyes are smudged with dark eyeliner, bringing out the golden undertones in them. She wears another suit like the one earlier today, only this one is tighter, and unbuttoned at the top to reveal finely carved collarbones.

Heat flushes my cheeks. I'm truly no better than a middle-school boy. One look of pretty skin and I'm painted crimson.

"Natalia," I offer, trying to lower my voice to a purr as hers was—sultry, seductive, and probably so forced. I've never been the bold type in the talking stages of a relationship. I prefer to be flirted with over flirting myself. Natalia did not seem to mind earlier, nor do I mind that she brought out this more confident side of me. Who am I and where did Addie Collins go?

Natalia smiles with a look of cunning amusement and settles on the seat beside me, letting her hand drift from the back of my chair to her side. The wisp of contact when her skin skims past my bare shoulder sends goose-flesh prickling across my arms.

Natalia only smirks. "Cold?"

"Just tired," I lie.

She nods as if she believes me. She's humoring me.

She rasps her knuckles on the bar, then holds up two fingers. Before long, the bartender brings out a refill of my drink and a new glass for Natalia.

"Probably from carrying the weight of everyone's stares," she says, then leans in my ear to whisper, "or maybe just mine."

If I wasn't blushing already, I definitely am now. This woman is more than beautiful—she's powerful, her every movement graceful yet rippling with strength. Even beneath the finely tailored suit, I can see the curve of her muscle and her control over each one. My mouth goes dry at the sight.

I glance over her shoulder for Maddy, but Natalia places her hand over my wrist.

"Your friend is fine," she murmurs before dropping her hand to my knee. "Just fine." That hand traces trai-torous circles around my knee before drifting upward to my thigh. She squeezes gently, and I fight the urge to clench my legs together if only so she won't notice. Those fingers begin to move again, sketching my skin with her fingertips as she leans closer—close enough that I can smell the musk drifting from her neck, mingling with the scent of leather. Her mouth forms words I don't hear as my gaze latches on to those fingers, sliding further up until…

"Addie."

My name is a prayer upon her lips. I've never thought of my own name as being sensual before, but from her lips, it might as well be the hottest thing I've ever heard. She leans closer, her lips just above mine. I can taste the spearmint coming from her breath.

"What are you doing here?" I breathe.

"What I'm doing and what I'm *supposed* to be doing are two different things, love," she whispers against my lips.

Quickly, my back straightens and I swallow thickly. "What are you supposed to be doing?"

"Something I'd enjoy far less than this," she whispers, before plunging her lips to mine.

My hands find her hair, my fingers weaving through her short, silky strands. I've been dying to touch her hair since I first saw her in the café, wondered what it would feel like. It's soft—unimaginably soft. Her hands cup my face, callouses scraping at my jaw in such a way that I lean in and let her mouth swallow my moan. This earns a low sound of approval from the woman whose tongue has taken to searching the entirety of my mouth, my lips.

I can feel my dress riding up, but before I can move to pull it down, one of those hand slips to hold it in place. Natalia's eyes are open now, a predatory gleam in them as if to say *mine*. As if she doesn't want others in the room seeing any more of me than I do.

"Come with me," she whispers against my ear, sending her breath skittering across the shell. Then she places a kiss against my jaw, just below the lobe. A promise.

Wordlessly, I take her hand, letting her throw her jacket over my shoulders and lead me towards the back of the club where a lone black door and security guard stand.

Natalia sends a quick message on her phone, then nods to the man, who opens the door then lets it click shut behind us, encasing the room in darkness.

"Do you own this place?" I ask, part awe and part fear. I know she has to have at least some money, but I'm way out of my depth here if this is the case.

She chuckles lowly, cupping my chin with her hands. "No, but I know the owner," she says before planting a kiss where her hands were. She begins trailing the length of my jaw with her lips when I push my hands against her chest. The action does not do much, only leave an extra inch of room between us.

"Do you think he'll mind?"

Natalia huffs, then runs her hand over her jaw. "No, I texted him."

"But—"

"If you're finished," she grounds out, grabbing my wrists with one of her hands, "the next sound coming out of your mouth won't be anything about this room, or the man who owns it."

Before I can respond, she lifts my wrists above my head, pushing me until my back hits the wall, and pins them there, her body pressed against mine. Her lips find mine again as she slides her knee between my legs, giving me the friction I need with each movement.

Her fingertips press sweet bruises into my wrists, her other hand flying to my waist, then up my ribs to the underside of my breast. It lingers there, teasing me. I whine against her lips and she laughs, a low, rumbling sound that goes straight to my core. She lowers her hand back to my waist and pulls her lips back as if in punishment, but before I can protest, they immediately lower again to my neck. She trails deep kisses along the slender column of my throat, alternating between sweet kissing and sharp nips. My head involuntarily tilts back, offering more skin to her.

That hand slips lower behind me, cupping my ass and pulling my leg over her hip. I gasp as her thigh shifts between my legs, the position allowing me to roll my hips against hers. She moans against my neck, the sound going through my throat, straight between my legs. I buck my hips, and she smiles.

"Greedy," she murmurs, but pushes in further.

That movement hits exactly where I need it, and my knees buckle.

Her hand flies up, teasing my breasts over my dress. "Too many clothes," she murmurs.

I would have to agree. I roll my hips again, craving the release I'm so close to. My core tightens and my head tips back again. "Natalia," I moan, her name tasting like fine wine on my tongue.

She pauses her ministrations, looking at my face with heavy-lidded eyes clouded with lust. Finally, she removes her hand, letting it drop low, beneath my dress. Her fingers trail upwards and my hips still as I feel her drawing closer—close enough that she should realize I'm not wearing panties tonight.

"Fuck," she groans before crashing her lips against mine again.

Her hand is so close to where I want it—where I need it.

"Natalia! Oh, Christ!" A male voice nearly yelps as light streams through the now-open door.

Natalia shifts, covering me as I right myself, my face heating instantly. "I texted you that I was busy, Riven," Natalia grinds out between clenched teeth.

My face flushes even further. This is the man who owns the club. And I was caught nearly fucking his friend in his office.

"That was twenty minutes ago. You tend to fuck them quick then come back out." He shoots a glance over to me where I stand, still protected behind her. "No offense, love."

Like anyone could not take offense to that. My face warms with shame and embarrassment as I right my dress, ripping my hands from where Natalia still holds them gripped above my head, her fingers digging protectively into my hip. Possessively.

"Just give me five fucking minutes, Riven."

"Sure, sure," he mutters, then shoots a glance over to me. "Sorry about that."

I offer nothing more than a tight-lipped nod.

The door clicks shut behind the man, once again leaving us alone in the darkness. Natalia groans and runs a hand over her face, shifting away from me. Her absence leaves my skin chilled instantly, only the few bruises she left emanating any warmth.

Stupid. I'm so incredibly stupid to think this was anything more than a quick hookup. I don't know what I was thinking—or if I was at all. This was just an instant attraction that led somewhere physical. I shouldn't have expected anything more, don't have the right to. Yet anger simmers in my chest as I straighten myself.

"I'm sorry about Riven. He doesn't know what he's talking about. That was—"

"No, I think I know well enough what that was," I reply hotly, my heels already clicking their way to the door. It was a mistake—a stupid fucking mistake made by too much alcohol and too little sex.

As my fingers close around the door handle, a scarred and tan hand covers mine. Natalia towers over me now, squaring her shoulders and coming to her full height over me. Her presence alone is domineering, but the feel of her pushing into my back, knowing how much space she can take up of mine, knowing how easily she claimed me against the wall only moments before—the thought almost douses my rage with a deeper heat.

Almost.

"Say it," she whispers, her voice lethal. "Say it was a fucking mistake. You don't believe it. I don't either. Say it was a lapse of judgment and you never want to see me again."

This is ridiculous. I don't even know the woman. I've only met her once before. I shouldn't be having these feelings, this possessiveness that seems to crawl over my skin and scream, "Mine!" at her touch. I wanted her to want me, and I shouldn't. Not in this way.

A shuddering hiss.

"It was a mistake," I breathe.

I twist the knob.

The door clicks shut behind me.

I raise my chin, square my shoulders, and march towards the dance floor to find Maddy, ignoring the tug of emptiness pulling me back towards that office.

My best friend is right where I left her, in the middle of the crowd, the weight of everyone's eyes feather-light to her. She loves the attention, bathes in it. Her golden hair tumbles over her shoulders as she moves to some early 2000s song, swiveling her hips in tune. Someone steps close behind her, his hand snaking towards her waist. I use the opportunity to slide in, placing my body between them and my hands on her waist.

She immediately leans back, resting her head on my shoulder and peering up at me from under her thick lashes. "You look freshly fucked." She laughs, smoothing her fingers through my tangled hair.

I cringe and shake my head, and her face is immediately serious.

"Do you want to leave?"

I move to shake my head again, not wanting to ruin her night, but she spins, grabbing my hand. "Of course you want to leave. Come on, I'll text Donovan where we went."

The crowd parts as we walk through, Maddy trailblazing the path ahead. Her grip is firm on my hand, and her death glare equally sharp towards anyone who steps anywhere near the two of us.

Most people know Maddy as the wild friend, the extrovert, the friend who drags me places I'd rather not be. But she's the protector—the one who, yes, will have a good time, but will have a good time anywhere. She's my biggest advocate and supporter, and if I said I wanted to leave the fucking Met Gala, she would say goodbye to DiCaprio and hail a taxi immediately.

The cool air is a kiss across my exposed neck, licking away the sweat that pooled at my nape. I've never been more thankful for a cool October night than right now. The ringing in my ears dims as we walk further from the club. Our apartment is close enough to risk the walk, the pathways well lit. Maddy still walks ahead, marking each passing stranger with a predatory glare, her chin held high. I hold my phone against my chest, switching it on for the first time since before the bar, just as we walk through the doors to our apartment complex.

The screen is still loading as Maddy slides the key in the door.

Then the first buzz comes through.

Then the second, and third and fourth and...

Twenty-seven missed calls. Fifty-two texts.

The first few texts are the same as the first ones I received—taunting, demanding I answer. A few more reveal large blocks of text. All one word.

Addie.

Unknown number:

Addie Addie Addie Addie Addie Addie
Addie Addie Addie Addie Addie Addie
Addie Addie Addie Addie Addie Addie
Addie Addie Addie Addie Addie Addie
Addie Addie Addie Addie Addie Addie.

Over and over, they wrote my name. A damnation.

My heart begins to beat faster. The last one arrived only one minute ago.

I don't realize my hands are shaking until Maddy places her hand on my arm. I swing at her, my blind punch missing, just barely brushing the shell of her ear.

She freezes, pretty eyes wide and lips parted. Almost instantly, her shock disappears, wiped away, leaving a cool countenance. "Can I see your phone?" she whispers gently—so gently, my heart could crack.

I offer it with shaking hands—no, my whole body is shaking. I can't get a breath in.

Dying.

I'm dying.

Maddy turns off my phone and pockets it, guiding me to our couch first. "Do you feel like you're in danger?"

A nod. Only it's that I feel like I'm in danger.

I am.

Maddie nods back and rises slowly, letting me see her every movement. She walks to the front door and turns the lock, but doesn't engage the dead bolt. Then she picks up the bat behind the coat rack and stalks to our curtains, pulling them back and letting me see there's nothing there. The sound of shower curtain rings scraping across the rod sounds next, and she calls out, "Clear!" When she emerges from both our bedrooms after thoroughly inspecting every pantry and cupboard of our kitchen, she locks the dead bolt and settles next to me.

"Can I look?"

Another nod.

Maddy pulls out my phone. I can see her fighting the

urge to gasp or show horror when reading the messages. "These started this morning."

Yet another dip of my chin. It's all I can do, the only movement I can force my body into.

"Addie, this isn't okay. I'm going to go call the police, see if there's anything they can do."

"Okay," I croak, my tongue loosening enough to utter the two syllables.

This is pathetic. I groan, dropping my head into my hands and forcing myself to take deep breaths. The tightening in my chest only worsens when Maddy reenters with a tight-lipped grimace.

I cringe. "Bad news?"

"No." Maddy's tone is clipped as she scowls. "They said this number has made no indication of causing you any form of harm. The best they can do is try for harassment charges, but it's a weak wall to stand on. You'll need to bring your phone to the station tomorrow morning to see if they can trace the number, but they said they'll probably just block the number and it'll go away on its own."

It never goes away on its own—not these types of people and crimes. This will persist until I am a statistic on the Monday-morning news. "Twenty-four-year-old Addie Collins found face down in a ditch, cold to the touch."

Mads gnaws at her lip. "Donovan's friend works at this security company that specializes in private security." Before I can protest that in no world, this or another, could I ever afford that, Maddy holds up her hands. "I know it sounds pricey, but maybe he can get a discount? Friends and family, maybe?"

I fix her with a dry look. "I don't think they do those in private security, Mads."

"Well, it's better to try that that do nothing. I'll text him and arrange a meeting tomorrow for after you head to the police station. Two birds with one stone!" She tries to stay positive, but I can see her trembling hands and the fact that she keeps eyeing the baseball bat.

I swallow the bile rising in my throat and force a smile.

Maddy links her arm through mine and switches on the television. "I was in need of a movie night anyway," she giggles, even though we both know she'll fall asleep before the first act even ends.

CHAPTER 4
ADDIE

Unknown: If you go to the police, I will know.

The double glass doors are cool to the touch as I push them in, the AC of the Mancini Security building blowing my hair away from my face. The police were as unhelpful in person as they were over the phone. After taking one look at my messages and saving both the numbers and the messages themselves, they dismissed me with a helpful reminder to call them if anything worsens or develops further. I wanted to tell them to go fuck themselves but a part of me remembered at the last second that if this stalker is to show up, then they'll be the people who can save my life, and thought better of my previous aggression.

The entryway of the building is massive. Each of the walls are lined with bulletproof glass, allowing outsiders a view of the inner workings of the business but without posing a danger should a threat see their target seeking help. Intricately carved stairs spiral up the sides of the walls towards a second floor that boasts what can only be described as an incredibly gaudy café. There, men and women mill about, dressed as if they're attending a press conference with the president, sipping from glasses and eating decadent pastries off of fine plates.

The base level features a plush, green carpet and a single receptionist's desk where a pale young woman sits clicking at her keyboard. Behind her is a single elevator that requires a key card to open.

I approach the desk, doing my best to walk with square shoulders and convince the others that I have the funding to be here. "Hi," I say sweetly. "I'm here for an appointment with Jon Michels. My name is Addie Collins."

The woman glances up with a sneer creasing her lips before looking back at her computer. I smooth out my pencil skirt, meeting the receptionist's cool gaze with a warm smile. She clicks the space bar three times then squints at the screen before shaking her head. "I don't have you on the list."

My smile falters just slightly. "Would you mind checking again?"

"Still not here," she says without glancing at the screen.

"Then why don't I call him? He's a mutual friend, so—"

"Yeah, I've met plenty *mutual friends*. This isn't a charity case, sweetheart."

My face burns at the snide remarks. A line has started to gather behind me, all important-looking businessmen wearing suits worth more than my apartment. I offer a stiff nod and turn to leave when a hand lands on the small of my back. The warmth sends small flicks of calming energy up my spine.

"I'll take this one, Maria," Natalia purrs.

I would recognize that smooth voice anywhere. But why was she here? The fingers that roamed my body only hours before now trace small circles across my lower back.

"But you have meetings all day," the receptionist tries to protest, but Natalia silences her with a single look.

"Then clear my schedule. If this woman *ever* shows up at your desk again, are to direct her personally and directly to me. If I am not here, she can be left in my office. I trust that you'll treat her with the same level of authority you do me." Then she peers at me, her smile softer than one I've seen her wear yet. "Come with me," she murmurs against my ear.

I follow her, her hand sliding from my back to my wrist.

The receptionist, Maria, shoots a glare my way that looks purely venomous, but I only brush back a strand of hair from my face, highly relying on my middle finger to do so.

Natalia remains silent as she leads me down endless corridors, dipping her chin in acknowledgment every so often to men and women in suits nearly as nice as her own. None of them look as good in them as she does. As we walk I slowly develop a better picture of the woman guiding me, and what her role might be here.

Natalia's gait is long and elegant, every inch of her exuding calm power and refined strength. Her suit is black, as it was yesterday, but the shirt beneath is white this time, contrasting nicely with her tan skin.

She pulls me towards another elevator with a single button which also requires a key card. She pulls hers from her pocket and swipes it. When the light turns green, the doors open to another glass elevator that over-looks the entire office. Hundreds of employees mill about doing their tasks, appearing more and more like floating specks of dust as the elevator climbs higher and higher up the building. On the inside of the gold paneling is only one button, which Natalia promptly clicked with her knuckle before the elevator shot skyward.

"Where are we going?" I finally ask.

"My office."

When we stop at the top floor, the doors open to an office without any glass walls. Each of the walls are white and pristine, yet bare save for a few pieces of art that are probably each worth more than everything I own combined. I realize with a sinking feeling that it's far too lavish for an employee of the company.

My mouth is dry as I turn to Natalia, who has removed her coat and is pouring a mug of coffee. "You like sugar in your coffee, don't you? I apologize. I'm not much of a barista." She laughs softly, a beautiful and rich sound. "I'm almost embarrassed to serve you this."

I shake my head. I do like sweet coffee—I actually have a massive sweet tooth and hate black coffee with a passion—but I feel as if I've already inconvenienced this woman enough. Still, I watch her discreetly slip cream and sugar into the cup before handing it to me. I accept it gratefully while she pours herself a plain black cup.

"So, do you... own this place?" I ask with a cringe.

Natalia smirks over the lip of her mug. "Natalia Mancini, at your service."

My sharp inhale stings my teeth. It was bad enough when she could have been the owner of the bar, but the owner of the largest security company in America? I'm way out of my depth.

"Well, thank you for the help, but I should probably get going."

Natalia's eyes shutter and darken. "Why were you here?"

I scoff. "I don't think I need to tell you that."

"You show up at my company claiming to have a meeting with a man who no longer works for my company only a few hours after showing up at a nightclub he used to own. So I *do* actually believe that it is my business and that you do need to tell me."

Used to own. Something happened after I left last night, and my gut told me it wasn't good. A chill runs up my spine but still I cannot stop myself from blurting out, "I need help and have nowhere else to go."

It's true, as broken and weak as it sounds. The police can't help me—flat out refuse to—and Donovan's friend, as sleazy as he was, had connections that could keep me safe. But now he's gone and I'm left with nothing but this infuriating woman.

Natalia's hand rests atop mine over the mug. I look down to see ripples in the coffee. My phone buzzes in my pocket.

"Who's trying to hurt you?" Her voice is deadly calm, yet I can hear the strain in it, as if she's trying to hold herself back from snapping completely.

I slide the phone out of my pocket and unlock it,

revealing the 200 texts I've received in the past twenty-four hours, some now including pictures of me from this morning. One shows me entering the police office, with a message that reads, *Leave the police out of this or you will regret it.*

"It seems silly," I laugh, tears flowing freely down my face now. "These are threats people would use in middle school. 'Stop it or you're gonna get it.'"

A rough thumb brushes over my cheek and I bite down on my lip. I've known this woman for as long as I've had a stalker. She could be the stalker for all I know, and yet something tells me she isn't. While I'm with her, I'm safe. Protected.

"It's not silly," she murmurs with heartbreaking softness. "Those are children, and this is a sick individual who will do god-knows-what to you."

The soft hush of her voice is too much, too kind for someone who was so unkind yesterday.

I snap, pulling my hand from hers and pursing my lips. "I don't have money. I was meeting that man because Maddy said he could get a discount somehow. The police can't do anything."

Natalia snorts. "Of course they can't."

"And I'm out of options. So—" God, I hate this. I push back from the counter and sink to my knees, kneeling before this powerful woman, and bow my head.

"What are you doing?" she snaps, eyes wide.

"I'll do anything you want. I'll do anything, just please—"

Her hand reaches out, latching under my chin and pulling my face to meet hers. She crouches, still towering over me despite almost kneeling herself, and glowers.

"Don't you ever kneel in front of anybody every again," she grinds out between clenched teeth. "I will protect you, no cost. No payment. Just get up."

Embarrassment stains my cheeks. "Back at the bar, you propositioned me and—"

"Sweetheart, I'm not offering to protect you because I want to have sex with you. I 'propositioned' you back at the bar because I wanted to hear you scream my name in a more private place. This—" she gestures to the yawning space between us, "—is purely business."

Liar. She's a liar and we both know it. Not about the protection part, but the key words—*purely business*. Even now, I can see her eyes casually drifting over the curves of my body, drinking the sight of me like a fine liquor. She doesn't bother to hide it, not when her lips curve into a feline smile as she says, "The offer stands—outside of this office, of course."

Then the reins are back in her hands, snapping taut around my neck as my lips part and want creeps up my spine.

No, I can't have this woman, can't even borrow her for a night. Because she would live up to her promises and it would be the best damn night of my life, then she would move on to the next pretty barista and I'd be filled with gnawing want for the rest of my days.

Before I can embarrass myself further, her face softens and she guides me back to the chair. Her motions are stiff and forced, as if she's still poorly concealing that rage from earlier.

Something warm pools low in my stomach at the thought of her protectiveness. and I wonder how bloody she'd be willing to make those hands for me, even in the short time of knowing each other.

"Hand me your phone." Her voice is sharp, domineering.

I pass her my phone without a second thought.

Natalia finds my messages app and opens it, inhaling sharply at the slew of expletives, threats, and photos. I watch as her face darkens with each swipe of her thumb, each vulgar message read. After a while, she puts the phone down silently. Then she grabs her coat and my hand, interlacing her fingers with mine.

"Come on, we have a date."

CHAPTER 5

NATALIA

Unknown: I thought you were a docile little bitch. We will fix that.

*W*hore. *Bitch. Slut.*

Addie.

He had called her all of those things, whoever he is. As infuriating and gut-wrenching as the first three were, the fourth was the worst. Her name should never be uttered from his lips, or pass through his mind at all.

A quick message sent to Riven confirms what I already know—the texts were sent from a burner phone, the line nearly untraceable. Just as it was for the other two victims.

Rage was the first fire to course through my veins when I read those texts. Terror was the second, a more foreign feeling in my blood. I cannot recall the last time I felt its icy hands clawing up my throat, but I felt it when I saw the first tear slide down her cheek. Saw the parallels. Whoever has been killing girls in the city doesn't intend to stop at two victims, and whoever he is, he now has his sights set on Addie.

I don't tell her, not as we drive in silence. Not as I ask for a table for two in the most popular restaurant in the city. Not even as we peruse the menu and I tell her to order anything she wants. It's on me. She just sits there quietly, those pretty blue eyes red and swollen. The waiter watches her with something like pity and I want to gouge out his appreciative eyes.

I choose that moment to speak, raising my voice just enough that the waiter's eyes widen slightly. "Do you want me to call the chef out for his recommendation, love? Or we can order one of everything until you find something you like."

I suppose I speak too loudly, as there are some sneers at the word "love," others gazing at her with jealousy, some trying to measure my watch with their eyes.

Addie blushes and shrinks as if to hide behind her menu. "That won't be necessary," she huffs, blowing a curl from her face. "Just a Caesar salad, no chicken, please."

"And two veggie burgers with extra fries."

Addie frowns. "I didn't see that on the menu."

I stifle a laugh. "It's on the menu if I ask for it. Chef is an old friend of mine, and I saw you looking up vege-tarian options."

In the car, I had watched as she took note of the address on the GPS and immediately looked up the menu. She had paled at the prices, and paled even further at the carnivorous meals. She likes to be prepared, and is clearly vegetarian. I'm not, so I don't know why I ordered the same thing. Maybe it's because I hate the way the waiter looks at her, or because I have this increasing need to understand her. Maybe then I can get her out of my head.

"I don't like meat," she says under her breath with a pointed glance towards the waiter.

He blushes scarlet and I laugh, a full belly laugh. My cheeks hurt by the end of the bout. I haven't laughed hard or loud in so long, I literally can't think of when the last time was. She's perfect, too fucking perfect. I hate it— hate that she has this grip over me that so many have coveted yet failed to achieve.

The waiter disappears, and Addie slams her face into the menu, a silenced scream obviously building in her throat.

"That was the best thing I've heard in a while."

"Don't bring it up," she murmurs over the lip of her water glass. "So embarrassing."

"Far from it."

A bit of the color dissipates from her cheeks and she hums, contented.

We still haven't spoken aside from this short conversation and the silence creeps in all too quickly. Suffocating —it is suffocating not to hear her voice.

"I know you told me a bit back at the office, but I need you to tell me everything you know. Any potential enemies who could want to get back at you?"

Addie swallows another sip, her eyes holding mine in challenge as if to say, "Here?"

"They aren't here. Everyone is too busy figuring out how to get *with* you, not get *to* you."

No one has shown any sign of maliciously watching her. I'm not surprised. She had arrived at the office via foot. If anyone had seen her, they would have assumed she was leaving the same way she came. And if they had spotted her with me, they wouldn't be able to track us by my car. My windows are completely tinted and my clientele is wealthy enough that my car could have belonged to any number of them. We have at least an hour until they discover we aren't at my office anymore—an hour to cover all our bases before we send my intended message to her stalker.

Addie recounts everything in hushed, hurried breaths —rom the first text to when we left my office.

I clench my fists. Her roommate, Maddy, has a boyfriend who is supposedly friends with my mole— Jon. He worked at my company, like most of my men do, covers for the real work they do for me. Especially for my hitmen, working in security gives them a reason to explain the blood on their clothes to family and spouses.

Jon double-crossed us, smuggled weaponry to a smaller rival gang who had hoped the weapons would give them a chance to overthrow me. Jon's last words were giving me their location before I killed him in his own office. I had to replace the rug and come up with an excuse about a trip to have "sent" Jon on. Meanwhile, my men had boated out past our country's borders and dumped the body somewhere in the ocean.

I'd need to look into this Donovan, and her roommate. Usually, there are no correlations between Mafia members and their outside relationships, but Addie was also an outsider when she was dragged into this. I will overturn every stone to keep her safe, even if some might be considered overkill.

I should be surprised by how quickly I am ready to kill for this woman. Not only to kill for her—that is my job—but to personally protect her. But I'm not. Being drawn to her feels natural, as she's magnetic. Sitting at this table with her feels more like home than any family meal I've ever attended.

This same woman who now sits across from me, eyeing me with something like suspicion as she stabs at her house salad. She does not pick it up with her fork, but stabs it as if it were responsible for the threatening texts she's received. She waves a speared piece of lettuce around on her fork for emphasis as she stares me down. "I have a question for you now," she purrs. "Why did you take me to lunch?"

"What? You mean our date?"

"This is not a date."

"Like hell it isn't," I grind out. "From this moment forward, we are going to pretend to be in a relationship. That way, your stalker knows you aren't alone. And before you argue, if I am to personally protect you, I will need to have a reason to be around you as much as possible without raising suspicion. Most stalkers will be deterred if their victims are nearly never alone, especially if they're with the head of Mancini. Either that, or it will provoke them enough for them to make a bolder move. Or their rage will embolden them enough to maybe take a swing at me and I can deal with them head-on and be done with it."

Addie hums, taking another stab at her salad. "This sounds too much like a romance novel."

"What are you implying?" I ask through my budding grin. I'd love to get my hands on one of those romance novels she reads. To learn exactly what makes her tick.

"Fake dating turns to real dating nonsense." She fixes me with a stern look. "Am I supposed to believe you *don't* have ulterior motives?

"Do you want me to say this is a selfish ploy to keep you close to me? Because I won't tell you otherwise. Should I deny that I've been undeniably attracted to you since we met?"

"And what if I'm not into women?"

A dry laugh. "Our rendezvous in the nightclub tells me otherwise. Not to mention that little jab at the waiter."

Addie only shrugs. "I could be experimenting."

"Oh? And tell me, what did you think of your experiment?" I rock forward, bracing my elbows on the table.

Addie mimics my movements with a feline smirk. "I suppose it was adequate."

I clench my jaw. "Have I ever told you just how vexing you are, Addie Collins?"

"No, tell me. Tell me just how much I vex you."

There is a seductive purr to her voice when she speaks, but before I can offer to show her instead, the waiter returns, dropping two veggie burgers before us.

Addie rolls her shoulders and clears her throat, the smallest of blushes covering her cheeks. She cuts her burger in half with slow, deliberate motions and I choose to not say anything about the way her knife shakes.

"So what's the plan now? We fake date, then what?" Her gaze drops to her lap, her brows furrowed.

As if on instinct, my hand reaches across the table for hers. It felt natural, holding her hand in mine like this. "I will keep taking you out on dates and keep someone posted at your apartment and job. You'll have my number and theirs, and if you ever feel unsafe, you call. In the meantime, I'll take another look at those messages and see if we can't figure something out." When she appears unconvinced, I add, "We'll figure this out, Addie. Day by day, okay?"

"I just don't understand why you're helping me," she breathes.

"Day by day," I promise again.

Addie looks up, her hair blowing from her face as she exhales sharply. "Right. Day by day."

CHAPTER 6
ADDIE

Unknown: Stay the fuck away from Natalia Mancini. You're mine.

"Our plan worked." I inhale sharply, looking at the text on my phone. "I got another text, this time telling me to stay away from you."

Natalia snorts and I can practically see her roll her eyes through the phone. "How original."

"Can you at least try to act concerned? I can barely put my key in the lock, I'm shaking so bad." I'm not lying. My hands do shake with each motion, and I've missed the lock to my apartment at least five times now. Maddy probably thinks my stalker is trying to pick the lock and is waiting with her baseball bat on the other side of the door.

"Addie," Natalia says again, this time in a soothing

tone. "I'm right downstairs. I have someone at the stairwell. I won't let anything happen to you."

My heart stutters in my chest. Heat floods my face. Am I dying of a butterfly-induced heart attack?

The key clicks in the lock.

"Right, well, I'm inside now, so I'm going to hang up."

"Aw, no 'you hang up first's?'"

"Goodbye." I fight the blush on my cheeks and close the door to the apartment with my hip.

Maddy sits on the barstool at our kitchen counter, her hair pulled away from her face with a claw clip. Relief floods her face at the sight of me, and she jumps up and throws her arms around my waist. "I was starting to get worried! What happened? Can the police help?"

I shake my head and watch as her face falls. We both knew this would happen but still, we'd hoped that they would care even the tiniest amount.

"There is some good—slightly weird, but good—news, though." I force a smile to my lips and tell Mads the whole story.

Maddy can't control the grin that splits her pretty face in two. "You're dating the hot bar hookup?"

"*Fake* dating, and *half* hookup," I correct with a cringe.

"Nuances." She waves me off with a well-manicured hand. "If she wasn't interested in you, she wouldn't be helping you."

I settle my elbows on the cool island counter, letting the chill ground my emotions. "I offered to sleep with her and she wasn't interested. There's got to be something more."

There has to be. Strangers don't do this for other strangers, not without a catch. No one is that kind, let alone someone like Natalia Mancini. She has a reputa-tion of being cold and brutal—being a young woman can't be easy to overcome in her industry. Still, she has to have ulterior motives.

"Sometimes a blessing is just a blessing and we need to take the wins where we can," comes Maddy's soothing voice as she lays a hand on my arm.

"Right. You're right." I force a smile to my lips then excuse myself to the shower.

When Natalia dropped me off at my apartment, she didn't say anything about my less-than-stellar living conditions, but I saw the slight crinkle between her brows as we drove into the complex parking lot. After seeing her office this morning, I can't quite blame her. If her office is that immaculate, I cannot imagine what her home must be like.

Still, I refuse to be embarrassed. I worked my ass off to get here, to have a place of my own, and even if it's a far cry from her expensive taste, it's just fine by me.

Well, everything but the broken water heater is fine by me.

After an unsatisfying cold shower, I find myself seated in front of my computer, the browser open to an empty inbox. I've been querying my latest book for a year now, and still have no takers despite my agent's optimism. Writing has always been my true passion, as wonderful as it is making coffees for a grumpy man. Publishing a book is a dream that followed me to the city when I moved, and comforted me years before when my father passed. Still, four books later and no takers.

I don't understand what I'm doing wrong. The story falls into the genre specifications of word count and prompt, it's marketable, the writing is good enough, and yet each day goes by with no publishing company banging on my door to publish it.

My head falls into my hands. Time. These things take time, and I just have to be patient.

I'm not very good at being patient. I never have been and have never claimed to be.

A week has passed since Natalia and I started fake dating, and still no news on my stalker, just more creepy text messages and threats. I thought they'd get easier to read but they haven't, and Natalia told me to just stop looking at them, like that advice ever helped anyone.

Not knowing what else to do, I go for a run in the hopes of clearing my head. This is yet another bad idea because I hate running with a capital H-A-T-E. I'm pretty sure it's blood I taste in my mouth on the last block of my pitiful jog, but I elect not to think too hard about it.

"Did you have a good run?" Mads beams from the couch. She holds a cup of steaming coffee in one hand and a photograph in the other. The table in front of her is littered with other photos, all of them ones I recognize from her latest shoot. She has another gallery coming up soon and has to pick her catalogue.

I settle next to her on the couch and point to the photos I like the best. She nods and shuffles them into a separate pile.

"If I ever tell you that I'm going to run again, I need you to beat me over the head with Benny." I wince and nod my head towards the pink baseball bat next to the door. Mads decided it deserves a name given how much time we've spent with it since I received the first text, hence Benny was born.

Mads offers a toothy grin and mock salute. "Oh, by the way, you got a package while you were out. I put it in your room. It smelled a little weird so I don't know if you ordered anything organic, but you should probably check on it."

"Oh shit, thank you." I pick myself up off the couch, my groaning muscles already missing the sweet embrace of the worn couch cushions. I force my stiff legs to move towards my closed bedroom door and sniff. I don't remember ordering a package, but I wouldn't be surprised if my mom sent some weird cheese or fruits from her travels abroad. She tends to do that every so often—her version of a loving phone call.

The smell is strong when I push the door open, and I fight the urge to gag. I'll owe my mother one of those phone calls if this is from her. She can send something less smelly next time.

I notice the dark stain seeping from the bottom of the box onto my bedspread. Swearing lowly under my breath, I dash forward to pluck the leaking box off my bed. I eye the crimson stain on my white bedding with disdain. That is definitely not going to come out.

I pluck a pair of scissors off the small desk in the corner of my room and snip away the thin tape holding the box together.

Then I flip the lid open and scream.

Maddy crashes through the door, her eyes wide and lips parted with terror. I can vaguely hear her in the back of my mind, her voice ringing and asking if I'm okay, what's wrong?

Two open yet blank eyes stare back at me from the bird's severed head. It rolls around the box, the bleeding, headless body beside it.

Scrawled in messy handwriting and blood are three words across the inside of the lid—*I warned you.*

"The security feed had a glitch in the system. It's an older model, so it was easier to splice," Riven explains, flipping through the apartment complex's security footage showing everything in the past twenty-four hours. Conveniently enough, the time when Maddy said the package was delivered shows nothing but a system error and flashing lights.

Maddy taps her heel against our kitchen tile, her arms crossed over her chest. "Can't you just un-splice it?"

"Did I mention older model?"

"So what, the stalker is smarter than the right-hand man to the CEO of this nation's best security company? Glad to know we're in good hands," she responds hotly.

She and Riven haven't gotten along since they met twenty minutes ago. Their initial hostility surprised me. The two seem similar enough that I thought they'd be fast friends. Not to mention, now that I can fully see Riven somewhere other than the dimly lit club office, he's highly attractive, and with his tan skin and dark hair, he's exactly Maddy's type.

"I'll gladly just let you deal with then," he snaps back.

Natalia cuffs the back of his head. "You will not," she

seethes. "We'll figure this out. We have a team that can run forensics. Until then, I'll keep Marco posted outside your door. He'll keep you safe."

"That's great and all, but we have to leave for work," I say, nodding towards the door.

Natalia's mouth drops in incredulous shock. I can only shrug. I didn't have a panic attack like I did when the first few texts poured in two days ago. All the anxiety seemed to leave my body when I first opened the box and screamed. Now, I feel an odd calm, even though my hands shake and I know I've probably gone into shock.

"You're going to work?" Riven asks, matching Natalia's sentiments. "After all of this?"

"Not all of us have more than a minimum-wage job," I reply drily. "Even so, I'd rather not lose it and be left with nothing. So yes, we're going to work."

"Then Marco will go with you to Tella's and we'll finish up here." Natalia nods, and Marco echoes the movement. Then she turns to me, wrapping her fingers around my wrist. "Don't get yourself killed." Her voice is hard, bordering on uncaring, but beneath the hatred burning in her eyes, I can see something deeper, some-thing bearing the semblance of caution.

I can only nod and excuse myself to get changed.

The anxiety hits me in the car on the drive over. By the time we reach Tella's, my hands are shaking so badly I fumble with the doorknob for a good thirty seconds before Marco puts me out of my misery and pushes it open for me.

I force myself to fall into a routine. Froth the milk. Pump the cane sugar. Pretend there isn't a dead bird in a box in my apartment.

The first two are easier than the third.

Marco sits in the corner of the shop, sipping on a cappuccino I botched making for another customer when my hands shook too badly. Natalia sent him to watch over me while I work. She said that aside from her and Riven, he's next best, and she needs Riven to go track down a potential lead. She's running forensics on the bird, so I guess it isn't in my apartment anymore. That thought hardly helps.

Mads is up at the cash register per usual, her beaming grin plastered across her face. She answers with her usual cheerfulness, no signs of the terrified face that burst through my door once the screaming started. She's calm, her mask of cheer covering her true emotions. She's always been better at that than me.

By the fourth customer, my hand has stopped shaking enough to attempt a sorry excuse for latte art, and the shell-shocked terror of earlier fades.

Marco appears calm, occasionally glancing over his shoulder as if looking at the clock. He glances at the door each time the bell above it chimes, flinching just that it seems like a natural reaction. He looks for only a second, brief enough to be considered casual, but long enough that I know he's completely scanned their face and stored it in his mind. Marco does his best to be inconspicuous, but I have to laugh at the amount of attention he garners. The embarrassed pink tint across his ears tells me he notices too.

He's not unattractive, but a bit too lean and *male* for my taste.

I distract myself by fishing a cake pop out of the display for a child hanging on his mother's hip. I sneak a peek to make sure Daryl isn't watching, and when I see his door is shut, I slip the free treat into the child's small hands. He giggles happily and the mother offers an appreciative smile before leading them both out the door.

Closing doesn't take as long as usual either. Business has been slow and the messes small. We finish within fifteen minutes and I click the key into the lock. Maddy double-checks the doors after discarding the day's trash, then links her arm with mine. I hail a cab while Marco piles into his own car, content to tail us the entire way home.

Natalia hasn't sent many updates, just told Marco to let us know it's safe to come back and that the apartment has been cleaned. I send her a simple text letting her know we've closed up and left.

I felt a bit better knowing Natalia herself is working on the case. I can't quite explain it. Maybe it's the fact that she runs the country's most elite security firm, and that title has to come with qualifications, right? Or maybe it's Natalia herself, the woman a weapon in her own right.

Maddy bounces nervously beside me, the leather seats of the cab crinkling with the motion. She chatters idly from time to time if only to fill the silence, which I both appreciate and loathe.

"If you're not comfortable sleeping alone, you can stay in my room tonight," Mads whispers, squeezing my hand. "Me and Benny the Baseball Bat will keep you company."

I whisper a breath of a laugh, more for niceties than joy. I haven't thought much about sleeping in my room, nor have I considered what I'll do with my bedding. How far did that poor bird's blood go into my sheets? That's not something that will wash out, nor should I keep it, given the diseases they could have.

I suppose I'm going to find out when I get inside. Or maybe it isn't too late to get well acquainted with our couch.

I inhale sharply as I open the door to my apartment. Marco offers an apologetic glance before he brushes past me to clear the space—something Natalia strictly demanded he do, even though he sighed as if he already knew and has done it a thousand times before. He comes back out with a knowing smile and says the apartment is clear. Maddy fixes him with an odd look but lets me brush past to my room.

Everything looks exactly the same, if not cleaner, except for the bed. The original metal frame is there, but a completely new bedding set and mattress rest atop it. Sitting on the fluffy duvet at the bottom is a cream envelope, a black box, and a simple pink rose.

Natalia, of course. This has her dramatic flair all over it.

I reach for the envelope first, out of habit. As a kid, I was taught to read the card first before opening the gift, if only to appear appreciative and not greedy. I break the wax seal—who uses *wax seals*?—that binds the envelope closed. I find Natalia's clean cursive scrawled across the note and trace my fingers across the words.

Love,

I apologize for replacing your bedding. It was beyond repair, as was your mattress. I took it upon myself to replace them both with my personal favorite brands, as well as something to help you unwind. Before you argue, as I know you would if I were there in person, I have Marco stationed outside your door and other men around the building. He and Riven will switch before the sun rises, and Riven will drive you both to work in the morning. I have business to attend to tomorrow so I will not be around. I'll see you Wednesday for our second date.

Natalia

Something ugly burns in my chest at the note. I shouldn't have expected Natalia to guard me personally, especially not when she has a full company to run. Still, heat scorches my face at the words, "I will not be around."

Sounds a lot like, "Don't contact me."

I nearly pick up the phone to tear her a new one, or maybe just to text her a slew of words I'll regret in the morning to rid myself of this burning when a second note falls from the envelope.

Ps.
About the gift, don't fucking argue.

Ass.

I lay the rose gingerly upon my desk and slip the lid off of the black box. My fingers ghost over the swath of fabric inside, my eyes nearly rolling back when they feel the buttery soft silk inside.

Then my eye catches on the smallest scrap of lace I've ever seen.

Perverted ass.

I text Natalia as much before calling out to Maddy that I'm getting in the shower.

Natalia:

> You seem to be obsessed with my ass, love.

My lips instinctively curve upwards at the message when I step out of my shower. Finally refreshed, I dry my hair with a towel and slip into what must be the most comfortable pajamas I've ever worn. I have to admit, Natalia has taste.

> Do you treat every girl at the bar like this?

> Only the pretty ones.

> Glad to know I make the cut.

Then, because I'm still feeling a tad bit jealous and extra curious as to what would make her tick, I send another message.

> Marco is pretty cute. Does he have a sister?

> Don't test my patience.

I frown at my phone before turning it off. I hoped for a bit more of a reaction, but maybe she's busy. I set the phone on my nightstand, the clock flashing just past ten p.m. now. My frown only deepens. I have to be up early tomorrow for the opening shift, yet it would be an absolute sin to leave my latest romance novel sitting untouched on the bedside table. I crack open the book and get maybe a page or two in when there's a knock at my door.

"Come in!"

I expect Mads's blonde head to pop in and nearly

jump when I see Marco's pale face at the door instead. I should have known—Maddy would never knock.

"What's wrong?"

"I can't protect you if my boss kills me first," is all he says, holding up his phone to reveal a slew of expletive texts from Natalia regarding my teasing. Turns out he does have a sister, estranged at that, but he's not to introduce us under any circumstance.

I choke back a laugh at a particularly creative threat involving some blunt gardening sheers and his more private bits. "Sorry, Marco." My face warms and I curl up again while his phone continues to ping. My chest feels tight and warm at the same time—a foreign feeling, though not entirely unpleasant.

I've never been in love. I've had crushes, sure, but love? Completely foreign to me.

Not to say this is love—hell, I've only known the woman for just over a week—but there is an undeniable attraction between us.

It's the tattoos. I can blame it on the tattoos and the way they ripple across the length of her arm. Or maybe it's our halfway hookup, as Maddy so affectionately nick-named our moment at the club. Maybe if we fucked just once, I could get her out of my system.

I stop the thought as quickly as it comes. I can't. I can't risk falling for someone I can't keep. Natalia runs one of the most exclusive and successful businesses this genera-tion has seen, and I'm working a minimum-wage job for a middle-aged walking citation machine. We are in two completely different places in our lives, and I don't want to be indebted to her forever. For all she's done already, I might as well be.

No, it isn't love. It might as well be hate, for all the burning between us. Yes, we shall call it hatred with a dash of attraction. Nothing more, nothing less.

Marco nods his thanks before resuming his post by the door. Once I'm sure the door has clicked shut, I dive deeper beneath the silk sheets, running my fingertips over them and imagining Natalia picking them out. I wonder what could have been running through her mind, what she pictured us doing on these sheets. Maybe I can't keep her, but dreaming is free.

If I can't keep her in the waking hours, I'll hold her tighter when my eyes are closed.

CHAPTER 7
NATALIA

Unknown: Did you enjoy my gift?

Riven usually doesn't piss me off. Usually. He seems to be doing a fine enough job of it lately. First, he sends me into a trap, then he upsets Addie with his snippy remarks back at the club, and now there's this shit show with her best friend.

"Did you finish the background check on Madeline Yapon, like I asked?"

"It's already on your desk."

Great. Now he's the one irritated.

"You didn't find anything worth noting?"

"She moved to the city at the same time as Addie, despite not knowing each other previously. She's an only child. Both of her parents are still alive, but they have a tense relationship. Maddy visits them once a week on Sundays for brunch, and almost always comes home visibly upset. She's dating a guy, Donovan Larson—a new lawyer, fresh out of law school and already secured a well-paying job in the city thanks to Daddy's money and connections. No history of violence or crime with either of them."

I didn't think the best friend would be a threat— maybe only to my second's mental well-being, but not to Addie. I've spent long enough in the business learning how to read people to know just by looking at them if they're a threat or not.

"Good. Addie will need the support while we find this guy."

Riven runs a hand down his face. "I can't imagine being stalked by a serial killer is easy."

Silence.

"You did tell her she was being stalked by a serial killer, right?"

"Some of the details might have slipped."

Finding out you have a stalker is already a lot to swallow, but hearing that he's already killed two girls? That might push her over the edge.

"Jesus, Nat. He's already killed two people, and it started like this for both. Texts. Calls. Leaving things at their house. She deserves to know."

"Yes, and how do you want me to explain to her why I know when the cops don't?" I hiss through clenched teeth. "Explain that yes, I run with the Mafia. Actually, I'm their leader, and we're looking into a potential serial killer and can't go to the cops because it'll ruin everything? Did I mention I was leader of the Mafia? Can you see that going over well, because I don't, not for any of us."

"I get the point." Riven rolls his eyes.

My hands are tied. The Mafia generally wouldn't get involved with something like this, but then again, we've never been the traditional type. Besides, it's a challenge at this point. This serial killer thinks he can outsmart me, and I take that personally. I have more resources than the government and less hoops to jump through. In the time it takes for them to mobilize a task force, this fucker will be dead and they'll chalk it up to gang wars while I send condolences to the families.

"Any chance your brothers are tied to this?" I finally groan into my hands. I don't think they are—we've already checked that box—but everything else has been a dead end so far.

"Not their type of thing. My informant said they don't know anything about it, either, and I trust him."

I can't argue, not with the blooming headache behind my eyes. "So," I drawl, "back to square one."

"No, at square one, we had one body. Now we have two."

"Right. Square two then," I respond drily.

Nothing has come up yet from either of the bodies. As far as we know, the two girls didn't know each other, had no overlapping friends, didn't even run in the same circles. The only similarities they had were the times they were taken and killed, and their age. Both were in their early twenties, so at least we know his type. Too bad that doesn't narrow it down any, given that the city is filled with young adults trying to find a foot in this world. I can't put a unit on every young woman in the city. I'll just have to wait until he makes a move.

And I hate it.

We have reason to assume Addie is next. She fits the

mold perfectly, and again, she has no relation to either of the girls that died. Neither does Maddy or Donovan, so we can chalk everything up to wrong person wrong time.

"I don't like these odds." Riven runs a hand over his face. "If Addie is next, he would have made his move last week. Each girl was stalked for a week before she wound up dead. Addie is on week two."

"Approaching week three," I agree.

"What if they're not connected? There's plenty of stalking and murder cases every year, every month, even. Addie's could be completely unrelated and we're just running in circles."

"I have a gut feeling."

"Go get lunch then."

"I'm serious," I seethe. "The texts are too similar. The stories line up. If we aren't dealing with the same person, then we're dealing with a copycat who could lead us to the original. Either way, any lead is worth running down."

Riven throws his hands up. "I'm not questioning you, I'm just—"

"Questioning me?"

He grins. "Exactly."

I have to smile at that. Riven is a thorn in my side at worst, a brother to me at best. As swaggering and annoying as he can be, he's also the only family I have. Even if my parents were still alive, I'd still choose him as my own. We both know that family isn't defined by blood, and maybe that's what sets us apart from our own families—my father, his brothers. None of them understand that like we do.

"So Addie..." Riven asks tentatively. "Is this case really

about stopping another murder, or is there something personal here?"

"I'm going to pretend I don't know what you mean."

"I'm serious, Nat. I meant what I said in Michels's office. You don't do relationships. Distractions are dangerous." When I fix him with a glare, he adds, "Your words, not mine. Yet you're privately guarding Addie and going to her on a whim. Why?"

He's well within his rights to ask me this. It *is* uncharacteristic of me, sure, but it also affects his life and work. Still, the question strikes a chord of ire in my chest.

"I don't like being challenged, and this killer thinks he can do just that," I answer instead. The case is personal now, yes, but in more ways than one.

Why am I doing all of this for Addie?

I'm attracted to her—that is the simple answer, but since when does it run deeper than that? Is it because she made me laugh for the first time in what feels like a lifetime, or simply because there's something about her that I can't figure out, and that, in itself, is a challenge?

Or is it because the thought of Addie's body cold on the morgue table undoes me? Her face staring at me, unseeing through a file as we try to use her corpse to find clues as to who is next—the image sets my heart aflame. My ribs suddenly feel too tight for my lungs, my body too small for my thoughts.

"Alright, then." Riven's voice cuts through the air.

Oxygen reenters my lungs and I gulp it down greedily.

I make up my mind now. I will protect Addie, even if I don't understand why.

There is no other choice.

CHAPTER 8
ADDIE

Unknown: Looking for me, love?

Natalia looks like she's seen a ghost. "What are you doing?" She shakes her head in disbelief.

I sit hunched over my computer during my lunch break in the back corner of Tella's. Natalia swapped shifts with Marco about fifteen seconds ago, then found me googling "how to hack security cameras" and "how to trace phone numbers."

"I'm doing your job and hunting for my stalker." I beam like it is the most obvious thing in the world.

"You're insulting me," Natalia deadpans.

"Well, you have no new leads and I have a surplus of time and anxiety, so I figured I'd find him myself."

Natalia settles in the seat across from me, taking the coffee I left waiting for her. She raises an eyebrow in amusement and I try to ignore the way something in my stomach flutters.

"Okay, Nancy Drew, what have you got?"

My fingers still on the keyboard and I glower at her. "Nothing," I finally admit.

"Thought so."

"Last time I checked, you didn't have anything either."

"No, but I'm not relying on wikiHow to learn how to do the basic shit. Besides, we already traced the number as a formality, and so did the police. It's a burner phone."

I cross my arms and do my best to not look like I'm pouting. "Why does the government even allow burner phones to be a thing. It seems like only crooks use them."

"I haven't thought about it." Natalia shrugs, then takes a sip of her black coffee. To say it's black like her soul would be a cliché, but I have to admit that the line crossed my mind when she texted asking for one.

The truth is, I wish Natalia had a black soul, but she doesn't. She's overwhelmingly kind while also being a total asshole sometimes. My heart volleys back and forth in my chest like a damn Ping-Pong ball with her.

"You should leave this to me, and spend your lunch break actually having lunch."

"Mads is bringing me something back. Her boyfriend took her out today as an apology."

"An apology for what?"

"Who knows."

Natalia considers this for a moment before asking, "Then why don't I take you out?"

"Because I have fifteen minutes left until my shift starts."

"Minor details."

I huff a laugh. "Not all of us are crazy-successful millionaires—"

"Billionaires," she corrects with a smirk.

"*Billionaires*," I continue, "and we have to work on someone else's time."

Natalia rocks back in her chair, arms crossed in a way that does nothing good to my heart. Her black sleeves are rolled up today like they were the first time we met, showcasing the swirling tattoo sleeve up her left arm. Beautiful, thorny rose vines climb up her forearm as if it was a rail on a garden fence.

"How about after your shift then?"

I feel a wicked grin lift the corners of my lips at that. "Give me an hour to shower, then pick me up at the apartment."

"What the fuck are you wearing?" Natalia swears low as I lock the apartment door behind me, clad head to toe in all black, the look finished with combat boots and a beanie despite the heat.

"We," I say, pushing my finger into her sternum, "are going on a good ol' fashioned stakeout."

She sighs through her nose. "You've watched too many cop shows."

More like romance novels and trashy FBI movies, but I'm not going to correct her.

"Just indulge me."

"With tongue or teeth?"

"Fuck off," I bite, hoping the new flush in my cheeks can be blamed on wearing a beanie in late spring.

Natalia's grin tells me she knows it isn't. "Okay then, where are we staking out?" When I don't answer, she adds, "You know, people who go on stakeouts generally plan out these details ahead of time."

The crimson stain across my cheeks darkens further. "I got my first text at Tella's, so I thought we could go watch there?"

"You got the text while you were working there, though. Your stalker probably knew you'd be there and that's why he sent that message, or he just took a wild guess."

"Yes, but I was supposed to be on shift tonight until I swapped with someone else at the last second, so if he memorized my shift schedules, he probably thinks I'm there right now."

"Unless he saw you there earlier."

I throw my hands in the air. "I don't know, Natalia, but I'd rather do something than nothing."

"Right. I'm indulging you."

She flicks the ignition of her car on after opening my door. This is a different car than the one she picked me up in last time. The exterior is sleek and dark, with blackout windows that bar the inside from wandering eyes.

As the car roars to life, I look out the window. We veer onto a more crowded road, Natalia weaving in and out of traffic with the speed of a demon. Lights flash as the other cars fall behind us, buildings turning into nothing more that oily smears of color against the black sky.

At a stoplight, a man in the car next to us looks over. I pull a face. He does nothing.

"What are you doing?"

My body lurches involuntarily at Natalia's voice. "Just

double-checking that these windows are actually black outs."

"Why? Thinking of doing something you wouldn't want others to see?"

My mind chooses that exact moment to remember the night we met, her fingertips branding my thighs with punishing bruises, her lips claiming every inch of my neck. The feeling of her breath against my mouth and her body pushing against mine.

I wave a hand in front of my face as if I can push the thought from my mind. "No. Just want to make sure the stalker can't see us but we can see him."

Her mouth on mine.

Her knee between my legs.

Her thick voice practically purring my name.

I press my legs together and take to staring out the window again, my face flushed. This is not the time to be thinking these thoughts, not with Natalia sitting right next to me.

Natalia snorts. "If your stalker even shows."

"Can you at least try to be supportive?"

"I'm driving the car, aren't I?"

"Yes, with an attitude."

Natalia only smirks, and the sight drive my blood to a boil. How can one individual be so attractive yet so infuriating? The question chases me all the way to Tella's parking lot, where Natalia parks the car near the back entrance.

Then we wait.

An hour passes with little to no motion from the shop and Natalia now lays reclined in her seat, her arm crossed over her eyes. To any outsiders, she might look like she's sleeping, but I see the way her lip twitches as she withholds a smirk at my stare. She's annoyed, but also amused.

"If you're going to tell me I told you so, then please just get it over with and put me out of my misery."

"And why would I do that?"

"Because you were right. He never showed, and I'm an idiot. Happy?" My shoulders slump of their own accord. I hate this, hate every minute of being useless.

"Not in the slightest." Natalia finally uncovers her face, and those dark eyes shine with mischief. "I'm bored as shit."

"And what do you want me to do about it?"

"Tell me about yourself. Your wants, your dreams, all of it."

"No, ma'am, not so fast." I finally grin back. "If I'm baring it all, so are you. Let's play a game—twenty questions, or however many we get through."

Natalia's head lolls back with a groan and I have to bite back my laughter.

"That's so juvenile."

"Shut up." I swat at her arm. "You go first."

"Do you want me to shut up or go first?" My eye roll must be answer enough because Natalia asks, "What did you think you'd be when you were a kid?"

"An astronaut," I said confidently. "There was this character in a show I loved and she wanted to be an astronaut, so of course, I wanted to be an astronaut too. Then I learned I get motion sick and claustrophobic, so that was a no-go."

Natalia laughs lightly, and it's a beautiful sound that goes straight to my heart. I adjust my sitting position. If she keeps laughing like that, I won't survive our stakeout.

"Okay, my turn." I stumble through the words. "If you could be any fruit in the world, what would you be?"

"What?"

"You heard me," I said, refusing to blush again. "What fruit would you be?"

"Fucking hell," she groans, but I could hear the humor in it. "Probably a pomegranate?"

I nod. "You have a dark aura, so that makes sense."

"I have a dark aura?" Her eyes twinkle with mischief as she raises a dark brow.

"Not in a bad way," I explain, "just mysterious. And the pomegranate is used in the Hades and Persephone myth, and... never mind. Your turn."

Natalia takes her time choosing her next question, and I can't remember a time I felt more vulnerable. Where do I usually keep my hands? I don't usually fidget with them so much. Now my leg is falling asleep but if I uncross it, I'll disturb this quiet peace and—

"If you could go anywhere in the world, where would you go?"

The immediate answer is New York. I've always wanted to see where all the big publishers work, see Times Square, maybe watch a Broadway show, but if I could pick *anywhere*...

"London."

"Why?"

"That's two questions," I tease, but answer anyway. "I want to go at Christmastime and see all the lights. That, and London has been trending on social media for their hot chocolate lately, and I refuse to die without trying it."

"Noted," she says in a way that makes me think she truly did file the fact away somewhere in her mind.

"Have you ever been in love?" I blurt out. It's the question I wanted to ask from the start, but I didn't mean to ask as the second question—hence my dumb fruit question—and yet here I am, spitting it out a few minutes in.

Natalia stiffens and I almost apologize. I'm so stupid. This is all fake dating and I don't need to know about her past.

"No," she answers slowly. "I thought I was once, but it was just the high of my first crush. She was pretty and had big brown eyes, and teenage me thought that was all I would need in life."

"What happened?"

Natalia smirks. "Now look who's asking two questions."

"Sorry."

"Nothing happened. She went to college. I started Mancini Security. I went to her wedding last year as a friend."

"Oh," I breathe, not knowing whether to be relieved or disappointed in her answer.

We trade a few more questions, none of them nearly as personal as the first few. Soon enough, I can feel sleep pulling at my eyelids and fight the yawn that's climbing up my throat.

Natalia's hand lands on my thigh. "Come on. It's late."

"I'm not tired," I lie.

"Okay then, I am," she lies as well. "I'm taking you home."

I dip my chin, pretending not to notice how she doesn't remove her hand from my thigh. Halfway through the drive, she starts tracing idle circles across the thin material of my leggings, her callouses snagging every so often on the fabric.

The car is suffocating. Everything is Natalia—the air I breathe, the feeling of her touch. If I don't get out soon ,I might jump over the center console and do something I won't regret but will definitely be embarrassed by.

Before I realize it, Natalia has parked the car and opened my door. "Come on, sweetheart," she murmurs, holding her hand out. "I'll walk you up."

I'm not embarrassed by the way I drag my feet up every stair to my door—anything to prolong my time with Natalia. I tuck myself closer to her side than I would usually allow myself. It's because I'm tired and the world doesn't make sense when sleep deprived, I rationalize with myself.

That must be why I let my head fall against her shoulder and pretend not to notice the way her breath hitches in her throat. Or why I let myself wonder, just for a second, why I'm not asking her into the apartment that I just opened the door to.

Natalia pauses, one hand bracing on the doorframe above me. "One more question," she said.

"Yes?"

"If we were in that car for one more minute, I would have kissed you. Would you have let me?"

"Yes." It comes out as a plea.

Yes, please for the love of god, kiss me.

She nods, her dark hair bobbing with the motion. Then, with her hands still in her pockets, she leans in and presses a kiss against my cheek, just close enough to brush against the corner of my mouth. "Go inside and lock the door," she says.

Wordlessly, I nod and do as she said. The last thing I see before closing the door is the faintest tinge of red atop Natalia's ears before she spins on her heels and disappears into the shadow of the staircase.

CHAPTER 9

ADDIE

Unknown: Do you taste as sweet as you smell, Addie?

Three weeks pass with little to no commotion. Natalia continues taking me on "dates," but does nothing more than continue our dance of wit and banter. In the past week, she has grown distant, and a part of my heart screams that I should have known this would happen sooner or later. She's grown bored and will leave, never mind whatever moment we had outside my apartment after the stakeout. Besides, it's not like the mysterious stalker has been particularly active as of late.

Natalia walks in a lazy shuffle beside me, her stride languid as we walk through a garden, one of her more public outing choices, during my lunch break. I brushed on a bit more makeup than I usually would today in hopes that... well, I don't know what I hoped for.

I prayed that my interest would die as well, that I could forget whatever the hell came over me in the first few days of knowing her. It didn't. If anything, the flutter in my chest has grown to a full-blown roaring stampede.

Her knuckles brush against my bare thigh just below the hem of my dress as we walk. I trip, my breath hitching in my throat. Natalia says nothing, but the corners of her lips tilt upwards ever so slightly.

I sigh deeply through my nostrils. It's not like Natalia owes me anything. She's been doing me a favor, after all. One night, when I'd grown extra curious, I did a Google search as to what a private bodyguard might cost the average person. If I sold my apartment, all my earthly possessions, and then my body, I still probably wouldn't have enough.

"What's wrong?" she asks, her eyes piercing through my soul.

"Nothing," I snap.

"Addie, I don't speak sighing."

No, I suppose she doesn't. I don't know how to voice it any other way, though. How do I ask her why she would even bother helping me, or ask her about her feelings, or anything? We're more than strangers at this point. I could walk through a bookstore and pick which books she'd go to first, and I know she hates the color orange. I know how she likes her steak cooked and that she wishes she had a dog. But I can't tell anyone her middle name, the last time she cried, or what her biggest fear is. We're close enough to be casual, distant enough to not even be considered friends. Not that friends kiss or nearly fuck each other.

"Why did you help me?" When she doesn't answer at first, I ramble, "You hardly knew me, and you don't go this far out of your way to help someone on the basis of attraction. I never formerly asked, either."

Natalia's mouth is a hard line as she speaks. "The last girl I knew who had a stalker turned up dead days after the police wouldn't help her. I couldn't let that be you."

Oh.

I wish I could swallow my traitorous tongue. Wish I could swallow it and my stupid heart for breaking a bit when I realize this has nothing to do with me. It's a selfish thought—not to think that this could have been personal, but to be hurt because it isn't.

"We weren't close. To be honest, I didn't really know the girl. But I knew you. Knew you enough to know I wouldn't be able to live with myself if you were next," she continues, her shoulders tightening. Her eyes snap to the tree line beside us, to the parking lot behind us—ever vigilant, ever cautious.

My hand finds hers and I squeeze, trying to convey what words can't.

She smiles, then her phone rings.

I catch a glimpse of Riven's face flashing across the screen and she swears lowly.

"You'd better take that," I hum.

Her face twists with something like apology before she swipes her thumb across the screen and answers.

Deciding to give her privacy, I wander a bit further away towards a field of wildflowers. We aren't in a particularly good part of town but I assume it's fine. Natalia is only a few feet away, and a kid and her father are playing not too far off.

I reach the patch of wildflowers, crouching down beside them. This garden is mostly roses, which are stunning, obviously, but I love wildflowers. There is something so beautiful about wild things growing where they aren't supposed to.

I bend down and tap the center of a white daisy, smiling to myself despite the weight pressing against my chest.

My head snaps up at the sudden sound of deep male voices shouting. I look over to see another man has emerged from the tree line and is shoving at the girl's father while she watches on from behind his legs. I'm already on my feet when the first gunshot rings out.

The man falls heavily, blood spraying from his chest where the bullet went clean through. The others in the park run, screaming, and I can hear Natalia frantically shouting my name, but my focus is on the little girl who kneels beside her father, the knees of her jeans soaked with blood.

I throw myself between the girl and the man on instinct, shielding her body with my own when he raises his gun again.

"Move."

His pupils are nearly blown apart and his breathing erratic. He's high out of his mind, obviously, his finger shaking on the trigger.

"She's just a kid," I nearly sob through clenched teeth. "You already got her father. Let her go."

He sniffs. The gun clicks. "Move."

I close my eyes. I won't move, not as this child no older than seven clings to my shirt and weeps. Not as her father lays bleeding out next to me for god-knows-what reason.

A scream burns my throat when I hear the third

gunshot. I wait for the quick pain of the bullet blasting through my brain, for death to claim me. A heartbeat passes, and it doesn't come.

When I will my eyes to open, Natalia is standing there, her gun still drawn, pointing to where she shot the man in the back. He lays twitching on the ground as she shifts into action and ties his hands behind his back before she grips my arms fiercely enough that bruises are already blooming.

"What the hell were you thinking?" she gasps. "Do you want to die so badly? I swear, you make it so fucking hard to keep you alive."

The words sting, but I swallow my spiteful retort when Natalia's gaze drops to the kid, her father's blood splattered across her front. Natalia drags a hand over her face.

"We need to call an ambulance." I scramble over the man's body, pressing my hands over the bullet wound. So much blood. Too much blood.

"Jesus, Addie, again? Not without gloves," she hisses trying to pull my hands away by my forearms, but I don't budge. Instead, I push my full weight into stemming the blood flow.

"*Now*, Natalia."

I've never given her such a clear demand before, never dared it. But I see the tears streaking through the blood splatter on the girl's face as she freezes—freezes like I did when the heart monitor flatlined and the nurses rushed in, pressing paddles to my father's still-warm chest.

Natalia must see it in my face because she doesn't bite

my head off again. Doesn't do anything but sigh and pull out her phone. "They won't get here in time."

"I don't care." I grit my teeth. "*Do something.*"

"I already did."

Sirens pierce the air then, a black car bursting through the parking lot, sending rocks spraying across us. I can feel something sticky and warm sliding down my cheek but I ignore it. A woman emerges, snapping her gloves on, followed by a gurney. A young man follows close at her heels and helps lift the man from my grip. They load him in quickly, no sign of acknowledgment except a slight dip of their chin towards Natalia before they take the girl in the car with them and peel off.

"Come on," Natalia says, wrapping her now-gloved hand around my wrist. "We need to have a talk."

Something in her voice sends a shudder down my spine and makes my toes curl at the same time.

"Where did they take that man?"

"The hospital." She says it as if I should already know the answer. I probably should have.

The car ride to the hospital is silent despite this so-called talk we're supposed to be having. Natalia barely has the car in park before she pulls my door open and yanks me out, leading me towards the front desk.

"I need her cleaned up, now," she grinds out.

The receptionist balks for only a moment, then spots the badge Natalia flashes at her. "Of course, Ms. Mancini. I'll send the doctor right away."

"There's no rush," I butt in, and immediately regret it when I see the murderous look flash across Natalia's face.

Her stride exudes pure venom as she stalks towards

the room the receptionist points us towards. Nurses jump to the side, their faces going pale at the sight of Natalia prowling their halls, dragging my bloody form behind her.

A doctor is already in the room waiting for us by the time we arrive. He seems like a nice enough man, his face round and ruddy like an out-of-season Santa. He doesn't balk at Natalia's glare like the others did, but is professional as he cleans the blood from my hands first.

"Doctor, if you have more pressing matters to attend to, please go ahead. I can clean the blood off my hands myself."

He only shakes his head. "I'd like to take a look at that cut on your face before I go anywhere." Then, with a not-so-subtle glance at the dark presence in the corner of the room, he adds, "Plus, Ms. Mancini insists that I tend to you first."

"Yes, she does tend to be pigheaded that way."

"Just shut up and let the man do his job." Natalia glowers over the bridge of her nose.

The sight shouldn't excite me, but I'm just grateful she doesn't insist they hook me up to a heart monitor or she'd see just how much it does excite me.

"Well, it shouldn't need stitches," he says, prodding gently at the cut across my face. I hadn't realized that the warmth dripping down my face was a fairly large slice from a wayward rock back at the park.

"Thank you," I say as genuinely as I can once the man finishes cleaning and bandaging the wound. It feels silly to receive so much attention, especially when I know there was a man bleeding out somewhere in this hospital while his daughter waits with a lifetime's worth of trauma.

When the doctor finally leaves, I allow myself to glance back towards Natalia. Her face is an unreadable mask of poorly concealed fury as she fixates her gaze on the tiled floor. Her jaw clenches and her arms cross over her chest, her biceps bulging.

"If you're going to yell at me, get it over with."

"I'm not going to yell at you."

"So are you going to just sit there or…"

"You make it so fucking hard to keep you alive." She finally snaps her gaze up to mine. "Do you *want* to die that badly?"

I shrink inward for only a moment before my walls raise again, the barbed wire charged and ready to sink in to her insults. "I didn't die."

"That man could have had a disease," she growls, "and he could have given it to you through his blood. That gunman could have shot you."

"They could have died."

"*You* could have died." Her voice is a low rasp, blazing rage lining her dark eyes.

I lift my chin, refusing to be intimidated as she pulls herself to her full height. Her presence is domineering, but I refuse to back down. Refuse to let her overpower me with fear.

"If you're looking for an apology, you won't find one here," I say with lethal calm. "I won't apologize for saving his life, or that little girl's."

"You could have died," Natalia repeats again, her voice nearly cracking on the last word.

I won't let that soften my heart. I won't let her win this easy.

"Then it would be one less problem for you to deal

with," I say before I realize the words are leaving my mouth.

Natalia moves with a speed I did not know was possible for a human to possess. One minute she's peering at me from a few feet away, the next she has her hand planted firmly on the wall behind me. Her arms form a cage around my head and her hair falls to curtain her face.

"I'd rather you be a problem than be dead," she growls. "Stop. Trying. To. Die."

Any retort on how I wasn't actually *trying* to die dries on my tongue at the look of anguish that flashes across her face. She's all firm lines and taut angles, but for just a flicker of a second, she's soft. Afraid. It makes me reach my hands out as if to cup her face, but Natalia steps back, just out of reach.

She plucks her coat from the back of the small chair, then opens the door with a click. She doesn't bother checking out or paying, just dips her chin in the direction of the receptionist before passing through the automatic doors. I follow like an obedient dog at her heels, murmuring my thanks but not daring to slow for more than a second. There is a fury and tight restraint in Natalia's gait, and I won't push her any farther than I have already.

She flicks the ignition on her car and drives me all the way home in silence, leaving me with nothing more than a promise to call later in the week.

CHAPTER 10
ADDIE

Unknown: How's Maddy?

I hate the summer—the sweat, the bugs, the heat. All of it.

I especially hate when our dingy apartment AC goes out on the hottest day of the year.

Mads sits opposite of me on our brown leather couch, a pint of strawberry ice cream in her hand. I hold my own pint of Ben and Jerry's Phish Food, using a serving spoon to scoop copious amounts of the sweet cream into my mouth.

Mads rolls up the hem of her baby-pink tank top, exposing her tan and toned stomach. "So," she hums, nearly comatose from the heat, "no calls from your sex goddess?"

"Stop calling her that... and no."

Natalia has only come to see me once in the past three weeks. She brought me flowers at Tella's the week of the gunman incident, but other than that, it has been radio silence. It's just as well anyway. Maybe distance will cool whatever this raging fire between us is.

My cheeks heat as I think of how easily she was able to pin me in the hospital, how she towered over me and caged me with her arms. I allow the intense summer heat to take the fall for this blush.

Maddy narrows her eyes before pointing her spoon at me, wielding it like a weapon. "You need a plan of attack."

"I need a what now?"

"Do you want to climb this woman like a tree or not?"

That's it. The heat has finally made her lose her mind.

My response is to shove another bite of chocolate-marshmallow goodness into my mouth, swallowing down my bitter retort. It's no use lying to Maddy—she knows me too well—but my feelings for Natalia are confusing. No one can make my blood boil like she does, in every meaning of the phrase. She's gorgeous and charming, but also an aloof asshole who I would just as soon strangle as I would fuck.

Maybe I just need a good hookup, and then I can forget Natalia and her infuriating hot-then-cold act.

I shift on the couch, un-sticking my bare thighs from the leather. The result is a horrid suction sound. "Do I even want to know what's going on in that pretty little head of yours?"

Maddy grins devilishly. "I propose a challenge."

"This ought to be good."

"A challenge," Mads continues, "to discover just what makes Natalia Mancini tick. To get under her skin."

I bite back my retort that this plan seems like a sure-fire way to die. "Natalia is head of Mancini Security, in case you forgot. There's very little, if anything, that can 'get under her skin.'" I make air quotes over the repeated words, nearly dropping a glob of chocolate ice cream on our couch in the process.

Mads hisses a laugh but still taps her finger against her chin as if deeply thinking. "What if you made her jealous?" she asks. "You already know she's attracted to you, not to mention that alpha act she put on at the hospital."

Suddenly, I'm regretting sharing that information with her.

I clear my throat. "And how do you propose I do this?"

"Come with me," she hums, setting her spoon and dessert down. She pulls me to my feet from the couch, then heads to her closet. She rummages through the explosion of colorful clothes before fishing out the smallest scrap of fabric I've ever seen.

The dress is silver and shimmers with every beam of light that hits it. It would look like wearing a diamond.

But while Mads has a few good inches on me, I also have more curves than her, and that dress might not cover anything worth covering.

"My ass would be out."

Mads's answering smirk tells me that's exactly the plan. "We go to the club, someone will *obviously* try to make a move, and Natalia will lose her shit."

I swallow thickly. "And if she doesn't?"

Maddy just shrugs. "Then you have options of people to go fuck this out of your system with. Either way, Natalia realizes what she's missing and you get some form of satisfaction." Then she adds with a truly wicked smirk, "Carnal *or* emotional."

Maddy is either a genius or will be the death of me. My best friend left a few minutes ago with Donovan, kissing my cheek and promising to find me once we get to the club. Donovan and I managed to not swap any heated remarks, only glaring nods before he whisked her off.

I spin in front of my mirror, admiring the way the silver dress glows in the light. The garment rides up as I move, the hem just barely resting at the base of the curve of my ass. I twirl again to face Natalia, who does her best to look unaffected.

Lowering my voice to a sultry tone, I rest my hands on my hips, bending ever so slightly at the waist. "What do you think? Do I look fuckable?" I purr.

Natalia squeezes the arms of the chair. "No."

I mock a frown. "Maybe if I pull the dress up a little higher, someone else can come home and play protector for the night." Then with a wink, I add, "You could take the night off."

The arm of the chair cracks—*actually cracks*—as Natalia's knuckles go white. "Knowing your judgment, you might accidentally take home your stalker. We keep calling him a 'he,' but he could be a she."

"Then I guess you'll just have to wait outside the door until we're finished." I bite back the bile threatening to climb up my throat. It's a cheap shot, and I won't let it be the comment to take me down. I have the upper hand tonight, and Natalia looks... unwell. "You might want to bring some headphones, unless you wanted to listen as I—"

Natalia's hand shoots out so fast, I yelp. She grips behind my head, her fingers entwining in my hair and her thumb mindlessly brushing across my lower lip. "I have a new set of conditions to add to our agreement," she growls, her voice dangerously low. "While I'm guarding you, no one comes home with you. No one fucks you. Hell, no one even touches you. Any part of them that touches you, I will shatter beyond repair, got it?"

My breath hitches with each lazy swipe of her thumb across my lip, waiting for... I don't know what. Her stare burns my skin, branding me as hers. If I look in the mirror, I'm convinced I'd see it seared across my face for everyone else to see.

I wrap my fingers around her wrist and jerk my face away. "You're going to smudge my makeup," I hiss. Forcing myself to stalk to my mirror, I leave Natalia in the middle of my room. I brush another swipe of gloss over my lips, popping them with satisfaction.

Natalia's reaction tells me I look good tonight, but I don't need confirmation. I piled my curls to one side of my head, letting them cascade over one shoulder in a waterfall of ringlets. My eyes have been painted silver to match the dress, a flawless cat eye drawn on each. My bright-blue eyes pop in contrast to the dark lashes framing them. I look hot, if I dare to admit.

"If you're done preening, we need to go," Natalia snaps, slinging her jacket over her shoulder. She doesn't tell me to change or stay home like I thought she would. My heart twists and I'm not sure if I should be happy that the plan can move forward or disappointed that she doesn't care more.

I follow her out the door, triple-checking the locks before we head out.

Maddy is easy to spot once we walk into the crowded nightclub, skipping the line thanks to Natalia. She's dancing in the center of the club, her bright-blue dress stark against the sea of black mini dresses tonight. She is the center of attention, as she usually is.

Natalia brushes past me towards a man leaning against the bar. Once my eyes adjust, I recognize him as Riven, Marco sitting beside him. They hardly fit on the barstools, looking more like giants in a dollhouse rather than real men.

I move to push my way through the crowd to Maddy, trying to keep my head down. To my surprise, people part without much struggle, allowing me through with appreciative glances. Right. I'm here tonight to make Natalia jealous. I look good and everyone knows it.

Tossing a glance over my shoulder at the formidable woman at the bar, I smirk, then continue my walk to Mads, adding an extra sway to my hips as I walk.

Maddy whistles as I approach, her smile wide enough I fear her face may split. "You made it!" she squeals, throwing her arms around my shoulders.

I laugh into her blonde hair. Her skin is sweaty from an hour of uninterrupted dancing, her hair now three times larger than it was when she left our apartment.

She leans in close and shouts over the music, "How's our operation going?"

I can't help the blush that climbs up my neck, dousing my face in crimson embarrassment, and Maddy shrieks —*actually shrieks*—with joy.

"Come on," I laugh, pulling her towards the bar. "I need a drink if I'm going to keep this up."

"You don't have to ask me twice."

I laugh. I wouldn't say I hate going out, but it generally takes more of my mental energy than it does Maddy's. Not tonight, though. Tonight is all about me feeling confident in a tiny silver dress, and feeding off the looks Natalia tries to hide from her seat at the bar.

A few drinks later and Natalia's subtle glances have turned into full-blown stares as I allow myself to lose my body to the whims of the music. I dance with strangers, I drink for free all night, and I never stray too far from my bodyguards' line of sight.

I'm swaying to an old 2000s song when I bump into something solid. A hand lands a bit too low on my back.

The man's face shifts from irritation to lust within seconds of me turning around. He isn't unattractive, and if Maddy was single, I might have pushed him her way, but his assessing gaze feels like a sharp burn on my skin. I move to step forward but his hand stays firmly planted just above the swell of my rear. His tongue darts out to swipe across his lower lip.

"My bad!" I shout over the music.

Another attempt to shimmy from his grasp fails.

"You can apologize with a dance," he says in what he thinks is a seductive tone.

I roll my eyes. It takes effort to continue to believe he's just horrible at reading people and not blatantly ignoring my attempts to get away.

Maddy's eyes narrow in on the encounter and she begins to shove her way through her line of waiting dance partners, muttering colorful curses I can hear over the music.

"Sorry, I'm not interested."

"Don't you want to show me how sorry you are?"

Gag.

Before I can say anything else, the man's face melts into an expression of pure pain and his grip on me fails with a resounding crack.

Natalia's knuckles are white around his wrist and her expression is one of lethal rage. Her lips peel back in a near snarl and she moves her grip to his thumb, where it still lay resting against my skin.

Snap.

"You dislocated my thumb, you crazy bitch!"

Another snap.

"Now I've relocated it. I fixed the problem, but if you still have one, then take it up with my lawyer," she says as she presses a business card into his chest with one hand, the other intertwining with my fingers.

My heart thunders traitorously in my chest as she leads us away from the scene we've caused.

My unrequited dance partner is hurling furious taunts towards the bouncers, who do nothing but dip their chins in acknowledgment towards Natalia.

Holy hell.

A quick glance over my shoulder tells me Mads is okay, and she flips me a quick thumbs-up before making her way back into the fray of things. She seems smug enough that her jealous plot worked, though it might have worked a little too well.

I follow Natalia through the back door of the establishment, her face a quiet storm of rage and jealousy. The sight causes my stomach to flip and my hands uncon-sciously fiddle with the hem of my dress. I always thought anger was an unattractive look on anyone. It would appear to be just the opposite on my bodyguard. She's already the epitome of tall, dark, and handsome, yet with this brooding gloom, she puts all the characters in my romance novels to shame.

Wordlessly, she opens the passenger side door of her Pagani, the sleek red model opening skywards. I've only been in this car once before, as she usually takes a more inconspicuous vehicle to work—an *expensive* inconspic-uous vehicle, at that—but there is no going unnoticed in this machine.

"It's like a fucking bat mobile," I breathe, running my hands over the smooth dashboard.

The corner of Natalia's lips quirk up at this but she is quick to force them down.

It seems this is the only side I get to see of her lately. Between the incident at the hospital and now this, I wonder if there even is a softer side to this woman.

"So," I say, drawling out the word. "Where are we going?"

No response.

"Are you going to brood the whole drive?"

Nothing.

"Is it the dress?"

"It's not the goddamn dress, Addie," she finally snaps, her gaze darting from the road to mine.

I huff through my nose and purse my lips. "Then what are you so pissy for?"

"I'm just annoyed thinking of all the paperwork I'll

have to fill out after I kill everyone who stared at you tonight."

I suck in a sharp breath. "That's not a good look for someone in private security."

"Only security I care about is yours, sweetheart."

Right. Because I'm her client, and even greasy with his grabby hands could be my stalker. Anyone who looks too long could be a threat.

I need to stop getting my hopes up like this, and to stop praying for some miracle world in which Natalia views me as something other than a temporary distraction from whatever she has going on in her own fucked-up life. The thought of never being anything more to her causes my heart to give an audible crack.

I want to hate her, want to replace this longing with anything more realistic, but I can't. I can't hate her, just as I can't have her. She's become all-encompassing in my thoughts, my dreams, and all the dark matter in between. I'm falling for the one person I knew I can't keep, who just so happens to be the one person who will never feel for me what I feel for her.

I know Natalia is attracted to me, but it doesn't go deeper than that. She, herself, had proven as much. Her possessiveness will only be fleeting, and soon enough, this daydream will pass me by.

At some point in all my musings, the car had stopped.

Natalia's thumb circles across my thigh, burning the skin and sending my traitorous heart awry.

No.

No more flutters. No more foolish hopes.

"Thanks for the ride," I huff. Without another word, I

climb out and prepare to stalk up the stairs to my apartment alone.

I hear the lock click on the car and a second set of footsteps trailing behind me.

Natalia is nothing more than a whisper of a shadow as we climb. Her breath is hot on my neck as I force my own breathing to be even.

She breezes past me as soon as I unlock my apartment door, commencing all of her safety checks before nodding for me to enter. Right, that's part of her job description.

"Do you need anything?" she finally asks, her shoulders loosening for the first time since we left this apartment earlier. She's been here a few times now, but it still never ceases to amaze me how effortlessly she settles in. She knows where I keep my keys when I lose them, and that you need to kick the door for it to fully close.

"No," I reply shortly.

Her eyebrows pinch together in a harrowing glare. "Now *you're* the one who's pissy."

"I'm not pissy."

"Yes, you are," she says pointedly. "Are we going to go in circles all night? What do you want?"

"I want to know why you broke that guy's wrist!"

"Because he touched you with it and I fucking warned you what would happen if he did."

Un-fucking-believable.

I throw my hands in the air, frustration pricking my eyes with tears. "You're impossible to deal with," I groan. "You act like you want nothing to do with me one minute and then the next, you're breaking people's bones, for god's sake. Am I misreading things here?"

Natalia braces her arms on either side of me, one hand flying out to pin my wrist as I attempt to turn from her. Her dark eyes search my face, pleading with me while her hot breath warms my lips. "*Everything* I come to love is eventually taken from me. It would be safer to hate you—"

"Do it then." I raise my chin to meet her simmering gaze. "Fuck me like you hate me."

The words are out there now, and even if I could take them back, I don't think I would. Not as all of Natalia's muscles go taut and her mouth forms a hard line.

Checkmate.

She releases my wrist and takes a step back, her eyes still burning with unyielding flame. Then, before the mortification can set in, she leans down, brushing her lips across mine.

"That's just the problem. I *can't* hate you."

CHAPTER 11
NATALIA

Unknown: I haven't forgotten about you.

*F*uck me like you hate me.

Christ.

My office is usually my place of solace. The walls are dark gray, every inch of furniture polished leather or black steel. Any art on the walls is chic and minimalist, reflecting the very organization of my mind. I don't need clutter or color to think well.

Today, sitting behind this desk, I find it to be a prison.

Fuck me like you hate me.

Where the hell did she even come up with that?

I hate to admit the effect her words had on me, and the way my cheeks heat each time I think of her saying that last weekend. Never have I entertained the thought of hating her, only said it aloud to maybe convince myself to be done with this fucked-up mess I've found myself in.

However, taking her then and there had crossed my mind. Multiple times.

I took this job out of necessity. I'm drawn to her, but I also know that I have to stop her stalker from claiming another life. I've taken on too many jobs that hit close to home in the past, and every time, I manage to disentangle myself from them, yet with Addie...

One of our clients is due to drop by at any moment now—the vice president of some bank. Who he is doesn't matter to me so much as his money. He gives us blood-free money, and I gave him a security detail fit to rival a king's.

The old bastard is anal, though, and insists on monthly meetings to continue our assurance of his safety. He claims he needs to see the workings of my office and lay eyes on me to be sure he can continue to trust me. I've had plenty of client requests before, but this is one of the more ridiculous ones. Nevertheless, with him came other clients, friends of his that I would rather not lose, so giving in to his absurd request is the more favorable course of action.

Riven leads the man in moments later, his laughter rumbling through my office. The vice president was a wiry man, thin as a rail, with sparse hair atop his skinny head that he meticulously slicks back. He looks like a thread next to the hulking frame of my second, who looks like he wants to be anywhere but here.

"Sir," I say, plastering a grin on my face, "wonderful to see you again."

"Ms. Mancini." He beams.

I motion for him to sit opposite me as we begin our discussion. It's the same droll conversation we have every month. Yes, his payment came through. Yes, he's been confirmed for the same security team as the last month. No, he does not need to come in more than once a month to assure that this is the case.

I am nearly five seconds away from snapping the pen in my hand when my phone begins to buzz. Addie's smiling face, a photo I snapped on one of our first dates, flashes across the screen.

Addie has never called me during work hours.

"Excuse me just a second." I step back from the table. Riven's eyes narrow at my frown and the name he sees when I flash the phone screen at him.

I accept the call. "Addie."

There is silence for a moment, only the sounds of labored breathing and a creaking floorboard.

"Addie," I repeat. "What's wrong?"

Her sweet lilt joins the line a moment later, her words quick and frantic. "He—" Her voice wavers. "He was in my apartment."

My blood runs cold.

"I'm on my way. Just five minutes."

I was at least thirty minutes away.

"Please hurry."

"Stay on the phone," I growl.

The VP looks up as if he might protest as I sling my coat over my shoulder, but Riven nods. *Go.*

As if I need the permission.

I'm already on Riven's bike by the time the man has a moment to open his mouth. The colors of the traffic lights bleed into the rain as I speed down the interstate, weaving in and out of irate drivers. The sounds of their horns melt into the background as I leave them behind, all of it silence compared to the roaring in my ears. He was in her house, meaning he's not there anymore. Or at least Addie thinks he isn't.

My blood runs cold.

I can still hear her in my ear, her quick, labored breathing. She's alive, but there's no guarantee this fucker isn't still in there, waiting for her to turn the wrong corner and then...

"Fuck!"

I swerve as another car lays on their horn while attempting to merge. I'm maybe a minute from her apartment. I can't die now.

"Natalia, what was that?" she whispers.

"Don't worry about it." I grit my teeth against the speed. I've violated plenty of traffic laws at this point, enough that someone has probably called the cops. I make a mental note to have Marco wipe that from their records later. Right now, I have one priority—Addie. Get to Addie, while both of us are still alive. I can worry about dying once I know she's safe.

I barely have time to kill the ignition before I'm sprinting up the stairs, taking them four at a time, my gun drawn. Addie is just outside the door, her face pale, but unharmed as far as I can tell.

"Is Maddy home?"

A shake of her head. "I came home and the door was unlocked. She's at a gallery. There were scratches on the door, and when I went in..."

The roaring grows louder. She went inside without knowing if he was there or not.

"I'll deal with you later," I grind out, and her chin dips

in shame. She already knows without me saying anything. It was a pretty fucking stupid move.

"You stay outside." I fix her with a stern look before letting the barrel of my gun enter the door first.

"Like hell I will." Then, because she knows just what type of weakness she is to me, she adds, "I'd feel safer with you."

Fuck. I can't argue with that.

"Then you stay behind me. Do *not* take your hand off my back. If you do, I'm going to assume someone has you and start shooting."

Her face pales only by a fraction but she nods, dragging her bottom lip between her teeth.

I push the door open, cringing when it creaks. I make a mental note to fix that—or maybe not. If someone breaks in again, it could alert her. Not that there will be another repeat of this incident. Any fucker bold enough to try twice will be dead before his hand even touches the doorknob.

The lights are off when I enter. An image of Addie walking these dark halls and a gloved hand reaching for her floods my mind. I shut it off as quickly as it comes. Addie is behind me, her hand on my back. Her chest brushes just below my shoulder blades. My heartbeat thuds through my ribs.

I clear the hallway first before flicking on the light switch. No use for stealth at this point. If the stalker is still here, he knows we're here too. I'm hunting *him* for once.

Addie's breathing hitches as she takes in the sight of her bedroom in disarray. My jaw clenches so hard it pops.

Her sheets have been ripped from the bed and are strewn across the floor. Anything that might have been on her desk or bedside table lays scattered as well. I check the closet, under the bed, the bathroom. Clear.

Addie's hand leaves my back and my finger alights on the trigger. But when I spin, she's not at my back, nor does the killer have his hands on her.

Addie stands before her vanity mirror, her hands covering her mouth and smothering her gasp. The mirror has been shattered, but that isn't important. I can buy her a new mirror. The horror comes from the photos taped to the broken shards—photos of Addie at her job, at the club, our lunch dates. Then my eyes drift to the ones in the center. A cluster of images of Addie sleeping in her bed with a gloved hand drifting across her face, her arms, all while she sleeps, blissfully unaware.

Addie sinks to her knees, shoulders violently shaking.

Fuck, I haven't cleared the rest of the apartment yet.

"Addie," I plea under my breath. "Addie, come on. The house isn't safe yet. I need you to get up."

My words dissipate in the air when Addie's eyes remain wide and frozen, as if I hadn't spoken at all.

A click comes from Maddy's room.

I raise my gun again. "You, stay here. I'm going to shut this door and clear the rest of the house. No one is in this room. Lock the door and do *not* open it for anyone other than me. Do you understand?"

She manages a small nod, her breathing coming quickly now. She's near hyperventilating, her face going red and body shaking with full tremors. I need to handle this quickly.

Then, without thinking, I press a quick kiss to her temple. "I'll be back for you soon, I promise."

Something in my corroded heart cracks when I see

the hope in those silver-lined eyes—hope at my promise, and trust that I will keep her safe.

She drags her tongue over her lips and inhales shakily. "Okay."

It's small, but it's a start. A part of me knows it isn't just a truce to whatever pissing contest we've been having, but a promise for whatever is brewing between us.

We'll deal with whatever repercussions come with this quiet peace once I make sure the apartment is safe.

I clear the remaining rooms with predatory efficiency. I slip into my killing calm, ready to pull the trigger at any moment now that I know Addie was safely tucked in her room.

The living room. Clear.

The spare bathroom. Clear.

Maddy's room. Untouched.

Anything with Addie's touch on it has been trashed, strewn across the floor, or missing entirely. All of Maddy's stuff is perfectly in order, as if the stalker knew exactly where to look and where she would not be. I tuck that scrap of knowledge away for a later date. Right now, I have to deal with Addie.

I knock on her door. "It's me," I breathe, my heart hammering. "It's safe."

Addie opens the door slowly, her eyes puffy as if she's been crying. Her face is drawn and wan, no usual spark in her blue eyes. The sight nearly breaks my heart.

"Where do we go from here?" she whispers. I know she's not referring to the state of her apartment or the man out there hunting her.

I take the coward's way out, the feeling foreign in my

bones. "You can come stay with me. I'll set up the guest room in my apartment. It's in the company building, so it's the most secure place in the country."

She shakes her head. "I can't leave Maddy. Besides, this place is mine. I won't let some creep drive me away." She presses the heels of her palms into her eyes with a soft groan.

I pull them away and press another kiss to them both, slowly. Meaningfully.

"Then I'll stay here."

CHAPTER 12
ADDIE

"**T**hen I'll stay here."

Natalia's voice is smooth and assured, and yet I still must have heard her wrong.

"What?" I bluster.

She'll stay here? My gaze roams around the small apartment, barely large enough to fit the two people that already live here, let alone a third. Logistically, it won't work, but I can give a million or so illogical reasons more as to why it *really* won't work.

"And we'll need to start you on some training. Weights and self-defense," Natalia muses, her thumb and forefinger pressed to her chin.

My brain pauses on the word, "training," and I cross my arms. Sure, my body boasts some curves and I'm not the most athletic person in the room, but I'm not out of shape. I love my body and all she does for me.

"I'm in perfectly fine shape, thank you very much," I snap. "Besides, being skinny won't solve this."

"I'm not asking you to lose weight. Fuck, you look perfect as you are," Natalia says with a hunger in her eyes. I can read the genuine truth in them, in the way her hands clench at her side as she says it. "It's for strength, not aesthetic."

"Oh, really? What are all those muscles for then?"

Natalia bites back a smile at my pout, quite obviously fighting the urge to flex or show off. "Exactly what I said they were for. I like knowing that my body will do exactly what I say when I say it. I never have to wonder if it'll fail. If you sprained your ankle, would you trust it to hold your weight if you had to run from an attack? What about if running wasn't an option and you had to fight? Could you kick the assailant with enough strength to buy time?"

"That would hurt anyone, regardless of muscle."

"Yes, it would hurt, but that's not what I asked." Natalia pushes her thumb into the soft underside of my chin, forcing me to face her as she speaks. "I asked if you would be strong enough to do it. Would your body hold? Because mine would. I've trained my muscles to hold if the ligaments fail. I've built my body to withstand any attack. Your body needs to be a weapon so you'll never be without one."

My face heats as I can feel every hard line of proof of her work pressing into my softer, more pliable body. She's right. I'm strong, but not strong enough to save myself if, god forbid, she's too late. If I'm on my own.

The thought sends every nerve in my body prickling with unrest. If the stalker had been here when I walked in without Natalia, I would be dead right now. Maddy would have to be the one to find my body when she came home, and I'm not putting her through that.

"So that's what these are for," I murmur, daring to smooth my palms over the expanse of her torso, my fingers ghosting every hard peak of her muscles.

Natalia's hands hold mine in place, her lips curving up, mischief dancing across her features. "Yes, though I'll admit the appearance of them doesn't hurt."

I hum, leaning into the warmth that is Natalia. She smells distinctly of sweat and leather today, and I remember hearing her swear and the squeal of tires on the phone. She wasn't five minutes away earlier. She couldn't have been. And yet she got here all the same.

No one has done as much for me as her, let alone a woman I met only a few months prior.

Natalia continues on, unfazed as my brows furrow. "I'll have Riven bring some of my stuff by tonight. I'll move in, then we're start you in a training program. Once we've developed your core some, we can move on to self-defense."

It doesn't make sense. The more I think about it, the more my throat burns. My father died before I was old enough to face true hardship. When he was alive, it was all sugar treats, bedtime stories, and fuzzy feelings. When I was in high school, my mother started traveling, coming home only often enough to avoid suspicions from the neighbor and police. I was out the door by the stroke of midnight on my eighteenth birthday with a one-way train ticket to the city. I'd saved just enough for the first few months of this apartment with Maddy, scraping and saving every cent I earned from work and birthday cards from distant relatives. I had solved all my problems by myself, and Natalia just happens to waltz in when I finally meet the one problem I can't face alone?

It isn't fair. I didn't work this hard just to rely on someone who hates me. Not until she's honest with me about whatever the fuck this is that is stirring between us.

"Why would you do that?" I freeze, anger rising in my throat. "Why would you do any of this? We aren't friends. We aren't even fuck buddies. I've done nothing but make problems for you while you've done *everything* for me."

"Because I want to."

"Why?" I press.

I know this is the moment that will change every-thing, but I can't let go until she releases the answer to the question we've both been asking.

Silence. Nothing but silence and the burning that scorches my skin with embarrassment.

I knew I didn't make it up. The tension strung taut between us is more than just sexual—we both know it. I guess I'm just not worth enough to admit it. I not worth enough to give her a weakness to be exploited. I can't say I don't understand, but it hurts all the same.

I don't ask a second time, just walk towards the door with the full intention of throwing her out. Damn the fact that she had came all the way here and saved me. Damn the fact that she's still trying to save me, from both herself and this stalker. I care too much at this point to let myself fall any further, but as I reach out to fling open the door, her fingers lace around my wrists.

"Because you're mine," she breathes.

"What?"

It's killing her to admit it. The turmoil on her face is evident, her neck flexing as she swallows against the strain. "I've wanted you since I met you. It was the way you blushed before blatantly challenging me. How you could cry so easily, then call me a fucking moron in the next breath. This," she says, gesturing between us, "is no longer a want. You're a need."

I didn't expect this. Not the way her throat bobs as she admits she wants me, as if the fact terrifies her. Not how her eyes mist like some memory is taking her away from here.

My hands tremble as I lift them to cup her face. "But the stalker. He could come after you." *After he kills me.*

Natalia's lips lift in an arrogant smirk. "He'd be dead before he could try."

"And if he came again for *me*?"

That smirk disappears as quickly as it formed. Every line of her jaw is hard set as she searches my face with such intensity, my knees begin to wobble. "You're mine. And no coward who hides behind a burner phone is going to take you from me. Not through fear or death. You are *mine.*"

I inhale shakily. "But are you mine?"

"I'm yours just as the moon is the sun's. There's no light in my world aside from you."

The look of adoration Natalia shines my ways is just as poetic as the words she speaks, and I find myself grasping for her hand.

"I want you here in the light. With me."

I expect her to smirk and make some other analogy,

say that creatures like her are meant for the dark. But instead, she smiles and interlaces our fingers.

"Who am I to disobey the sun?"

CHAPTER 13

ADDIE

Unknown: All you've done is piss me off, whore. What comes next is on your head.

Maddy is awfully smiley for someone whose apartment was just broken into. I suppose it helps that none of her stuff was touched, but she still seems too joyful over this situation.

She kneels in our living room, clad in pink, rubber gardening gloves that go up to her elbows as she plucks larger glass shards from our carpet. I frown. My stalker had broken one of my favorite picture frames.

Bastard.

Natalia is in the shower. Riven had bumped into Maddy on the way up and dropped off some of her clothes. *That* Mads was not so smiley about. After long-winded ramblings about how it was a "shame for God to give such a pretty face to such an ass," she presented Natalia the clothes and told her to get in the shower because she smelled like tire rubber. Natalia did not protest, but promised to help us clean once she was out.

"Are you sure you're okay with her staying here?" I ask for what must be the fifth time.

"Yep." Mads grins, flipping me a thumbs-up. "Besides, it's not permanent. We'll find your stalker, you two will fall in love, get married, and move into a big, beautiful house with an extra tiny house in the backyard for me."

"Oh, is that so? And what if you marry Donovan first?"

That smile slips if only for a moment before it's planted back on her face. "Then I'll build our house next to yours and connect them via a path of secret underground tunnels."

A house connected to Donovan's? No, thanks.

I busy myself with righting our coffee table that had been overturned. Seriously, it's as if this guy just wanted to make a mess. What could I have been hiding underneath the single leg of a coffee table that would warrant flipping the whole thing?

The door to my bathroom creaks open and steam blows out with it, carrying a musky, spicy scent. Natalia steps out moments later, her blunt bob still damp and clinging to her high cheekbones. She's dressed in a tight black shirt and dark sweatpants, a look I've never seen on her before.

And holy hell, does she look divine.

Mads pokes me with her socked foot and winks before loudly announcing that she's starving and is going to step into the other room to order a pizza.

Once she's gone, I rise to meet Natalia where she stands in my kitchen making a coffee. The back of her shirt is warm as I rest my face against it, wrapping my arms around her waist. She's still a good foot taller than me, and I land at the base of her shoulder blades, feeling sheltered against her.

Her chuckle vibrates through me before she spins, leaning against the counter with her arms around me so that I'm cradled against her.

"You look good dressed like this," I murmur.

It's still surreal even hours later to see Natalia in my home, dressed down and holding me like I'm something precious.

Unable to resist, I lean up on my toes to press a sweet kiss against her mouth.

Admittedly, things got hot and heavy after Natalia's confession earlier. We didn't go past making out, but I was situated on the kitchen counter with my legs wrapped around Natalia's midsection when Mads walked through the door.

This kiss is nothing like that, nor the moment we shared at the club a few months ago. This is slow and tender, and Natalia takes her time exploring every inch of the kiss. I smile against her lips at her hum of contentment, letting my hands tangle in her dark hair.

"Oh gag, I only left for a few minutes." Mads laughs with a devilish light in her eye. "Pizza will be up any minute."

I blush but don't bother to step from Natalia's arms. Instead, I rest my head against her chest, folding my arms between us.

Natalia presses another kiss to my temple, then leans down to whisper in my ear, "We'll be finishing that later."

Natalia's words from earlier have been bouncing around in my head ever since I stepped into my darkened bedroom. I took a shower after cleaning up dinner, telling Natalia she could take my bed tonight. Maddy has already gone to sleep and I just need to grab some pajamas now.

Clad only in a towel, my hair damp down my back, I gently push the bedroom door open. I assume Natalia is asleep already after the busy day, given the silence, and creep towards my dresser in the dark.

Her hands wrap around my waist from behind me. "Are you trying to avoid me?"

"I thought you were sleeping," I admit. "I didn't want to wake you."

"I'm not waiting in your bed for a friendly sleepover."

"Oh, so we aren't just really good friends?"

All of my wit dies when I catch sight of Natalia's face, her sharp features outlined in the dim room. Her nearly black eyes darken as if they're pools that seeped from hell itself. Her voice is dangerously low as she leans close to my face, her lips brushing the shell of my ear. "I am going to fuck the word 'friend' from those pretty lips."

I tut my tongue. Dangerous—this is dangerous territory I'm edging towards, but I don't care. I love the thrill, the pit that forms in my stomach as I lean into her side. I can feel every inch of toned muscle stiffen at contact. "What are you waiting for then?"

Her grip is rough as she grabs my hips, spinning me so that I face her now. My towel falls away at the motion, falling to the floor around my ankles.

A low noise of approval settles at the back of Natalia's throat as she takes me in, her eyes trailing a slow path up my body. "Bed, now," she growls. "Before I take you right here."

I want to tell her she can take me anywhere at this point, but my mouth has gone dry. I gotten a taste of what tonight promises back in the club office, but this is all new territory. There is no threat of someone walking in and Natalia can take as long as she wants with me.

Once we make it to the bed, she lifts her shirt over her head, revealing two perfect breasts and her toned stomach. Anxiety flips in my chest. She's perfect, so fucking perfect, and I—

Well, I probably resemble a wet rat.

Natalia doesn't seem to notice, not as she finishes pulling off the rest of her clothes and crawls to meet me on the bed. Every inch of her is tanned perfection, and I feel my searing want wash over any trace of anxiety that lingers.

"I've been picturing you in these silk sheets since the day I met you," Natalia whispers against my skin, dipping her head between my breasts. "I want to see your curls on my pillow with you wearing nothing beneath me, while I give you pleasure like you've never known."

Desire coils tight in my core and my back arches off the bed as she closes her teeth around one of my nipples, then soothes the small hurt with her tongue. She swirls it over the stiffened bud while one of her hands trails lower. I let out a soft moan, and that hand immediately snaps up to cover my mouth.

"Quiet," she whispers, bringing her face close to mine. "Don't want to wake the roommate, now, do we?"

I bite down on my lip, and Natalia smiles.

"Good girl."

The praise goes straight to my arousal, and Natalia settles herself between my legs, that hand trailing lower towards where I want her. At the first sweep of her thumb across my clit, I buck my hips.

"You come when I say you can, or do I need to tie you down?"

She nearly laughs at the eager flush across my face. The wicked glint in her eye tells me I can expect something like that next time. Her fingers squeeze around my wrists, pinning me in place while she hikes my leg over her shoulder. Then after one final squeeze, she brings both hands to grip my ass and dips her head between my thighs.

I bite into my arm to keep from swearing at the first flick of her tongue. Tasting. Taunting. She alternates speeds, from sucking to stroking, and at one point, grazing her teeth ever so gently across the sensitive bud. I can feel release taut in my core when a soft moan escapes my lips and Natalia pulls away entirely. I nearly whine when she fixes me with a stern glance.

I clamp my mouth shut. Anything to get her back between my legs when release is so close. But she rises and crawls towards me until her legs are on either side of me.

"Something tells me you'll have trouble following my instructions," she breathes, then crashes her lips to mine right as she plunges her fingers into my center. Her kisses swallow my moan and she nips at my lip as she pumps her fingers in, then out again.

She groans against my mouth as if she's going to

devour me, and that is my undoing. I reach for her as my own release crashes through me. Our legs are entwined, my fingers stretching between her legs. Her skin feels like sin on mine and I can't resist reaching my other hand up to palm her breast.

"Fuck," she swears at the friction, but leans into my touch. I memorize her body by heart, searing every little noise she makes into my brain and what exactly I did to elicit such a response. I commit to memory the view as her head lolls back when she comes over my hand, and the taste of her neck as I kiss her through it.

When we untangle ourselves, Natalia's arms cage me against her, her heartbeat echoing against my own. "That was perfect," she breathes. "You're perfect."

I'm glad the darkness hides my blush. The woman was just inside me, for fuck's sake, and I'm blushing because she called me perfect.

Sex has always been a gamble with me. Either it's amazing or goes down in burning flames. I always second-guess myself—am I doing it right? Did that noise I just made sound too weird?

There was none of that with Natalia, only want and the need for her touch. I've never felt a desire so strong before. I need to be more than inside her. I need to be with her always, our sounds entwined, her breath my breath. I've never felt that for anyone, and it should scare the shit out of me.

But it doesn't.

In fact, it's the opposite. I snuggle deeper into her side, savoring the feel of her dark hair tickling my face and the way her long fingers trace shapes on my hip. If I could have this every night for the rest of my life, I could die happy.

"Makes me wish I hadn't stormed out back at the club," I agree.

Natalia laughs at that, and the sound turns my insides to goo. Seriously, I've only known the woman for a few months and this is the hold she has on me. The thought is as terrifying as it is lovely.

"I'm here now." She kisses the top of my head. "And I'm not going anywhere."

"I'd like that." I yawn despite myself.

Natalia's hand comes up to smooth the curls on the back of my head. "Sleep. I'll be here."

As exhaustion claims my consciousness, I know she means more than what she said, and I drift off to sleep feeling untouchable.

CHAPTER 14

ADDIE

Unknown: The hands you fuck her with are slick with that girl's blood. And the next. And the next.

"Another young girl has been reported missing. Dina Saffron, aged twenty-three, went out with a group of friends two nights ago only to never return to her apartment. Her roommates called the police, and as of this morning, authorities have officially ruled her as a missing person. With this being the third girl to go missing in the past few months, there are concerns that they may be connected and that there might be a serial killer on the loose. Authorities caution—"

I switch the television off with a heavy sigh. I heard about the other two girls and, like others, assumed it was just another unfortunate incident that befell a young woman. I slept with the baseball bat by my door and Maddy curled at my side those nights, but then continued on with my life as if nothing had happened. But a serial killer?

My mind flicks to my stalker. There's no way there's a connection. The media would have mentioned it. Their friends would have reported if the girls were being harassed or stalked before their abductions. The other two girls had been found dead, though, and if they had been stalked beforehand...

No.

No more thoughts of murder, stalkers, or the mess that is my life. Sundays are for my sacred couch-potato rituals, nothing else.

I take one day a week off from work but still follow a rigorous schedule. I'm more productive that way, a better functioning human. Just like every other Sunday, I sleep in, make myself a brunch of pancakes and a latte, then sit down to work on my manuscript. Later on, I bake and settle down with a good book, then treat myself to take-out. Maddy generally spends Sundays with her family and Natalia won't be home until later, so I have the whole apartment to myself to reenergize and prepare for the week.

As the afternoon crawls on, I settle for baking chocolate chip cookies, but with a twist. Mine are made with chopped Hershey's Kisses and the top is dusted with extra sugar sprinkles. Just looking at them would give a dentist a hernia.

I'm elbow-deep in cookie dough when a hollow rattle comes from the door. I blow a stray hair from my face. I'm covered in flour by this point, the white dust coating my curls and my loose-fitting top.

The knocking grows louder.

Screw it. Brushing my hands off on my jeans, I slide the lock out of place and pop the door open. Marco stands at the far end of the hall with a faint smile in my direction, but the face peering down at mine is less than friendly.

"Donovan," I say coolly. I pop my hip out against the door frame, bracing my weight against it.

"Addie," he responds with equal aloofness. "Can I come in?"

It wasn't a question.

Marco shoots me a warning look, his thick face now pinched with concern. *Should I remove him*? he mouths.

I shake my head at the man, and Donovan traces my gaze.

"You can call your guard dog off. I'm here to drop off some stuff Madeline left at my place," he says, holding up a bag that, from the sequins to the pink velvet, just screamed *Mads*.

"Fine."

"Wonderful." He brushes past me, making a pointed note to stare down his nose at me. He came dressed in one of his cheap suits that he gets dry-cleaned to appear more posh than he is. He breezes by my kitchen, ignoring the mess I've made on the counter, and settles on my couch.

"What are you doing?" I press, crossing my arms over my chest.

It's no secret between us that I don't care for Donovan. I made it clear enough to him after the first date when he honked for Maddy to come to his car. I nearly tore him a new one.

"You look a mess." He shoots a pointed gaze towards

my flour-dusted clothes. I narrow my gaze even further, especially when his eyes trail upwards towards where my shirt has dipped just a centimeter too low.

"You came to drop the stuff off. You've dropped it off, you can go now."

I hadn't intended to share my afternoon with anyone. Sunday afternoons are my quiet time where I can bake, read my smutty little romance novels unbothered, then spend hours in the bubble bath until my fingers turn pruny. Sundays are not for entertaining Donovan and his leering eyes.

"I'd rather wait for Madeline."

"I'd rather you not," I hiss between clenched teeth. "Maddy doesn't get back from her parents' for a few more hours and I have no intention of spending my day off with you."

"*Tsk*. So hostile."

"Only to those who deserve it," I seethe again. "We both know the way you treat Maddy isn't right, but she's my best friend, so I'll play nice in front of her if that's what she wants, but I made no promises to coddle you when she isn't around. So get out, before I call in that 'guard dog' out there."

Donovan remains sitting, holding my glare just long enough to have me shifting uncomfortably under his scrutiny. Then he rises, shoves the bag into my hands, and stalks towards the door. "Enjoy your cookies." He shuts the door hard enough to send the hinges rattling.

I drop the bag on the couch and head back to my dough. It takes a few moments for my hackles to lower, then I slam my mixing bowl against the table. "That motherfucker!" I seethe.

That's it. The zen of my sacred Sunday afternoon has officially been shattered.

The door cracks, and Marco peeks tentatively into my apartment. "Trouble in paradise?"

"Ha! He wishes," I scoff drily. "That's just Maddy's slimy boyfriend. God, I'd hang him by his dick from a flagpole if I could. Bastard."

Marco laughs through a cringe, subtly shifting his frame behind the door. "I hear cookies help with that," he says, nodding to my dough that's warming in the bowl.

I laugh, genuinely this time, tensions lowering. "I'll be sure to sneak some out to you when they're done. Thank you, Marco."

He nods, then grins that boyish grin that makes him look less like the seasoned killer I know he is.

The door clicks shut gently and I force my jaw to unclench. Drop my shoulders. *Inhale. Exhale.*

Before long, the scent of freshly baked chocolate chip cookies have finally replaced that of Donovan's cheap cologne. I inhale deeply, relaxed again. Once they cool, I transfer them to a plate and slip them out the door.

The clock blinks six o'clock from atop my bedside table when I hear shifting outside. Another rasp at the door, this one lighter and less demanding.

Riven's smirking face greets me. Balancing from his index finger are the handles of my precious Italian take-out. "You know this place is trash, right?" he hums with mock disapproval. "I could make better, and I burn toast."

"I'll ask you next time then, but for now, this is cheap

and yummy, thank you very much." I pluck the bag from his taunting grip.

He shrugs with a genuine smile lifting the corners of his full lips.

I don't know how Mads hadn't jumped this guy yet. Donovan would look like a shrimp standing next to Riven. Actually, he would look like a greasy shrimp next to the average man, and next to Riven, he would look like a gutter rat. Maybe I need to organize an intervention, especially after today.

I don't care what Riven said, my dinner is delicious. You can never go wrong with carbs and cheese, especially when garlic is thrown in the mix. I'm munching on my fourth cookie, bordering on a sugar crash, when my phone begins to buzz. I've grown less fearful of my ringtone since Natalia blocked all contactless callers, but still, I flinch at the first few notes of a pop song. The artist sings about the joys of going out in your twenties while I sit on my couch with takeout and cookie crumbs on my shirt. A joy, indeed, I think as I crack open a bottle of merlot.

I almost ignore the call until I see Natalia's name flashing across the screen. On the last ring, I swipe my thumb across the screen and put her on speaker.

Her low, sweet voice comes through from the other line immediately. "I heard you had a visitor today."

I roll my eyes. Always straight to the point when my safety is involved.

I take a sip, the wine not tasting great with my cookies but I'm beyond caring. "It was just Donovan, Maddy's boyfriend. He needed to drop something off," I say, trailing off and debating leaving out the detail of him wanting to stay until Mads got home. He hadn't asked to do that before, but it wasn't entirely out of character for him. He expects the world to revolve around his schedule, his wants. I take great pleasure in disrupting that order he craves.

She catches on quick—too quick. "But?"

I sigh, and before long, I'm recounting the entire interaction over the phone.

Natalia is silent on the other end until she speaks again, her voice gravely like cold death. "Did he hurt you?"

"Donovan?" I nearly laugh. "God, no. The man is as spineless as they come. I sometimes wonder how he became a lawyer. Must be the power of Daddy's money."

"Addie."

"No, he didn't hurt me. He was just... weird. Pushy. He's relatively harmless, unless you account for the rise in my blood pressure when he's near. And it was uncomfortable enough being alone with him for five minutes, I would *not* want to spend hours with him waiting for Maddy to get home."

Donovan is harmless for the most part. He's loud in a quiet way, the kind of disturbance where his voice is like a screeching car brake, but still soft and aloof. He's an asshole, for sure, and it takes serious effort not to break his nose whenever he's near, but he's not a physical threat.

"Do you want me to kill him?" Natalia asks.

I laugh. She could, I know that much, judging not only by her profession but the finely sculpted muscles I've had the mouthwatering honor of seeing. Natalia killing Donovan is no issue on paper, but still, the thought does not settle well with me.

"No, you don't need to do that. Like I said, harmless, just aggravating. But," I say slyly, "if you wanted to partake in my schemes to get Maddy to leave him, I won't protest."

"Oh? And what would that entail?" Humor highlights her voice, and I smirk.

"Is Riven single?"

Natalia chokes.

CHAPTER 15
ADDIE

Unknown: Would you rather I kill you and make this easier on both of us? Your play, Addie.

"Again," Riven rasps, easily avoiding my oncoming jab.

When Natalia mentioned picking up self-defense classes, I didn't think she meant I would be taking them with Riven. It isn't an issue, of course—I like the man well enough—but it would have been nicer to embarrass myself in front of a stranger rather than this hulking weapon of a man.

"Stop using your fists," he barks, dodging another swing. "You'll break your hand if you go in punching. Use your elbows or your knee. Your fists should be your last resort unless you want to fracture all your bones."

"Boxers use their fists."

"Boxers are trained, and probably used to a few broken bones. If you want to last long enough in the fight, you need to sustain minimal injuries. Knees and elbows are like shock absorbers, and they'll hurt like a bitch."

"I've seen you use *your* fists," I bite back.

"Do as I say not as I do. Now, again!"

We've been at this for nearly an hour now, and every muscle in my body aches and groans at me to stop. Sweat pours from between my shoulder blades, crawling down the nape of my neck and licking every vertebra of my spine. Riven, on the other hand, looks as if he just came in from a light stroll. His face is hardly gleaming with sweat, his dark strands of hair laying loosely across his forehead, damp with a light layer of perspiration.

"Where should you be striking?" he calls out again, his voice thick with amusement. Asshole.

In one quick motion, I drive my knee between his legs, a cheap shot that has him sprawling on the ground in surprise.

"Groin, eyes, underarms, and throat," I list, enunciating each letter of the word "groin," as if tasting the words.

Riven rises, a breathy laugh upon his lips even as he winces. "Not bad for a first session. Just don't be prepared to land another hit on me for a long while."

"Why? Because I'm a novice?"

"Because now I know not to underestimate you." He crosses his arms. "I just spent this entire session watching and analyzing your every move. I know when you're going to strike, when you'll wait, and what moves make you insecure. If that fight was real, I would have known in a few seconds just how to pin and kill you."

"Aw, congratulations. Want your alphahole award?"

Riven's eyes shutter. "This isn't a game, Addie. We'll

work on making you less predictable in time, but for now, go home and rest."

He's right—annoyingly so, but right, nonetheless. He slings an arm over my shoulder and passes my water bottle my way. I accept, taking grateful swigs from the teal bottle. The cool water runs over my lips and down the thin column of my throat, mingling with my sweat. Riven chuckles, a low and dangerous sound. He removes his arm from my shoulders the moment we step into the sticky wall of heat outside, and walks me the few blocks back to my apartment.

As I stomp up the stairs I pause at the sleek black camera mounted to the wall. That is certainly new, and far too nice to exist in a place like this.

I nod my thanks to Riven once I reach my door and pluck my keys from my pocket, nearly groaning in relief at the wave of cool air that slams into my body when I enter my apartment. Natalia sits atop one of the bar stools, her legs crossed smoothly as she intently studies a document on her computer screen.

In the past few weeks, she's made herself at home in our apartment. Mads doesn't mind the company, so long as we keep our more intimate activities quiet and Natalia continues to make delicious food for dinner.

"Hey," I hum, leaning up against the counter next to her. "When did the new security cameras get put up? I saw them as I came in."

"Last night?" she says it as if it is a question, rolling her tongue inside her mouth.

My brows pinch. "Weird. The owner is normally pretty fiscal and stingy about these sorts of things."

"Not anymore." Natalia grins impishly, shifting slightly to face away from me.

Weird.

I come up behind her and wrap my arms around her shoulders. "What did you do?"

"I... bought the apartment complex."

A breath.

What?

"You *what*?"

Natalia's smug face crumbles into confusion. "Your landlord refused to update the security system. Granted, he made the legal adjustments necessary, but this place is still only one step ahead of a human trafficking hub. I mean, the amount of stairs that lead directly to halls with blind corners and the gaps in the security footage?" Natalia scoffs, lost in her own world now. "So I bought the place from him and made the changes myself. Your neighbors came by earlier with thank you cookies."

"I—"

Frustration rises in my throat. *Un-fucking-believable.* After all my long-winded spiels on how this apartment is the first thing that has truly been mine, and how, for my sanity, I need to stay here? While my life is falling apart, I need to hold on to this constant, the one thing that I have accomplished in my life.

Then Natalia waltzes in and takes it all.

"I don't get why you're upset."

"Because normal people don't just buy apartment complexes when they have an issue with the landlord!"

"Have I ever promised you normal?"

I don't have a response to that, so I just throw my hands in the air with a guttural sound that borders on animalistic before stepping into the bathroom and locking the door.

One deep breath.

Two.

The shower faucet creaks as I turn the water on as hot as it will go. I step into the steady stream while it's still cold, goosebumps speckling my skin.

Tears prick at the corners of my eyes. It feels wrong to be upset. Natalia is trying to keep me safe, and clearly, everyone else in the building appreciates her efforts. She made this place safer. She did a good thing.

And yet she violated one of the first boundaries I gave her. This space was mine, and now it is actually hers.

Deep breaths.

I turn my face to the water, letting it stream over my face and down my body. Sweat is soon replaced by warm water and lemon-scented suds. I inhale deeply to calm the roaring in my head as I force myself to think it through again.

By the time I wrap myself in a robe and my hair is in a towel, Natalia is still seated at the counter, pouring over her computer. I pull out two stools at our kitchen table and stare pointedly until she takes the hint, stalking over to plop into the chair opposite of me.

"We need to lay some ground rules here," I say, lacing my fingers like an upset parent. "First rule, when I set a boundary, you need to respect it."

Natalia frowns. "And if it compromises your safety?"

"Tough shit. You talk it out with me first."

She swallows thickly. "Next rule?"

I blink. I didn't think she would agree so quickly.

Clearing my throat, I lean back leisurely in the chair.

"Second rule, we split time between my apartment and yours. This space is too crowded, and it isn't fair to Maddy."

"And you want to leave her alone?"

"No, that's rule three." I breathe again. Since when did the air have so much less oxygen? "If Maddy is alone, I want Riven or Marco with her. I'm almost always with you now, and when I'm not, I'm with her. She's already probably been identified as a way to get to me, so I need to know she's safe too."

"Do you want someone attached to your parents too?"

I shake my head. "My dad is dead and my mom is somewhere in Europe right now. She comes home maybe once a year, and that happened already roughly..." I pause, doing the math in my head. "Two months ago? Right before I met you, actually, so we should be set for at least ten more months."

Natalia inhales sharply, as if just now noticing the lack of family photos lining the walls. There are a few photos of me and my dad in my room when I was a kid, maybe one of my mom. Mostly any pictures hung are of me and Maddy, the occasional friends we hung out with. We don't know too many other people in the city, just odd acquaintances, but we've never found the need for other people.

"I'm sorry. I should have thought. I just—" She runs her hand through her short hair and I resist the urge to reach out and touch it. "I can't handle the thought of you getting hurt. Every moment I fail to catch this guy is another moment you're in danger."

I blow out a laugh. "Well, catch him faster then."

Natalia fixes me with a stern look, digging her toe into my calf under the table. "That's not funny."

"I can either laugh or cry." I shrug. "And I've cried too much lately."

That sets her mouth in a hard line. Displeasure lights her face but she says nothing, instead just filing that tidbit of knowledge I've ceded into her brain, storing it for later.

"Riven is an ass," I finally say to change the subject, rummaging through the cupboard for a snack. My stomach rumbles in complaint at my decision to shower before eating after that workout. Maddy just bought these pancake-mix-in-a-cup things that are actually pretty good, and I pop one into the microwave.

Natalia wrinkles her nose but again says nothing. "I'm glad you're now realizing this," she laughs drily. "But he's good at what he does."

I hum in agreement. My body might be one step away from shutting down in a storm of fatigue and lactic acid, but I feel accomplished. I know I'm somewhat safer than before, too, my own weak body no longer a prison.

"So about you moving into my apartment..."

"Part time," I correct, smiling mouth full of pancake. "And let's save that for later."

"Fair enough." She throws her hands above her head in surrender.

With my snack now in hand, I wander back to sit beside her. Her laptop is open to blueprints I don't recognize. There are electronic stickie notes all over the thing, some with paragraphs written on them and others that just say, *NO* in bold letters.

"Are you building an underground bunker?"

"No, that would be easier," she groaned. "My company has an event coming up soon. I'm trying to organize everything now that we have a venue. The VP of the Morgan group can't sit by the Jordan family because he has a thing for the president's wife, and the wife can't be sat near anyone because she has a thing for everyone."

"Even you?" I ask with a raised eyebrow.

Natalia rolls her eyes in response before clicking off of the page. "Don't you have work soon?"

I check my watch. Fuck.

Natalia catches my stool as I push it over in a mad dash for my bedroom. I totally forgot Maddy and I agreed to cover the afternoon shift for some of our more tolerable coworkers. Quickly throwing on my work shirt, the white one that I finally got the blood stain out of, I run to bang on Maddy's door.

"I know!" is the panicked response from the other side.

Natalia huffs in amusement. "Come on, I'll give you two a ride.

CHAPTER 16
ADDIE

Unknown: Nothing will stop me from making you mine.

I hate Donovan, hate him more than I've ever hated anyone. However, I love spending his money.

Maddy stole her boyfriend's credit card this morning and promised me a day of best friend bonding at Lunaluc, our favorite spa. I use the word "stole" loosely. She batted her pretty eyelashes a few times and he handed the card over with no complaints—no verbal complaints anyway, just a stiff nod in my direction.

Mads inspects her pretty white nails. She got them shorter than she usually does, something about almost scratching her eye out on accident the other night. I melt into the massage chair, letting the machine work out all the tension in my upper back.

"Have you found a dress yet?" she asks.

"Actually, I'm ahead of things for once. I've got a black

dress in the back of my closet that I've been saving," I reply, taking a small sip from my champagne flute.

Natalia has this big company event coming up, an anniversary gala celebrating ten years since she founded it. I was a little off on my initial guess on her age, and found out through a quick Google search that she's actually twenty-eight. Our age gap is small and doesn't concern me. No, what's more surprising is how she was only eighteen when she founded Mancini Security. I hadn't fully realized how young she was until I saw the number ten in front of the words "year" and "anniversary." Ten years ago, I was thirteen, still writing fan fiction and *picking* a random boy to have a crush on so I wouldn't be the only girl without a date to the eighth-grade formal.

"I found one yesterday. It's one I bought for an event that I wound up calling in sick to."

"Donovan coming?"

Mads shakes her head. "He was going to, but something came up at work."

I nod, doing my best to try to appear sympathetic. The only reason Donovan would have even considered coming was for the networking opportunities. Then again, if he had come, Natalia might have done well on her threat to kill him.

Not that I wouldn't enjoy the sight. I think.

My phone buzzes in my pocket as we leave, the vibration tone telling me not to answer.

Mads frowns, eyeballing my ringing shorts. "You're still getting texts?"

I sigh and pull up the text thread under "Unknown." "Every day. And letters, but Riven and Marco collect those and take them for evidence reasons. I don't even look anymore."

That's a lie. I look at every message and wish I hadn't every time.

"I know it's expensive, but why not get a new phone?"

I cringe. "This *is* a new phone. He got this number too."

Mads swears lowly, her steps faltering next to mine for a second. "I just hate how you have to sit around and wait for this guy to show up. It's not fair. I'm sorry."

My hands smooth over my arms, brushing down the hairs that have begun to raise and the goosebumps despite the summer heat. "It's okay."

It's not, and we both know it.

But Mads has a point. Why am I sitting on my hands waiting for my stalker to arrive at his convenience? Why aren't we baiting him and drawing him out? I've completed enough self-defense lessons with Riven now to know how to handle myself should something go wrong, and Natalia or Marco could easily take him out if they were with me.

Then there's the reason I haven't asked—the fact that Natalia will shoot down the idea in an instant.

But she doesn't have to know, right?

Maddy has a date with Donovan tonight and Natalia said she would be working late on something. She didn't say what, but I heard that a fourth girl has gone missing, and she probably knows something the news doesn't. If I could just sneak past Marco...

Marco doesn't so much as blink when I tell him I'll be spending the night at Natalia's apartment tonight. I've stayed over a few times now, mostly on Maddy's date nights so she and Donovan can have our apartment when they want it. Natalia will still have someone stationed outside to keep an eye on her for me, but they won't follow me if they think Marco is.

I smooth down my blouse and fight the urge to pick at my skirt. I've gone over my plan in my mind more times than I can count, but my nerves threaten to eat away at me regardless.

I steal a glance around the bar. There's a few people tonight, not enough to cause a stampede if something is to go down but just enough to have witnesses. My phone lays open atop the counter.

Me: I'm at Silver Crossings. Alone.

Ripples form in the liquid of my drink as my hands shake, and I'm forced to set it down. This has to be one of my riskier plans, but I refuse to wait for him to find and kill me. When he shows up, I'll text Natalia, Marco, and Riven, and see who gets here first to handle him. My money is on Natalia, but I'll keep him occupied in the meantime.

"Come here alone?"

The voice is smooth and cold, the type you would hear in old movies. It doesn't match his youthful face, and he can't be more than a year older than I am.

I switch my phone off and plaster a smile across my

face to cover my nerves and peer up at him. He's tall, broad-shouldered, and has a grin that tells me he knows just how attractive he is.

I shrug, feigning nonchalance. "Just for tonight." I will buttery confidence and seduction into my tone.

The man's eyes flit to my phone then back to my face before he settles on the stool beside me. "Addie, right? You work at Tella's."

My heart thunders in my chest.

"Yes," I say slowly.

My stalker extends his hand with a smile that shows all his teeth. "Ryan. Large cappuccino, triple shot of espresso."

That takes me aback for a moment. Ryan. I don't remember his name but I know his order. He's been a regular for a few months now, not too long before I received my first text message. Come to think of it, he was at Tella's the day I met Natalia.

"Yes! I remember you now. Ryan." I roll his name over my tongue. My mouth tastes like ash and my stomach begins to roil.

Now that I'm facing my stalker, I don't know how to feel. I always pictured a slimy man with greasy hair and a pale face that's constantly lit by the glow of a cellphone in a dark room. Maybe he'd wear a gray hoodie with suspicious stains on it. But Ryan seems normal enough, if you can overlook his heart attack of a coffee order. He wears a clean cotton shirt and casual blue jeans, and looks like he takes care of his appearance. He could be an actor in a Hallmark movie, for god's sake, not some *Matrix*-esque crime show.

Yet he sent a dead bird to my house. Broke in, and

made several threats against my life. He texts me incessantly, saying all the horrid things he wants to do to me. I can see Ryan sending the vaguer threats I've received, but I can't match his face to the one I got last night saying he'd stab Natalia then fuck me with the knife.

I hardly notice him getting his own drink until he offers a toast.

"To unlikely meetings," he says while the glasses clink merrily.

Unlikely, my ass.

I swallow a large sip and steel my nerves. I slip my phone into my pocket at the last second. It's one of those hidden pockets that women's jeans sometimes have. There's no way I'm letting Ryan grab it and take away my only contact with help.

The bartender brings out another drink right as Ryan lays his hand on my thigh, the conversation turning from friendly to flirting at some point in the night. What time is it? When did so many people leave?

My forefinger presses into my temple, a headache already blossoming. In the back of my mind, I register Ryan paying for my tab and helping me from my stool to a car out back.

Don't leave me with him! Call for help! my brain screams at the other unknowing patrons. But my lips won't form the words, and my muscles drag like lead against my bones. I can barely hold my head up, let alone put up a fight.

My drink.

He put something in my drink.

Fuck, I should have thought of this. I'm an idiot. I'm a...

I'm in the back seat of his car, somewhere on the highway from the looks of the lights. I don't know how long I'm out for, nor where we are. Slowly, my fingers inch behind me to my back pocket where I find my phone. Lifting my gaze, I try to find the door lock through blurry eyes and streaking lights.

My head clears a bit at this small victory, enough that panic starts to creep back in. I'm alone, in my stalker's car, being taken god knows where.

I sit up slowly, careful not to make a sound. Not that Ryan notices. He's busy on his phone, talking to someone with a tone that says he knows he's about to get what he wants. I can hardly distinguish the words, something about bringing a girl home and that he'd be late for something tomorrow. Trying to piece the words together make my already pounding head *throb*. I look out the window. Fast—we're going too fast. Ryan is staying just slow enough to not get pulled over but still drives with urgency, his eyes darting the sides of the highway.

I follow is gaze to see trees lining the sides of the road. There's plenty of other cars on the street, but not a single building in sight. That's not too uncommon around here, but we could be on any number of highways going in or out of the city. The thought has my stomach churning with anxiety. If I scream can someone hear? Probably not from their cars.

He turns on his blinker and I spot the exit sign. He's leaving the city.

No.

No, no, no, no.

Without thinking, I throw open the door closest to the side of the road.

Ryan drops his phone, craning his neck in shock. "Don't—"

It's too late. I jump.

I should have known jumping out of a moving car would hurt. I should have, and yet the pain still takes me by surprise as the asphalt tears all the skin from my knees, my hands, my legs. I roll down into a grassy ditch, dirt and gas-covered grass sticking to my bloody limbs.

Ryan peels off, not even bothering to stop and see if I'm still alive. He won't, not when the police see the traffic cameras and ask what he did to make me jump out of a speeding car.

I grit my teeth against the building sob in my throat as I flex my wrists, then my ankles and legs, double-checking that I didn't break anything. My wrist smarts and sports a new purple bruise, but shows no signs of being otherwise broken. A sprain at worst, a nuisance at best.

Headlights blur past in spears of light that burn my eyes. My vision remains fogged from the drug in my system, whatever it was. Blindly, I fumble for my phone in my back pocket. Gone.

Searching on my hands and knees, I dig my fingers into the musky ground before they wrap around something solid.

And completely shattered.

"Please turn on, please..."

The phone turns on.

My fingers fly across the screen, punching in a number I know by heart now.

Natalia answers on the first ring. "Where the hell are you?" she all but growls. "I come home to Marco saying he expected you here, and Maddy saying you're not at your apartment. I swear to god, Addie—"

"I don't know where I am," I whisper. I hate the way my voice cracks and how the shattered glass of my phone screen scratches against my cheek as I hold it with trembling hands.

Natalia goes quiet, then breathes in a voice like cold death. "I'm tracking your phone. Stay on the line."

"He was trying to leave the city. I jumped near the exit, but he was going so fast and I think I rolled down towards the woods. I'm in a ditch so it'll be hard to see me, and I think I might have hit my head?" The last part comes out more as a question than a statement but Natalia doesn't question it. I can hear the tires of her car squealing and Riven's voice in the background. He's shouting at someone.

Marco.

Guilt coils in my gut. I didn't think about how this would affect him, and he's been so kind to me. I'm a lousy friend, if that's what we are.

"Do *not* move. We're almost there."

I don't think I could force my body to move if I wanted to. Not that I would tell Natalia that. Instead, I let myself fall back, laying my head against the wet grass and trying to focus on anything other than the burning pain that sears my whole body.

It would truly be a competition to see who kills me first—my stalker, Maddy, or Natalia.

My money is on Maddy.

I don't know how long passes between me calling Natalia

and the time she arrives. It could be a few seconds or an hour, I'm not sure. What I am sure of, however, is the emotion written across her face—concern, fear, and murderous rage.

"Who?" she breathes.

"Ryan. I don't know his last name. Small black car? I don't know what type, I'm sorry."

"Don't apologize." She tucks a stray curl behind my ear. "I'll kill him for this."

"I know." I believe her. Without a doubt in my mind, I know Natalia will find him and kill him. For every mark on my skin, I know she'll make him feel ten times the pain and fear I do.

She moves swiftly, scooping me into her arms with a gentleness that could break my heart. I wince and try to hide it from her. I'm not fast enough.

"What hurts?"

I laugh, my ribs aching. "Is *everything* an acceptable answer?"

"Yes, but I need specifics."

"My head, mostly. He put something in my drink. I don't know what, but my head is throbbing. I don't think anything is broken, but I think I'm bleeding."

"I know you're bleeding, sweetheart," Natalia murmurs.

I glance down to see her hands already soaked with blood, and my head swims.

She nuzzles her nose to my neck and the soft of my jaw, pushing my head up. "Don't look."

Too late. The sight of all the blood sends my eyes rolling back in my head and my remaining flesh lights with fire.

Fuck.

Fuck.

I try not to make a sound, cautious to not even breathe too loud. This is mortifying. I started with this stupid plan to prove to everyone that I don't need saving and to put this mess behind me, yet what happened? I needed to be saved. Again.

Natalia settles me in the back seat of her car next to Riven before taking her place behind the wheel. Marco sits in the front, her glare plastered on the side of his face that is cast downwards in shame.

"How're you doing, kid?" Riven asks softly. There's no hint of his usual cocky tone in his voice.

I ignore him and turn to Natalia. "It's not his fault," I say, nodding to Marco. "I lied to him. It's *my* fault."

"Addie, love, I'm trying not to be mad at you."

"And you're doing that by being mad at him instead? Bullshit."

Natalia grits her teeth and her jaw pops from the strain. Beside me, Riven smirks, but covers it with a disapproving tut of his tongue.

Natalia's knuckles are still white on the wheel when we pull into the hospital I recognize as the one we went to after the gunman incident. Natalia parks in front of the entrance, the same doctor already there. I take the time to read his name tag this time—Dr. Park.

"I can't say I'm happy to see you again, Ms. Collins," he says with a courteous nod. "And in worse shape than before."

The nurse cringes at the sight of my blood-crusted clothes and the grass stuck to my wounds. I want to murmur a ,"Same, sister," but keep the thought to myself as they lead me into an examination room.

"Well, this time, I'm actually injured, and Natalia isn't just making a big deal out of nothing."

Natalia bristles at that but Dr. Park is already beginning his examination. His latex gloves make a suction noise when they pull back from my wet, crimson skin, and I bite back a gag. "This is some serious road burn. Want to tell me how it happened?"

I blink against the light he shines in my eyes next but keep my gaze straight ahead. "I jumped out of a car on the highway."

"A man drugged her and stuffed her in the back seat," Natalia supplies. "We have no idea what it was."

Dr. Park frowns but nods again, like a student trying to convince their teacher that they're still paying attention. "We'll get a blood test going and keep you here for observation. How're you with needles?"

The nurse steps forward and my stomach churns like a roaring tempest. "Can't you just scrape some blood of the million other cuts on me right now?"

He huffs a laugh that tells me that's out of the question.

A hand laces its fingers through mine. Natalia squeezes lightly, the thumb of her spare hand hooking under my chin. Her lips are soft as they press slow and gentle kisses to mine. "Where's my brave girl now?" she murmurs as the needle slides in. "The one who jumps out of cars and stands between a kid and a gun."

"I thought that made me an idiot."

"Yes, it does. But it also makes you incredibly brave."

"All done." The nurse steps back, handing the vial to Dr. Park.

"I'll be back shortly with those test results. In the meantime, Amanda here will clean those cuts out and patch you up."

"And that would be our cue." Riven sketches a bow.

Marco follows him out the door, skipping the bow altogether.

Natalia stays and watches the nurse with sharpened eyes and a narrowed brow as Amanda helps me out of my clothes and into a hospital gown.

"Congratulations," I say pointedly, nodding towards the sparkling ring on her finger. "How long have you been engaged?"

Natalia takes the hint and settles into the guest chair, albeit reluctantly, while Amanda begins listing off a long string of dates and venues and family members who are not invited to the wedding. I welcome the distraction it brings from the searing pain as she cleans out each of my cuts and scrapes. I lost a lot of skin, and I try not to think of the scarring that will follow. I wouldn't call myself vain, but I take great care of my skin, and those scars will just be a reminder of this horrible night. It's strange to think that I spent my morning in a spa with Maddy, and now I'm ending it in a hospital bed. My pink toes remain perfect against the cool tile floor.

"The doctor will be back shortly. In the meantime, we'll get you into bed."

"Any ideas on what the treatment for all this might be?" I ask, gesturing to my body as a whole.

"We get a lot of burn victims here with the chemical

plant close by. That, and sometimes kids playing on their parents' treadmills who fall and rub their skin off. We've got a cream that works wonders and should take care of any lasting scarring before it starts." Amanda smiles reassuringly as she settles me against the scratchy pillows. I miss my silk sheets and soft mattress already.

Natalia waits until Amanda closes the door to approach, her fingers finding mine. Her lips press a firm kiss to the inside of my wrist, her eyes locked onto mine the entire time. "We're going to have to talk about it, you know."

"I know, but can I just rest first?"

"I have to go take care of this, Addie," she huffs. "I can't just let him walk away. So we need to talk about it now."

"Natalia, I already feel like shit. You're not my keeper, so if you're going to lecture me, save it. Just let me get some rest." My voice comes out harsher than I intend for it to, and Natalia's mouth hardens.

She releases my hand and rises, her steps clipped as she heads for the door. "I texted Maddy where you were. She said she'd be here soon. I'll see you in the morning."

And just like that, she's gone. Only a hint of her perfume lingers in the air, woodsy and bold, before that is carried out by the stale air conditioning as well.

I try to fight back against the tears of frustration that prick at my eyes. Natalia is going to handle what I failed to, as usual, while I sit worthless in this cold hospital bed.

I close my eyes against the thought. My heart burns. Is it so much to ask for, to be capable? If Natalia had tried my plan tonight, it would have worked. Why didn't it work for me?

And why is that all I can think of now that Natalia has gone to "take care of" this problem?

Gooseflesh prickles my arm. What is she going to do to him?

CHAPTER 17
NATALIA

Unknown: I am going to kill him.

I'm going to kill him.

Not in the way I usually promise to kill Marco or Riven, but truly strip the flesh from his body. I will flay him piece by piece until there is nothing but the ash of his bones beneath my boot.

Finding Addie in that ditch was even more terrifying than when she called me during my meeting with the vice president. Her body was so crumpled and blood-soaked, I feared she had died on my way over. Until she lifted her head and saw me, and gave the smallest smile. I'm not even sure she knew she had done it.

My knuckles turn white on my steering wheel.

My car reads off Riven's text—"We've got him"—and an address.

I turn down a back road off the highway and follow the road signs. I don't dare use my GPS for this, not when data leaks are so common and I only have so many secluded spots left. Riven switches the houses around every so often to avoid detection, and this is a new one. It's close enough to the last one that I can get there just fine, but I keep my eyes on familiar landmarks just in case.

On the outside, the house looks like a cozy suburban home—pretty yellow shutters, rose bushes out front, and it's even topped off with your classic white picket fence. It doesn't get more greeting card aesthetic than that. The house will be listed for sale in a few weeks after a thorough cleaning and we'll find a new one, but for now, it houses all my toys and victims.

"Ryan Thilden," Riven introduces as I enter. "Meet Natalia."

Ryan sits tied to a chair in the center of what will become a beautiful living room with an open-floor concept. He sports a black eye already, and my gaze drifts to Riven.

He shrugs in response.

Ryan spits at my feet. "Isn't it stupid to reveal your name to me?"

"Not when you won't be leaving this room alive."

I can see the switch in his eyes—the moment his eyes widen and a stain blooms across the front of his jeans. That one second is all it takes for arrogance to turn to fear—the moment he realizes he's going to die, and I'm going to be the one to kill him.

"I have money," he pleads.

I scoff. "So do I."

"My dad's a politician. Whatever you want, you can have, you just need to let me live first."

I pretend to listen to him as I reach into my blazer, but all I see while he pleads for his life is Addie, broken and bleeding in a ditch on the side of the road. Addie drugged in the back seat of his car. Addie in his arms, unconscious.

I flip a business card out of my pocket. It lands perfectly on his knee. "Marcus Thilden is your father, and a client of mine," I say with a serpentine smile. "I already get whatever I want from him."

And there it is, his last bargaining chip.

That tiny scrap of hope fades from his face entirely as he sees my name scrawled in neat calligraphy across the card. It's while his eyes are still glued in shock to the card that I reach for my first tool. It's new, a gift from Riven, apparently, after the past few fuck ups. It's one of those serrated blades that goes in easy and kills on the way out.

The blade dives into his kneecap with a sickening pop.

Ryan screams, the business card now pinned to his leg with the blade. Blood spurts across my hand as I pull the knife out, bits of flesh and joint hanging from the serrated edges.

"Please!" he begs. "Please!"

It's always the same words, the same manners that have been ingrained in most of us since we were children. "Say *please* and *thank you*, tiny child, so that one day, the Mafia doesn't kill you."

It never works.

"What do you want from Addie Collins?"

He coughs, the action shaking his body against the restraints.

I bring the knife closer to his neck and glare point-edly at his knee. The message is clear enough.

Talk.

"She's hot, that's all. I visited her job a few times but she's always busy. She was at the bar and I'd had a drink, so I made a move. That's all!"

"Except—" I press the tip of the blade into the junction of his thick neck and shoulder, "—you failed to mention drugging her, putting her in your car, and trying to leave the city after she sent you a text with her exact location."

His face pales, but for a moment, confusion flickers across it. "What?"

"Did you do the same thing to Anna Russo, Dillon Lars, and Dina Saffron? Did you stalk them, drug them, then kill them too?"

"I didn't stalk anyone," he cries out. "I saw Addie a few times at work. I didn't know she'd be at the bar. Check my phone."

"He could have a burner phone," Riven adds.

"You go search the car for it while I finish this then."

Riven nods and stalks out, the door slamming shut in condemnation.

Ryan sags against his restraints, sobbing. "All of this for one bitch," he seethes. "I would've kept my hands off had I known she was fucking gay."

"No, you wouldn't have," I say, wiping the blade off on his jeans. "Cowards like you love the challenge."

"I didn't stalk the bitch," he protests. "Those murders on the TV, those weren't me."

I plunge the blade deep into his gut this time. I've

most definitely hit something vital, and he jerks forward, blooding dribbling from his mouth.

"You're lucky I'm being quick tonight. Because that girl you kidnapped is sitting alone in a hospital bed with most of her skin missing. You know as well as I do that the minute I take this knife out, you're going to bleed out, so buy yourself a few miserable seconds to make peace with whatever god you believe in and tell me the truth."

Blood, piss, and tears mingle across the floor. It's a dishonorable way to die, a disgusting, lonely, and terrifying way to go, and he deserves every second of it.

"I didn't kill them. I didn't stalk them. You have the wrong guy."

I remove the knife.

And I believe him.

Riven walks back into the room empty handed and shakes his head. Ryan is already slumped over, dead or about to be dead.

My second whistles. "You were quick tonight."

"I was."

"I'm guessing you want me to deal with this mess while you go see Addie."

"I do."

Riven claps me on the shoulder. "On it. You should shower first, though. I doubt they'll let you in the hospital looking like that."

I don't need a mirror to know what he means. I'm covered in blood. The red splatters across my face, streaking my short hair, coating my hands. I know if I look, there will hardly be an inch of me left untouched by the evidence of my sins. Heaven would look at me and laugh the day I showed up at those gates.

Addie is asleep when I walk into her room, her face pale against the papery sheets. I move quietly, shutting the door with my back turned.

"You're back."

Damn it, I thought I was quiet. "You're supposed to stay asleep," I admit, closing the door fully with a click. When I turn around again, Addie is sitting up with a sort of hope on her face. Even covered in bandages and bruised, she's radiant. I make my way over to her, settling beside her on the edge of the bed.

She forces a dry smile that stretches the skin of her lips to the point of splitting. "Knowing you're in danger twenty-four seven makes you a light sleeper," she admits.

"You're never in danger when you're with me."

"I know."

The question hangs so obviously in the air. Did I find him? Did I kill him? Still, she continues making her way over until she's only a step away from me.

"Dr. Park came back. The drug was Rohypnol. Thankfully, there was nothing else, and my headache is from a concussion I got from jumping out of a moving car. Go figure." She gives a huff of a laugh.

Even in this moment, she's trying to comfort me, to put my mind at ease, when she's the one in the hospital gown and I'm the one that failed her.

Again.

"He's dead," I whisper. "I thought you should hear it from me first before it's on the news."

Addie inhales sharply. She's trembling with what must be fear. I deserve as much. I finally showed her the monster lurking beneath and this isn't even half of the blood on my hands. Not even close.

Addie leans forward, her chest brushing against my shoulder, and cups my face in both her hands. Then she tugs lightly until I'm facing her and presses a kiss to my forehead. "Are you okay?" she asks.

Her scent hits me so strong then that I nearly crumble into her. The smoky tang of asphalt and the sterile scent of the hospital all but covers the soft whisper of lemon that is so distinctly Addie.

I rest my forehead against hers and inhale deeply. "I'm okay. Are you okay?"

"Was he... you know?" she asks instead of answering my question. My shoulders slump.

"No. He wasn't your stalker. I'm sorry."

She brings her hands down to rub her arms. "Well I'd feel better if that had actually been my stalker, not just another random guy who had it out for me."

"I'll find him," I promise.

"I know," she sighs. "But I kind of wanted to be the one who did it."

There's more weight to that sentence than she lets on, so I waits a moment before she catches my probing stare.

She inhales softly, then crosses her legs to rest her elbows on her knees. "When Maddy meets people, she tells them she's a photographer. When I meet people, I tell them I'm a barista," she starts, brushing a stray strand of hair behind her ear. "I've written two unpublished books, had multiple short stories in the local magazine, and have had a literary agent for over a year now, but I won't call myself an author. I haven't had any offers on the book I'm querying, either. Maddy tells me I can just self-publish it, but I can't bring myself to do that."

That takes me aback for a moment. She's mentioned her writing before but we've never spoken on it for long. Usually she blushes and brushes it off or something else steals our attention away.

"Why not?" I ask, crossing my arms casually. "Traditional or self-published, they're both real authors, right?"

She sits upright hurriedly. "Of course they are. It's not about the validity of the title. If it was just about being an author, I would have self-published years ago."

"Then what is it about?"

"They're braver than I am," she whispers. "I need a publishing house to tell me I'm good enough to be an author. I need someone to read my story and give me the validation that I'm good enough to do this. I can't take that leap of faith on my own like others can." She pauses, and I think she's done, but she continues. "My father died when I was young. My mother lost her mind—it nearly killed her. She took to traveling and partying, going on dates with rich men and stringing them along to receive lavish gifts that she could pawn. Somehow, money always showed up to feed and house me, and I never questioned it. She took care of me the best she could, but made it clear I had to take care of myself."

I knew her father died already and that her mom isn't in the picture, she told me as much herself, but I never knew to what extent her childhood sucked until now. I lean closer involuntarily, drawn to the pain in her heart that mirrors my own.

"She'd come home just enough that the neighbors wouldn't be suspicious, and taught me how to drive the car when I was twelve so I could move it in and out of the garage so people would think she was there. I forged her signature on all my school documents and took care of myself every day until I moved out. I worked hard to prove to her that I was good enough, and yet she never stayed more than a few days. She missed my graduation, every birthday, every first. But I never blamed her. It's my fault."

I swear under my breath. I know where this is going, and know I have to have a chat with this woman if we ever meet.

"So when my stalker showed up, he was just another problem that I was going to solve on my own. The police knew the case wasn't good enough—that *I'm* not worth enough to protect. So I was going to save myself, only I can't. He's been one step ahead of us all, and it's killing me. I thought if I could just trick him into meeting me and end this for myself, then maybe I wouldn't be a failure at this too. Maybe just once, I could prove to myself that I'm good enough. Only I'm not. I needed saving this time too." She looks up then, tears rimming those blue eyes. "I'm not an author. Not a daughter. *Not enough.*"

CHAPTER 18
NATALIA

Unknown: Ryan should be lucky Natalia killed him and not me. Does she know how he touched you at the bar? He still had his hands when they burned him, so I guess not.

*N*ot enough.

Two words I've heard my entire life from everyone I I've loved.

"She'll never be enough to take over the family name," my father had said when my mother failed to give birth to a son.

"Love is not enough in the face of power," my mother had confessed to me on her death bed. Her death was a tragic accident—at least that's what everyone else was told. But I was there when she swallowed the pills. I was there when she took her own life. I was thirteen and she had left everything to me.

I invested and I slaved away, creating my new empire. When I was fifteen, I repeated those words back to my father when he pleaded that he loved me, and I put a bullet in his head.

"It won't be enough," Riven had tried to argue when we were twenty and I thought I could solve all his issues with bullets and bills. So many men died that day. To Riven's mother, his name was on the death toll. He hasn't seen her since. He *can't* see her.

Not enough, I've told myself every day since the first body came in. I'm not doing enough to avenge her death. I'm failing every murdered girl by failing to catch this guy.

And tonight, failing to keep Addie safe, even from a lowlife whose body is now rotting somewhere.

How the hell can someone so perfect think she's not enough?

"Bullshit."

Addie startles. "What?"

I stalk towards her, gripping her shoulders tight. She moves to her knees as if she could stand on the bed just to tower over me, but I hold her still.

"That's bullshit," I growl. "You're more than enough. So your mom's a deadbeat. That's her loss that she doesn't get to see how far you've come, how beautiful and wonderful you are. I've watched you face down the barrel of a gun without flinching. I've seen you manipulate and lure a fucking stalker into your trap."

"That didn't work."

"It should have." I run my hands through my hair. "It was smart and it would have worked if you'd had backup. If you were anyone else, I would have suggested it already, but I can't—"

"Can't what?" she presses, staring up at me from

under those thick lashes. She looks so innocent, yet she knows exactly what she's doing.

"I can't put you in danger. I can't put myself in a position to lose the most valuable thing I've ever owned. I told you you're mine, Addie, and I don't intend to lose you."

There's a sudden beep on her heart monitor. I look over to find a spike in her heart rate.

Addie stares at me undeterred, before lifting to her knees and crashing her lips into mine.

The machine beeps again, but it's lost to the roaring in my ears as she wraps her arms around my neck, slipping her tongue into my mouth.

I'm over her in a second, laying her back down on the bed and pulling the privacy screen closed with me.

Addie moans as my hand slips beneath her hospital gown, but jumps when there's another protesting beep from her machine. If it wasn't literally monitoring her vitals, I would have pulled it from the wall by now.

"Nat," she pants, her hands pushing back on my chest. "Wait. My heart monitor. It'll go off and the doctors will come in." Her eyes are wide and her face flushed enough that her freckles are nearly obscured.

Cute. So fucking cute.

I drag my teeth over her lower lip with one glance back at the privacy screen separating us from the unlocked door. "Well, sweetheart. I guess we'll have to see how quickly I can make you come." I push one finger into her swiftly, and the line on her monitor jumps. "Think you'll be a good girl and come for me before Dr. Park comes back?"

That line jumps again as she nods. I'd like to have her

long and slow, but not tonight. Not when I have a job to do and anyone could walk in at any minute.

Addie is shaking, her every nerve alive and ready to come undone underneath me. She tangles her hands in my hair, pulling at the short strands. I slide a second finger inside her, pausing only when a set of footsteps shuffle past the closed door. We don't dare breathe too loud.

When they pass, I continue, faster and harder now. My thumb circles over her clit and I withdraw my fingers completely to pinch down.

Her heart monitor goes haywire as she gasps.

We only have seconds now until someone comes in to see what's wrong.

It's exhilarating, the flush in her eyes as I pump in and out of her at a punishing pace, the way she covers her mouth to keep from being heard. Anyone could walk in at any moment and see this, see her. The thought makes me move faster, and I know it's what pushes Addie into a shattering release that has her biting my shoulder.

The door suddenly opens and the privacy curtain is ripped to the side as Dr. Park runs in, the nurse from earlier hot on his heels.

I sit in the chair beside Addie, magazine in hand. I raise an unamused brow at them.

"Is everything okay?" he asks, his eyes moving right to Addie's flushed face.

"Yes, why wouldn't it be?"

He eyes me incredulously. "We heard her heart rate monitor in the hall."

"Oh," Addie squeaks. "Hospitals make me nervous." I can hear the strain in her voice as she tries to keep her breathing even and note how her thighs clench beneath the thin hospital sheets.

I flick my brows up again at the doctor.

"Right," he stammers. "We'll discharge you in the morning, so not to worry. Please click the pager beside your bed if you need anything."

"I will. Could you flick the light off on the way out? I'd like to try and sleep." She mocks a yawn.

Clever girl, but such a bad liar.

Dr. Park nods and the two file out, lights clicking off behind them.

From within the dark, Addie releases a breathy laugh. "I hate you."

"Your vitals say otherwise."

Beep.

"Damnit."

It's my turn to laugh then. I find my way to her in the dark and press a kiss to her forehead. "You should sleep," I say, a shade gentler.

Her head shakes beneath my lips. "How am I supposed to sleep after that? I feel like I just had a coffee. Are we sure my pulse isn't racing still?"

"Is Dr. Park rushing in again?"

Another head shake.

"Then I think you're good."

There's a beat of silence and all I can think about is how an hour ago, my hands were slick with blood, and now they're covered in Addie.

And she doesn't care.

Her fingers wrap around my wrist. "I'd sleep better with you next to me."

"You've got no skin on you, baby. I don't want to hurt you."

I can practically hear her no-nonsense glare in the dark as she says, "You fucked me just fine. I think you can get in bed with me."

I can't argue with that logic.

Addie slides over to make room for me, and I curl beside her, carefully wrapping my arms around her midsection where I know the least damage was done.

She hums contently, quite pleased with herself, before nestling her chin in the crook of my neck. "I love seeing you like this," she admits. "All soft and vulnerable. Just for me, so don't let anyone else see you this way, okay?"

I doubt anyone else ever will, nor will I let them, but I nod in the dark, nonetheless. It doesn't dawn on me until after I do it that she can't see it, but I know she felt it and knows my intent.

"Just get some sleep."

"M'kay."

"I love you."

She's asleep before she can hear it.

I flick the TV on in the quiet of the morning. The clock on the wall reads 5:02 a.m. Addie is still sleeping, curled around me with a small smile on her face. I press a kiss to her forehead.

Mine.

Mine to protect. Mine to love. Mine to kill for.

"— a car crashed off the interstate early this morning.

The driver has yet to be identified given the fiery nature of the accident. The victim has yet to be identified. The only clue to any identification authorities have is the license plate, which was one of the only things left not mangled from this tragedy. Back to—"

I switch the TV off just as I see the text from Riven.

Riven: It's done.

I rest my head atop Addie's as she stirs in her sleep.

Mine.

CHAPTER 19
ADDIE

Unknown: You're choosing one killer over another. This is your only warning to choose the one killing FOR you.

I'll never get over how stunning Natalia's apartment is, if a little monochromatic. From the glass walls overlooking the crowded city below, to the clean, steel kitchen in the center of the open floor plan, everything is organized and sterile. It's gorgeous, an interior designer's dream, but it doesn't look lived in. The thought of Natalia up here alone makes my heart hurt.

I've stayed in the apartment with her for the better part of the week since I was discharged from the hospital. The nurse wasn't lying when she told me the ointment they prescribed works miracles. Where there used to only be bloody road burn, my body is covered in tender pink flesh within a few days, and while the areas are still sore and healing, there's no sign of scarring.

I turn my body in front of the full-length mirror and frown. There are no scars, but the new pink skin is noticeable and patchy. The black dress that I planned to wear to tonight's anniversary gala is strewn across the bed, utterly untouched since I stepped out of my shower. It's beautiful. It hugs every perfect curve and hollow, but it's sleeveless, with a low, dipping neckline and a slit up the thigh—perfect for exposing all my new wounds.

Before my shower, I tried the dress on with a pair of opera gloves, but even that does little to conceal the walking battlefield of my body.

My phone buzzes on the nightstand. Maddy.

A few moments later, the doorbell rings. I wrap myself in a towel and go to greet her.

Natalia left a few hours ago to oversee some final details for the event and told me to call Maddy over. She promised us full use of anything and everything in the apartment, including the expensive wine she keeps locked away for special occasions. I told her that It'd feel too guilty to drink them, but promised to help myself to some of her less aged collection.

Maddy stands in the doorway, a smile on her face that spans the whole lower half. Her arms are loaded with pink gossamer, makeup bags, and a camera. My stomach churns at the sight of the last object. Mads has been going on about how excited she is to get photos at this event for her next gallery, and I promised to be her model, but to say I'm feeling less than confident at the moment is an understatement. I know she could Photoshop out my cuts, but knowing that the raw file exists somewhere...

I smile anyway and take her bags to set them on the counter. "What's this?" I ask, nodding to a large black box.

Mads's smile widens. "Natalia had it sent to the apartment so she could surprise you. Go try it on!"

I raise an eyebrow but open the box anyway and nearly gasp. The dress is the most beautiful thing I've ever seen. The main body is comprised of glittering gold fabric that's form hugging, then stretches out at the skirt for an elegant mermaid silhouette, yet my eyes drop to the sleeves. They're a shimmering gauze that's just opaque enough to hide the worst of my road burn, but sheer enough that the material is still light and sexy.

"She had it custom-made, of course." Mads beams, unable to help herself. "If you don't go try it on right now, I might just die of anticipation."

Laughter forces its way to my lips and I nod, unable to hide the swell of emotions. Damn her, she knows me too well at this point.

Maddy shares my sentiment, jumping up and down on the balls of her feet with excitement. Before long, she's ushering me into the bathroom to finish getting ready.

"Are you excited or nervous for tonight?" she asks after applying a pink shimmer to her eyelids.

"A bit of both."

Tonight is the tenth anniversary of Mancini Security. Natalia invited both me and Mads to attend weeks ago when it was still in the organizing stages. She has been spread thin between preparing for this and finding my stalker, so Riven and I put together a surprise for her after the gala.

Our relationship is still new, even though it feels like

I've known Natalia for my whole life, and I wanted to do something nice for her. She's always been so good at taking care of me, so it's about time I return the favor.

"She's going to love it," Mads says with a wink before passing me a tube of lipstick. "Use this one. it looks better on you than me."

Natalia sends a car to pick us up from her apartment, along with a lengthy apology that she can't be here to pick us up herself. I merely brush her off with an honest "It's fine," and think nothing of it. Still, she insists on sending a car before her investors pull her away again.

The driver already has the address of the venue plugged in to the GPS when we climb into the car. I recognize him from afternoons spent in Natalia's office. He always holds the door for me with a smile.

It doesn't take long to get to the venue, a five-star hotel not far from the Mancini Security offices. Outside, glamorous cars worth more than my apartment building are pulling into the driveway, their even-more-glamorous occupants spilling out in a flurry of diamonds and designer shoes.

An emerald-green carpet has been laid out down the steps leading to the ballroom of the hotel where a kind concierge checks our invites and takes our coats. Upon seeing my name, he calls for someone to escort us inside to where Riven is waiting, a cocky smirk planted upon his lips.

"You two finally decided to show up," he says.

"Fashionably late." Mads smiles, baring her canines.

"Emphasis on the *late*," he murmurs.

I pretend not to see the silent pissing contest the two are having with their eyes as I survey the ballroom. Natalia spared no expense. Every inch of the place oozes wealth and class, from the champagne tower in the corner of the room to the diamond chandeliers dangling from the ceiling. I came here with her a week ago to survey the area and those were not there before.

A butler dressed in all white hurries by, his footsteps nothing more than a silent flurry of motion across the polished floor. Small shells stuffed with caviar rest upon a tray that he passes around to the patrons. Lavish, expensive—and gross.

"Natalia is finishing up appeasing a few clients down the hall, but she sent me to escort you two for now." Riven extends both his arms to us.

Maddy reluctantly lays her arm over one while I take the other, letting him lead us into the fray.

"Everything is set up," I tell him. "I just need to leave a little early to finish the rest."

"I can occupy Nat while you leave." When he sees my pale face, he adds, "Don't worry, she's going to love it."

I smile through the queasiness invading my stomach. Gifts and kind gestures already require a certain degree of creativity that I do not have. The task of planning them only gets harder when your girlfriend is one of the wealthiest and most successful people in the country. There's nothing I can offer her that she can't get herself.

"Here's to hoping."

An hour passes and Natalia still has yet to make an appearance. I stand with Riven by the champagne tower, nursing a flute while scanning the room for any sign of her.

Maddy glides across the ballroom, her soft-pink gown fluttering behind her like a cascade of rose petals. She tosses her head back and laughs, her hair a golden flame that curls down her back in long waves. She pays no mind to her dance partner—he's just the fifth of many more to come—but he's looking at her as if he can already hear the wedding bells. I smile. Maddy tends to have that effect on people.

I'm not the only one who's noticed, given the way Riven is clutching the stem of his champagne glass with white knuckles. I fear he may snap the fragile crystal.

I lean back against the wall beside him. "She has a boyfriend, slimeball as he is," I huff, crossing my arms over my chest.

Riven's eyebrow raises slightly, the only indication of shock evident on his face. I figure I should warn him now —that, and Natalia immediately shot down my genius matchmaking plans. Her second, she warned, has some dangerous enemies and a twisted history that Maddy would be smart not to get involved with. I thought that was an unfair assessment, but she was adamant.

"Good for him."

Him, not her, I note.

The lethal rage emanating off of him sends a wave of cold down my spine.

"I need a dance partner," I say suddenly. "You seem adequate enough."

We both could use the distraction right now.

Riven looks at me like I grew a second head, but only for a moment before his shoulders loosen and a smirk lights his face. "Promise you won't step on my toes?"

"I promise nothing," I say, accepting the arm he extends.

He chuckles, a low sound like rumbling thunder.

We glide onto the dance floor, my heels clicking against the cool marble with each step. The golden dress hugs my every curve and hollow, reflecting the light that bounces from the chandelier. It lights up each carefully placed diamond, turning my body into a dancing wildfire. Riven steps forward and my feet yield to his, letting him lead the waltz. I force my weight to the balls of my feet, trying to keep my heels from catching on the polished floor.

Riven lifts my arm, allowing me to spin out. I'm aware of the eyes on us as I move, but I couldn't care less. The only person I want to be dancing with right now is god knows where, while my partner has his eyes on my best friend.

"You know, I think you'd be a better fit than Donovan."

Riven raises a well-manicured eyebrow. "Donovan?"

"Her boyfriend."

Something akin to recognition flashes across his face. "That's a shitty name."

I bark out a laugh. "I agree. Riven is much better."

Riven doesn't try to hide the smirk on his lips as he spins me again, faster now. My heel nearly catches on his dress shoes and I hiss beneath my breath. He laughs again at my red face, and after a tense moment, I allow myself to smile.

"What is going on here?"

Natalia's voice is lethal as she rips me from Riven's grasp.

Her second stumbles for a moment before righting himself, his eyes wide. Natalia's shoulders are squared and her eyes darkening by the second.

"Enough of the territorial bullshit," I hiss, elbowing her gently. "You left me bored by the champagne so I asked him to entertain me."

Natalia grunts, and that smirk appears back on Riven's face. He and Natalia have a conversation with their eyes, one that leaves Riven laughing and Natalia fuming. Maddy appears right as I think Natalia might shoot him, her face flushed and eyes sparkling.

"How many marriage proposals have you gotten so far?" I jest.

Maddy links her arm in mine and dramatically rests her head on my shoulder. "Don't be ridiculous. It's only been one."

Riven's jaw clenches so hard it pops.

"Do you mind occupying my dance partner?" I ask with a coy smile. "I need to go soothe Natalia's ego."

Natalia's mouth flies open as if to protest my statement, but Maddy is already sizing Riven up like a predator trying to decide how to take on another predator.

Riven holds her stare with a scoff. "I think I'm done dancing for the night," he says.

Maddy shrugs. "Just as well. You would have been a shit partner."

"Oh, really?"

"Yep," she says, popping the "p" with her glossy lips. "You have two left feet."

Without another word, Riven's hand snaps out, gripping her wrist gently and dragging her to the center of the dance floor. Maddy's face is flushed as she keeps pace with his quick tempo, nailing every spin and dip as if she were simply walking.

"So are they fighting or dance-fucking?"

"Don't even start," Natalia groans, her hand alighting on the small of my back. Electricity shoots from the small touch of her hand on my bare skin. She must feel it, too, her movements stiffening with each second of contact.

Finally able to look at her fully, I notice just how beautiful she is in this moment. Natalia is always gorgeous in her work suits, but in a tux, she's deadly. The look is fully black, coating her features in sleek elegance.

"Are you done staring?"

My face flushes crimson as she takes me in. I dip my chin in a poor effort to hide it, and cross my arms in a pout. "You're late."

"I'm sorry, love."

"What, no excuses?" I have to admit she's piqued my interest at that, but all I'm left with is a bored smile.

"None worth your time. Just had to go play politics with a client for a little while."

"I see."

"Now," she says, that grin curving into something more feline, "I'd hate to leave you bored by the champagne, although I'd love to hide you away from everyone else's gaze."

I tug at one of the sleeves self-consciously. I felt the

stares as I danced with Riven. They intensified each time my neckline dropped too low, revealing the healing burns across my skin. The dress hides most of them, but a quick view slips through every now and then.

Natalia captures my hand in her own, and places a kiss against my palm. "The word *beautiful* pales in comparison to you."

Her wine-red lipstick leaves a stain across my heart line, and I fight the urge to drive to a tattoo parlor right now and have them immortalize the mark. Still, I accept her arm and let her lead me out to the ballroom floor.

"Wait." I frown down at the lipstick mark when she tries to take my hand. "I don't want to mess it up."

Natalia drops her gaze to my open palm and the red splotch across it. She smirks, taking my hand regardless and whispering against the shell of my ear, "I can give you more later in places no one else can see."

I let my head tip back as I laugh. "Is that a promise?"

"More like a warning."

"I look forward to it then," I say as I accept her hand.

The music guides our steps as we launch into the first dance. In truth, dancing is far less complicated than people think. The waltz we do is only four steps, and the only embellishments are the added dips and spins Natalia throws in.

I watch her as we move, my eyes lingering on her face. I'll never get over how attractive Natalia is, but tonight, she is simply beautiful. She wears makeup to work and on our dates, but usually minimal. The dark lashes framing those nearly black eyes only draw my gaze to her crimson lips. They aren't the cherry red that I sport tonight with my soft glam look, but a deeper red, like the wine I know she prefers.

"You're beautiful," I breathe.

Natalia's steps stutter, and her face flushes crimson.

"Oh my god," I all but squeal with glee. "Are you *blushing*?"

"No."

"You're beautiful."

"Stop saying that," she mumbles, regaining her place in the music as quickly as she'd lost it.

"No. Clearly I don't say it enough."

Her blush only deepens, and she executes a perfectly timed spin that has me back in her arms by the time her cheeks have returned to their usual olive color. "Where'd you learn to dance?" she asks suddenly.

"I've been to a few balls. Mostly book-themed, of course. There was one in the city about two years ago that Mads got tickets for for my birthday. We taught ourselves the basics in our living room."

"That's a better story than mine. I just had to learn for my father's events."

That sours the mood just enough that I don't respond, don't know how. Her father is lucky he's dead, or he'd be dealing with me. Not that I would stand a chance against anyone related to the powerful woman before me, but my last few moments on this earth would be spent making his very inconvenient.

The hours slip away between champagne flutes, long talks with investors interested in Natalia's arm candy, persuading Natalia not to murder said investors, and stealing tiny snacks with Mads. We're exploring the rest of the old hotel—a sort of alcohol-fueled adventure—when a security guard forces us to return to the ballroom.

"Do I want to know what you two were doing?" Riven asks as said security guard escorts us back to where he and Natalia sit.

Mads flashes an award-winning grin and playfully pats the guard on the shoulder. "Just taking in the views."

The guard sighs through his nose as if he doesn't get paid enough to deal with us. "Please keep all guests inside the ballroom."

"Of course." Natalia can't hide her smirk. "We plan on heading out soon anyway."

That thought sobers me up quickly. That's right, the plan I have for Natalia tonight.

I side-eye Riven, hoping he'll take the hint.

He coughs then clears his throat loudly enough to garner some attention. "Before you head out, the president of the Wallace group wants to speak with you," he lies smoothly.

Natalia's irritation blooms on her face. "He can wait."

"It's fine," I say, perhaps a little too quickly. "I'll meet you at home when you're done."

She looks at me with a hint of concern hardening her features. I know she doesn't love the idea of me going home alone, especially when Maddy is staying at our apartment and not Natalia's. "Are you sure?"

"It's fine," I say again, more forcefully now.

"Okay," she relents, "but text me the minute you're inside the apartment. I'll be quick." She presses a kiss to my cheek, staining me again with her dark lipstick. A possessive smile creeps into the kiss and I fight the urge to grab her by the collar of her suit and make out with her in the middle of the ballroom.

Riven slowly leads her away, and once her back is turned, his eyes widen as his mouth parts in a silent, "Go."

I run out of the ballroom.

CHAPTER 20
ADDIE

Unknown: Wrong choice.

Everything is a disaster. Natalia will be home soon and all I've managed to do is burn pasta and make a tiramisu that looks more demolished than deconstructed. I'm a terrible cook—it's why I stick to lattes and Daryl never lets me work the bakery portion of our café. We learned during my first week on the job that I should only be passing out the muffins, not making them. It took two weeks to get the scent of smoke out of my work shirt.

I took Riven up on his offer to learn how to cook true Italian pasta, and he had thrown the tiramisu recipe in there as a surprise. His lessons were wonderful, but my skills were not.

I changed into one of Natalia's shirts, one of the ones she bought oversized for comfort. It falls to my mid-thigh and is thoroughly covered in flour, espresso, and cocoa powder.

The keys turning in the door send my senses on high alert, but before I can cover my mess, Natalia walks in. Her shoulders are nearly to her ears with tension and her face is weary, but her eyes widen at the sight of me, sprawled across the counter trying to hide my mess.

"What flour bomb went off in here?" She grins, dropping her coat onto a chair. She runs her finger through the white powder on her counter, then drags her thumb across the cocoa smudge on my face.

Cheeks blazing crimson, I explain everything from Riven's lessons and my failed attempts to make her a dinner that reminds her of home, to thoroughly coating myself and her kitchen with tiramisu ingredients.

Before long, Natalia is laughing, clutching at her core and doubling over, pressing kisses to my face. "You're wonderful." She holds my face in her hands. "But you know I wasn't born in Italy, right?"

My blush deepens. "No, but I assumed with how much you said you travel there, and honestly, your name..."

Natalia laughs again, a sound I usually find beautiful —when it isn't directed at me. "My grandfather was born in Italy before he moved here for... business. I'm usually over there checking on a family friend, not any of my relatives. I do appreciate a good tiramisu, however."

"I wouldn't eat that." I cringe as she takes a bite.

"Yeah, I won't be finishing that." She jumps out of the way when I swat at her. "I plan to have something sweeter anyway."

"That will have to wait."

Natalia's eyebrow raises, but I don't say another word as I lead her out onto the balcony. One of the first things I noticed when I came to her apartment was the balcony. Natalia is on the top floor and her balcony overlooks the whole city. She's high enough up that no one can reach us, or see us.

That is what made me choose this as the place to lay out candles and a few throw blankets I brought from my apartment. I ran out of time to grab roses earlier so I had to forgo the rose petal trail, but something in the way Natalia's eyes soften tells me she doesn't care.

"What's this?"

"You've worked hard your whole life—this gala is just proof of that." I slowly undo the top few buttons of her shirt as I speak. "Tonight, I want to reward *you*."

Her shirt slips off her shoulders easily, falling among the pillows and blankets as she sinks to the floor. My hand pushes against her sternum, gently lowering her until her back is flat against the ground.

"Addie," she breathes.

My lips find hers as she undoes her bra and I swing my leg over her hips until I'm straddling her. Heat pools in my lower stomach as her hands climb up my stomach and my palms press against the sides of her face. Her fingers inch towards the waistband of the lace set I slipped into once I got home, and I push back.

"Let me have you first."

Her lips part in a whine almost immediately as I slowly peel off her shirt to reveal what I wear beneath. With painstaking slowness, I lower my lips to her jaw, marking a trail from the column of her neck to her sternum.

Her breasts are smaller than mine, but peaked and tan. A breeze pebbles gooseflesh across them as I wrap my teeth around a dark nipple and lightly scrape them across. Natalia's breathy moan goes straight between my legs.

Continuing to swirl my tongue across each breast, I let my hands trail lower until I find the button on her pants and undo it. Natalia takes the hint and peels them away, leaving nothing but a scrap of satin between me and her. It's torture not to taste her right away, but I force my hands to be slow as they trail up and down her inner thigh, moving ever closer, then trailing back down.

Something like a growl settles at the back of Natalia's throat as I sit back, dragging my lips down her stomach as I go. My thumb swipes over her clit once, then twice, each time lighter than the one before it. Just enough to tease her, yet not give the friction she needs.

"Are you going to torture me or are you going to fuck me?" she grinds out between clenched teeth. Her head is thrown back, leaving her tan neck exposed to the moonlight.

"Both."

I press the flat of my palm against the apex of her thighs while I slip two fingers inside of her. She gasps, her body rocking as I pump in then out again, rough, just how I know she likes it. She grinds herself against the heel of my palm as I work, bringing herself near a climax, but I pull out before she can come.

"Addie. Now," she moans.

I feel my thighs clench involuntarily at the heady

need in her voice. Then I allow my head to dip between her legs as I lay my tongue flat against her center.

My eyes drift to her face as I fuck her with my tongue, her eyes rolled back and dark lips parted. Heat coils between my legs and demands release. Her moans stroke the fires of my ego as I watch her come apart under my mouth. She's the most dangerous person I know, and I have her writhing beneath me. My own fingers slip beneath my panties and I touch myself as I touch her.

"Fuck," she breathes right as I groan against her center. My own orgasm rocks through me as she comes apart on my tongue.

Then her arms are wrapped around my middle, pulling me to her side as she plants a firm kiss on my lips, tasting herself. "You're perfect."

"And you're beautiful," I respond.

And she is. Her dark hair sticks to her sweat-damp face and those dark eyes nearly glow with otherworldly light under the moon. She is my own death goddess, dragged from heaven just for me.

I love her.

The words are on my tongue as she stares at me like I hold the key to the stars. No one has ever looked at me that way before.

Instead, I say, "Next time you go to Italy, can I come with?"

Her face softens, and I feel my heart turn to a puddle within my chest. "Of course. We can go anywhere you want."

"Anywhere?" I say with a devious grin. "Like the moon?"

Her laughter rattles through my ribs. I'd do unspeakable things to be able to bottle that sound and keep it forever.

I rest my head against her chest and her fingers trace idle shapes over my hip. Then she folds a kiss onto my forehead and I swear I hear her whisper back, "To the moon, my love."

CHAPTER 21
ADDIE

Unknown: Secrets never bode well in a relationship. I've been honest with you from day one. Can you say the same of your lover?

I push open the glass door to Mancini Security with my hip, cradling two iced coffees in my hands, and Marco close behind. The cool of the glass chills my skin through my thin cotton dress. The city's summer heat has lingered with a vengeance. I'm of the personal opinion that July should be dedicated to beach days and beach days only. The universe, apparently, does not share my sentiments.

I'm grateful I chose to wear bike shorts beneath my dress today, especially as sweat begins to drip down my back.

Marco excuses himself to go speak with a colleague while I find Natalia, and I brush him off with a smile.

The secretary from my first day here, Maria, sits at the

receptionist's desk. Her nails click angrily against the keyboard as if she holds a personal vendetta against it. The aggression towards the poor computer only continues to grow with each step I take towards the woman.

"Good morning, Maria," I chirp with sugary sweetness.

Maria forces her gaze to mine, her glossy lips peeling back in a courteous smile. "Miss Collins," she preens. "How can I help you?"

"Natalia left her phone at her apartment this morning. Do you know where I can find her?"

"What, you don't know already?" she says with a darker edge to her voice.

My eyes narrow and I force myself to imitate Natalia's quiet rage, drawing my shoulders up and widening my stance. "Unless you'd rather I tell her you were unhelpful again, I'd appreciate it if you could tell me where to find her."

Maria hesitates, blanching before she plasters that cool mask onto her face again. She pulls out a map and taps on a room near the back of the building. "You'll need Natalia's card to get back there. I assume you have one?"

I fish the card out of my wallet, carefully balancing the two coffees in one hand. I flash it at the receptionist before storming towards the other door, trying to keep my steps even and light. There's no reason she should get under my skin so much. I don't even know if she likes women or just doesn't like me. I can't bring myself not to care, though, not with the way she smugly ignores me every time I come into the building—unless Natalia was with me.

The corridors are cold as I walk further, the AC on full blast and screaming through the halls. I can hardly hear my echoing footsteps as I stalk toward the room in question, my anger slowly dissipating, replaced with curiosity. I've never seen this part of the company before, nor do I understand why this hallway is darker than the others. It feels like an alternate universe, like something out of a dystopian horror film.

Voices grow at the end of the path, mostly male and speaking in hushed tones. A metallic clang soon follows, then a few laughs before Natalia's tenebrous tone rings out amongst the group. Her words are obscured by the roaring air conditioning, and I strain to hear her.

The door where the noise is coming from is slightly ajar, and I peek in. She must be in a meeting of some sort, and I don't want to interrupt.

"The money has already been wired over."

My heart hitches in my throat.

"Are you sure it is untraceable?"

"It's a ghost gun—it's in the name."

That was Riven. Guns? Money wiring?

Against my better judgment, I lean forward, pressing my cheek against the wooden door. There are three men in the room, all dressed in suits and wearing ear pieces. The one in the middle holds an assault rifle. A quick glance shows that he's searching for a serial number, and by the look of satisfaction on his face I know he doesn't find one.

Riven stands opposed them, the sleeves of his dress shirt rolled up to expose tan, corded muscle. Beside him, Natalia leans against the wall, her arms crossed over her chest.

"And we won't expect any trouble from the Barones?" The larger man spares a glance in Riven's direction.

Barones. I knew the name sounded familiar when I had first met Riven. They're gangsters, Mafia that works in the shadows of the city. They're nearly a myth at this point, a nightmare.

No one who crosses the Barones lives to tell the tale.

No one except...

"Riven is mine," Natalia states coolly, "and the Barones won't step foot in my territory. They know what we have."

"And if they do?" the man counters. "Last I heard, you had a mole in your ranks."

"Jon Michels is telling his story to the fish at the bottom of the ocean as we speak. He's been dead since I landed back in the country. After seeing his body, I doubt after any others will be willing to cross me again," Natalia responds with a biting edge in her voice that I don't recognize.

The other man laughs. "I suppose the rumors about the head of the Mancinis are true then."

My stomach roils. Jon Michels—Donovan's friend that we went to the club with the night I met Natalia. He was the man I was supposed to meet my first day here, but Maria said the name wasn't familiar and then Natalia showed up and I...

Oh my god.

Natalia killed him, in the room she was about to fuck me in. I was there, in the room. The signs were there all along.

All the pieces begin to line up too quickly, and the room begins to spin.

Mancini Security. It climbed the ranks quickly and no one batted an eye. All the times Natalia had dried blood under her nails or only wore black for days. The resources she has that the police doesn't.

What, you don't know already?

My eyes burn and I spin to flee when my heel catches on the floor. I stumble, my hand flying out blindly to brace myself. I land against the door, pushing it wide open and baring my shaking form to the room full of armed criminals.

"What the fuck?"

The large man has the assault rifle trained on me immediately, but as soon as he raises the weapon, a barrel is pressed to his temple.

"Raise a weapon to her and I will blow your head off," Natalia seethes. I've never heard her voice so low, so lethal before.

My feet slip in the coffee I spilled as I try to back up, and I land on my tailbone on the cool floor.

Riven disarms the man as Natalia rushes to me, but I flinch.

"Addie..."

"Don't," I gasp. "Just... don't."

Her eyes flood with anguish and her hand flexes as if reflexively reaching for me, and now that she can't, her body doesn't know where to place itself. "I didn't want you to find out this way."

"Find out what?" I snap. "That you're Mafia? That you're a killer?"

"Yes," she says unflinchingly.

I scoff, scrambling to my feet, not caring how foolish I look. I don't bother picking up the crushed coffee cups, or bother being embarrassed about the coffee staining my light-colored dress.

Natalia's phone buzzes in my pocket and I shove it into her hands. "Don't call me. Don't come near me."

"Addie, please," she pleads. "You can hate me, but it's not safe."

"Oh, and *you're* safe?" I laugh. "At least I know what the stalker wants with me, but you? You're worse. You made me—"

The word dies on my tongue. I won't let her hear it. She doesn't get to know I fell for her just as hard as she fell for me. She doesn't deserve that, not now.

"You're more dangerous than he could ever be. Just... just stay away."

I can hear her calling my name as I leave, but it's drowned out by the roaring in my ears.

Mafia.

Natalia is Mafia.

My mother worried about the Mafia presence in the city when I moved here—one of her only motherly moments I could remember—but I assured her it was mostly safe. They didn't operate here like they did in movies. There wouldn't be any violent shootouts or kidnappings in my life. From what I had heard, the main Mafia gang in the city dealt with weapons, and the Barones with drugs. Considering I didn't cross into either of those circles, I had thought I was safe.

But Natalia is Mafia.

The thought keeps ringing in my head, louder and louder, until I can barely hear Maria wishing me a good day as I push open the glass doors that lead to freedom. The hot air hits me like a wall and I stagger for the sidewalk, the tears on my face drying instantly, only to soon be replaced.

Natalia, who is charming, kind, and protects me when no one else will. Natalia, who held me, fucked me until I forgot everything but her name. Her scent. Her warmth.

I stagger again, nausea roiling in my stomach.

I was so willing to pass off her easy violence as something that came with the territory of working in private security. I was so enamored that I missed all the warning signs that now scream at me.

My fingers dial Maddy's number before I know what I'm doing. "Come home," is all I say before hanging up.

The walk back to the apartment is a blur. One minute I'm pocketing my phone, the next, I'm standing in my bedroom shoving everything into boxes.

Maddy crashes through the front door. "Addie!" Her voice is breathless as she kneels beside me. "What's happening?"

"We need to leave."

I've never heard my own voice so devoid of emotion before. Now that I've had a moment to notice, the room seems darker, too, as if all the colors in the world have just gone out.

Maddy's face is flushed, her eyes bright with worry as she moves to hold my hands. "Why are you crying?"

"It's not safe."

"Is it your stalker?"

"She owns the apartment."

"Who, Natalia? Addie, what's going on?"

"Madeline."

Maddy's face blanches. I haven't used her first name since we first met and she immediately told me to just call her Maddy. She said before Donovan only her grand-mother still used that name for her.

"Okay, we can go," she says slowly, "but first, you need to tell me what's going on." She rocks back on her heels, taking one of my sweaters with her and folding it neatly in her lap before placing it in my open box. Her eyes are wide, full of trust and fear.

I tell her everything.

Thirty minutes later, we're in the back of Donovan's car driving to Maddy's parents' house. Donovan, much to his credit, says nothing to me the whole car ride, just sighs and turns on the radio station that I like and he hates. It's as close to a peace offering as either one of us has ever given the other.

Maddy sits in the back seat with me—to which he initially grumbled something about being a chauffeur, but one look had him quiet. Donovan never does well with tears. I don't think he really understands them.

Maddy's mom is the first to embrace me, and I do my best not to feel stiff. Maddy and her parents have a complicated relationship, to say the least, and while Mrs. Yapon has always been kind to me, I know enough about the woman to make me resent the embrace.

Mr. Yapon hangs back, helping Donovan unpack his car where we had stuffed just the essentials for the time being. Maddy brought up that there's no need for Natalia to steal anything from our apartment, so I didn't worry about leaving some things there. She promised to go back and get the rest later this week with Donovan once we find a more permanent place to stay.

Mrs. Yapon rubs my arms warmly and leads us to

Maddy's room, telling me to take and long as I need to unpack while she has a talk with Maddy downstairs.

My friend smiles in a way that doesn't reach her eyes before closing the door and leaving me alone in the room.

Mafia.

It sounds like a fake word, something that shouldn't be uttered in the real world, only on movie screens and books.

Mafia.

Natalia isn't just in the Mafia—she's the leader of it. Or at least this one in the city, however that works. I don't want to think about it.

Deciding to leave my boxes in the middle of the room, I quietly wander towards the staircase where I can hear Mads and her parents talking in hushed voices.

"There was mold growing in her room. A pipe burst or something and it got into the walls, that's why her eyes are all red and we left as soon as possible. Donovan and I are going to get the rest of the stuff later this week once it's safe enough to go back."

Then her father speaks. "Why didn't you stay with Donovan then?"

"You know he and Addie don't get on the best."

"Addison could stay here and you could stay with him," her mother supplies as I creep my way down the stairs.

I can hear the dejected tone of Maddy's voice even from my position halfway down as she says, "Wow, trying to get rid of me already?"

The joke falls flat, mostly because it's true.

I peek my head around the corner right as Mrs. Yapon

opens her mouth again. "Sorry to interrupt." I smile. "I just wanted to thank you again for letting us stay with you on such short notice."

Maddy mouths a silent "Thank you" as her mother embraces me again, then leads us to the living room to discuss new apartments.

CHAPTER 22
ADDIE

Unknown: Smart girl.

Three weeks. It's been three weeks since Maddy and I moved in with her parents, and three weeks since I cut all contact with Natalia.

I thought Natalia's big reveal would help soften the blow of our separation, but I was wrong. My anger does nothing but quickly warp into sorrow as I deal with our breakup, or whatever this is. We'd never explicitly said that we were dating, but I'd assumed it ran deeper than that with us. Dating sounds too casual for what was. I suppose it doesn't matter now that it's over.

She hasn't come by Tella's, either, and I don't know whether or not to be thankful for that. Part of my heart shatters further, knowing that she isn't even going to try to fight for me. The other part is glad that she has finally chosen to listen to me when I put up a boundary. Still, I watch for her as I stand behind the counter.

"That's a sad-looking latte," Daryl hums over my shoulder.

"It's because *I* am sad, Daryl, and I can smell your disapproval from here."

I don't usually snap back at the man, but today, I'm not in the mood. I've come to realize that loving Natalia was an addiction, and I've just cut it cold turkey.

The older man's gruff demeanor shifts for a moment and he stuffs his hands in his pockets. The lunch rush is tapering off now, with only a few customers waiting on their drinks. Slowly, he takes the cup from my hand and motions for me to give him my apron.

Fuck.

Fuck.

I'm getting fired.

I've lost Natalia, my home, and now I'm going to lose my job.

My brain begins to spiral to all the worst-case scenarios, from being found dead in a ditch after my stalker has his way to one of Natalia's hitmen gunning me down. Or worse, going back to my mother for help.

Panic flares in my ribs.

My mouth opens, but no sound comes out, not that it would do anything as Daryl holds his hand up.

Then he slips my apron on over his head and begins brewing a new espresso shot. "Take a break, kid, and tell the second circus monkey to do the same."

Tears well in my eyes, the invisible dam I placed over my weepy emotions now breaking at the sight of an old man in an apron that says, "Addie" in pretty swirling letters. As he hands the new latte to the customer, they squinted at the name tag but say nothing, and a small laugh escapes my throat. It might be a sob.

"Thank you," I croak.

He only huffs and tosses a muffin my way. "If your blood sugar drops and you pass out, I'll get sued. Go get it together."

Once Maddy is sure I'm okay sitting out behind the building alone, she heads back to the break room to make a call. She said she finally found a new apartment and the landlord just texted asking for a phone call to iron out the details.

The wind is picking up now, August slowly coming to a close. It's still hotter than is comfortable, but the breeze has the brisk bite of an autumn chill behind it now. Only one more month and the leaves will start to wilt and change color. Maddy talked about us going to the mountains, a trip to just get away from everything. I told her I saw a horror movie that started that way, but agreed, nonetheless.

"Addie?"

My heart hammers in my chest. The voice that called my name is soft, tentative, as if by breaking the silence, she'll break the fragile peace of the moment.

"I'll scream," I say, not bothering to look up at Natalia.

Judging by her voice and the new patch of shade that drops by my feet, I know she's far enough away. She's fast, but I still have time to get into Tella's and call for help if she tries anything.

"You don't need to do that."

"But I will, so don't come closer," I say, hating the way my voice shakes. My hands are, too, I notice with no small amount of ire. My whole body is shaking.

Mafia.

Natalia.

My mind and heart are at war and I force my hands into fists at my side. Three weeks. it's been three damn weeks and still, my heart breaks for her.

"Why are you here?" I finally ask, keeping my gaze trained on a blade of grass growing through the cracked concrete.

Natalia inhales sharply as if in pain. "Because I can't let you go," she admits.

"Why? Because I know too much? Are you going to torture and kill me too?" Admittedly, throwing what she said in her face probably isn't the best idea, but I'm too angry to care, too heartbroken to feel bad for the way I see her shadow flinch from the corner of my eye.

God, she fucking *flinched*.

"Please look at me, love."

"Don't call me that." I snap my head up, realizing my mistake all too late.

Natalia's face is gaunt, her eyes adorned with dark smudges and a bleary haze. Her cheeks are tear-stained, and a part of me fears that if the breeze returns, it will knock her off her feet.

My heart softens if only a fraction. This isn't the ruthless Mafia boss I now know her to be. This is Natalia, my Natalia, standing broken before me in a way I've never seen her before.

But she's both, I remind myself, and set my jaw. "What do you want?"

"Are you scared of me?" she breathes.

"Yes." Maybe?

No, I'm not. I could never be.

"You never have to be afraid of me. Hell, you're the only one in this world who never has to be afraid of me."

"Then why?"

"Because I love you."

I love you.

All the air leaves my chest as if the heat has stolen it away. My heart pounds in my ribs. *Breathe*, it screams at my useless lungs, *breathe.*

I can't.

I expect her to pause, to wait for me to say it back, but she continues, "It wasn't supposed to be this way. I was attracted to you, yes, but it wasn't supposed to go further than that. Then I had you, and you were mine and I couldn't stop thinking that if I wasn't yours then I was nothing. This empire, this world, it means nothing without you in it."

I love you.

It floods away all traces of the word *Mafia*, all notions of fear and anger.

I love you.

Maddy was the last person to say those words to me. Before her, it was my mother right before she left for a trip five years ago. She stopped saying it after that, and had stopped meaning it long before. My dad said it to me seconds before he died, one last act in his final moments of clarity.

When Natalia says it, I know she means it to the same degree my father did. Not in the same way, but the same intensity, the same fire. The way they both had to say those words before they lost the chance to ever say them again.

I love you.

"What do you want me to say to that?"

Natalia's face crumples and I feel a droplet hit my cheek. When did it start to rain?

"How am I supposed to ever believe a word you say to me now? How can I trust you when you lied to me for *months*? And don't you dare say you did it to protect me, because you did it for yourself. Because you're selfish and—"

Natalia's thumb brushes over my wet cheek. "Don't cry over my selfish heart, love."

My hand comes up to where hers is. I look up at the sunny, cloudless sky.

Oh.

"I *was* selfish," she continues. "I didn't want to lose you, and I knew I would the minute you knew the truth. But this is the only lie I have ever told you. All of it was real, and I will do *anything* to prove that to you."

Then she kneels.

"I will do *anything*," she repeats, tears shining in her eyes. "I will grovel for the rest of my goddamned life if I have to. I'll load the bullets and put the gun in your hand. I will give you the keys to everything I've ever built. I will kill everyone who stands in our way and leave this bloody business if it means you'd never cry a single tear over me again. Just please—" Her voice breaks, too thick with emotion as she bows her head.

I rise to my feet and wraps my arms around her neck.

Natalia, my Natalia, weeps into my shoulder, her hands bunching in the fabric of my work shirt. I run my fingers through her hair and inhale deeply the scent that is so strongly her that my knees tremble.

"Where were you?" The words comes out as a whimper.

Natalia grips me tighter. "Trying to stay away like you asked."

I laugh then, and it turns into a sob. "You're a terrible listener."

"I know."

"The worst."

"I know."

"And for that crime, you'll have to help me and Maddy move all of our stuff back into the apartment."

Natalia laughs, and it reverberates through my face as I nuzzle my nose to her neck. I missed her more than I'm willing to admit, more than I probably know, and now, having her back in my arms, my emotions wash over me in vicious waves. My legs buckle beneath me.

Natalia's arms secure around my waist, holding me up. "Don't break an ankle on me now, Collins. I'd hate to move all those boxes by myself."

Behind me, the staff door to Tella's swings open.

Maddy's mouth opens then closes of its own accord. "So I'm guessing I'll need to call that landlord back and tell him we won't be moving in this weekend?"

Before I can answer,, Daryl pops his head around the corner, his eyes narrowing in on my teary face. "I'm swamped up here. Break time's over. Addie, splash some water on your face, and you—" he grimaces, looking at Natalia, "—go sit in the booth or something. I've had enough weepy headaches today."

"Yes sir." I grin, wiping my eyes on the back of my hand.

Daryl glowers in a way that warns me to scrub my hands raw before I return to the espresso machine, then heads back inside.

Maddy pops her hip to the side, her arms crossing over her chest. "I've got a call to make. Addie, you get to cover for me." With a mock salute, she dives inside.

Natalia slips her hand in mine. It feels right.

Even with a million questions swirling in my mind, having her beside me feels right.

CHAPTER 23
ADDIE

Unknown: You were warned, and my patience is wearing thin.

My fingers trace idle circles across Natalia's bare stomach, my arms wrapped around her middle as we lay in her bed. We moved back into my apartment a few weeks ago, but Maddy is out with Donovan tonight and I figure she'll want the place to herself. Riven is stationed outside our apartment, nonetheless, a task I'm sure he enjoys.

"So your grandfather moved here and brought the business with him, which then passed on to your father before you..."

"Yes," Natalia admits. She's spent the past hour recounting how she wound up where she is in life, what happened to her parents, and the barest bones of how she met Riven. Whenever I asked her about it, she said I would simply have to ask him, as it is not her story to tell.

I know he and his brothers aren't on good terms anymore, and decide not to press.

"And you deal in weapons to your allies, but never narcotics?"

"That's more the Barones' thing. We stick to our own circles and do our best not to cross paths."

"But if something were to happen, you'd be the one to win, right?"

Natalia smoothes her hand over my hair. "Yes, but it isn't worth taking them down. The bloodshed on both sides would be catastrophic and someone would just rise up to take their place anyway. The Barones are at least in agreement with me that a turf war is the last thing either of us needs."

"What does Riven think of that?"

"He respects it."

I hum, contented. I can't imagine having family who hates me as much as his seem to. My mother doesn't hate me, she just doesn't love me.

"What about his mother? You mentioned his father is dead, but his mother is alive?" I ask.

"She's in Italy. I go visit her every few months to make sure she's doing okay. His brothers don't speak to her anymore."

A memory appears in the back of my mind—Natalia mentioned being jet-lagged our first lunch date on the drive back to my apartment.

"Were you in Italy visiting her right before we met?"

Natalia nods, her chin brushing against my cheek as she does so. "Riven heard that she had been hurt from someone in our circle. I went to make sure she was okay and was ambushed by a smaller group trying to catch me off guard."

My heart thuds in my chest. She was alone and a group tried to kill her. I picture Natalia, her against a group of trained and armed Mafia in a foreign country.

"Why didn't he ask her himself?" I force the shake from my voice.

"Because she thinks he's dead."

What?

Natalia continues, her voice solemn. "When shit went down between them, his brothers told her that he had been killed in a shootout. Said the body was too mutilated for an open casket funeral. They held a fake ceremony and everything, then told him if he ever tried to contact her, then they would kill them both. She moved back to Italy not long after."

The room around me becomes blurry as my eyes mist over. Riven is an ass at worst and a loyal friend at best, yet he always seems to drag with an invisible weight. Every joke is slightly guarded and meticulously planned, even if it seems like the wit is waiting on the tip of his tongue. It's almost as if he fears that one wrong move would drive us away from him, that if he was too smart or too irritating, another target would be placed on him, so he contends with always drawing the short end of the stick.

"Don't cry for him," Natalia says. Her knuckles graze my cheek. "He wouldn't want that."

"I suppose it's also a bad look to have me cry over a man in your bed."

"You're naked in *my* bed, so who you cry over is no cause for jealousy. I've already won."

I scoff. "I underestimated your confidence."

"I'm used to being underestimated." She says it so casually despite there being a greater weight behind her words. Her father underestimated her, and it led to his demise. My stalker has underestimated us, and it will lead to his ruin.

"Doesn't it bother you?"

Natalia waits a beat before answering. "It used to. Now, I realize it's a weapon."

"Do you enjoy it?"

"I enjoy the fear in a man's eyes before I put a bullet between them. Love that tiny flicker of realization between the moment of believing he's safe because I am just a woman, to the moment of reckoning with the pretty monster behind the barrel."

There's nothing I can say to that, so I simply lay my ear against her chest and listen to her heartbeat. If she's a monster, then she's my monster, and I'll learn to love her, claws and all.

———

Natalia in the morning is my favorite Natalia. Now, don't get me wrong, I love her at night—more specifically, *all* night—but there is something about waking up to find her in the kitchen. She always wears light-blue sweatpants and a gray sports bra while she cooks breakfast and nurses a mug of black coffee. I think those sweatpants might be the only pop of color she owns, and the pastel looks good on her. The blue settles nicely against her tan skin and seems to breathe life into her—a life that is easily forgotten when she is forced to wear black to hide bloodstains and bruises.

Different bruises litter her neck and chest now as I approach and I place a light kiss atop one near her shoulder.

"Morning," she hums. She has opted for eggs this morning, scrambling them to perfection, no brown bits.

I grunt back a less-than-human response before shuffling to the kitchen counter with my plate. Once I settle in my seat and reach for my fork, Natalia slides a folded piece of paper over to me. I can see the faint outline of bold letters through the paper, and raise an eyebrow. Usually, my heart would be racing with the fear of a new letter from my stalker, but Natalia wouldn't hand that to me first thing in the morning, let alone without any warning.

"What's this?"

"Something I put together while you were still sleeping."

"Someone was up early, I see." I wink.

Natalia only shrugs. This is nothing new. As trained as my body has become to early hours thanks to opening shifts at Tella's, nothing compares to how light Natalia sleeps. She'd hear a tree branch crack several stories below us from within the apartment, and bolt upright, hand reaching for her gun. I suppose that's what happens after so many years of having lethal enemies.

With careful fingers, I unfold the piece of paper, vaguely aware of Natalia's gaze pressing into me. I read the words written across the sheet and slam it back onto the table. "Shut up."

Natalia smiles into her mug. "Honestly, not the reaction I was expecting."

Italy.

Natalia is taking me to Italy next week.

"I'm going to have to call Daryl."

"I already did."

"And buy all new clothes."

"I thought we could go this afternoon."

"I need to tell Maddy."

"When you do, give her this." Natalia passes a second sheet of paper my way.

I didn't think it was possible for her smug grin to grow any wider, yet somehow it does when I read the second sheet and throw my arms around her neck. "Thank you, thank you, thank you!"

Natalia sets her coffee mug down to brace herself against the counter as I pepper her face with kisses.

"I need to go see Riven's mother anyway and you asked to go after the gala. She lives in Rome, so obviously, Riven can't be there, but we have a house in Positano that he and Maddy will meet us at after a few days."

After the gala... that was over a month ago, and even I had forgotten that I'd asked her to visit Italy. Natalia didn't forget—she never does.

I need to see a cardiologist at this point, after all the emotions this woman has subjected my heart to.

"You're incredible. Thank you. I mean it."

"I love you." She smiles into the kiss she places on my forehead.

I feel my stomach drop a bit as I keep my lips pinched together in a tight grin.

Natalia told me she loves me when we reconciled, and while I feel the same, I still haven't been able to bring myself to say it back. No moment feels right, and I know she's patiently waiting, but I can see her dim a bit each time she tells me and I say nothing.

"Before we head out later, I do have a favor to ask," I say. I prop my chin upon her sternum and use my best doe-eye impression on her, even though I knew there's no need.

"Anything," she says, and I know she means it.

"I got a text…"

Natalia's smile drops, but I press on.

"And I saw on the news that another girl was killed. Isabella Marx."

"That's right." Natalia's words are slow, deliberate. Her eyes squint, as if she's trying to see the plan unfolding in my head.

"I want to be more active in this investigation. I know you have meetings all this week, but do you think Riven would have time to take me to the coroner's office?"

"Addie—"

"I know it'll be hard to see," I swallow thickly, "but if we don't catch this stalker, then that could be me on that table next."

"I won't let him hurt you," she swears. "So if this is because you're scared, don't be. I'll protect you."

But who protected them?

Anna. Dillon. Dina. Isabella. Who swore those same words to them when the first text came through? Who is at home, sobbing, with the door locked and a kitchen knife in their hand because we haven't caught him yet?

I shake my head. "I owe it to myself and to those girls to try to find him. I won't do anything stupid to put myself in danger again, but I want to help. Let me help."

It isn't a request anymore. It's a demand.

Natalia saw what will happen if she tries to keep me out of this. This case is more mine than hers, and I refuse to be kept in the dark any longer.

She sighs through her nose, then shakes her head. "He has a break in two days. I'll ask him to take you then."

"Thank you."

My throat burns. Two days until I comes face to face with what could be my fate.

Two days until I meet my failure.

Two days until I meet Isabella Marx.

CHAPTER 24
ADDIE

Unknown: Would you like another gift?

I know Riven has arrived when suddenly, every woman in Tella's appears to be distracted. The woman in front of me nearly drops her macchiato as I try to hand it to her. Only Maddy crosses her arms and levels him with a glare.

"We're closed."

"Sign says you're open, ma'am."

Maddy walks out from behind the cash register and flips the sign. "Now it says closed."

Riven flips it back again with a wink.

Before the two of them can break the damn sign, I slip out of my apron and pat my friend on the shoulder. "Our shift is done. Kelsey and Trey just clocked in. I've got to go take care of some stuff with Riven. You good heading home alone?"

Mads waves me off with a small huff. "I'll be fine. I'll be stuffing my suitcase."

"We don't leave for another week," Riven notes unhelpfully.

"Don't remind me I have to spend twelve hours on a plane with you."

"Okay, and we're going now." I beam and all but push Riven out of the door. It was sweet of Natalia to decide to bring Maddy with us to Italy, and while I understand why she invited Riven, I fail to see how putting the two of them on a plane together is a good idea.

The drive to the coroner's office is near silent. I haven't seen Riven since Natalia told me about his mother, or his brothers who want him dead. It's harder than I thought it would be to not let it affect how I see him. He's still the cocky and kind Riven I know, but the sadness within him is all the more evident now that I know some of his history.

"I'm sure Natalia tried to talk you out of this," he says as we pull in to the parking lot.

"She did, but she was supportive when I put my foot down," I respond. "She also told me this is the private Mancini office, not the city coroner."

Riven nods and holds the door open for me. "I'm not taking you to see the body. It's hard enough talking about what was done to her, let alone seeing it in person. I'll show you the files and everything we've come up with so far."

I purse my lips at that but secretly, a wave of relief pushes my shoulders down. The idea was less scary when it was just an idea, and I'd thought I was braver than I am. But seeing the real body...

Panic clamps a fist around my chest.

In through the nose for five. Out through the mouth for five.

Riven scans an ID card against a metal disk next to the doors, then holds them open for me. When he scans the card again for the second set of doors, I rush forward and take the handle before he can.

"Chivalry isn't dead," he says with a small bow.

I let myself grin, then follow close behind. The hallway seems to get colder the further we walk, and a sinking feeling settles as a pit in my stomach.

"Here," Riven calls as we enter a final set of doors into a small office. It has no windows or second exits. On one wall is a cork board covered with red pins, but there's nothing pinned to it. It looks like a deconstructed murder board. Leaning against the other wall is a filing cabinet with a multitude of locks on each drawer. Riven grabs the key ring from his pocket and selects one before unlocking the second drawer from the top.

Motioning to the small metal desk in the center of the room, he spreads four files across the table. Water rushes in my ears as I see the initials.

A.R.

D.L.

D.S.

I.M.

A manila folder slides my way. It's identical to the other three in all ways save for the initials that act as an identifier. Riven settles on one of the metal chairs across from me and begins pulling out notes. His folder reads *A.R.*—the first victim.

I leaf through the file he handed me. I recognize the

name as the third victim: Dina Saffron. I'd heard her name on the news in my apartment right before Donovan interrupted my sacred Sunday ritual. I had been too busy being pissed at him to even think about the girl who will never feel anything again.

Riven glances up from under his furrowed brow. "Her file is pretty graphic. The photos are hard to look at, so don't force yourself."

"No, I need to find this guy," I breathe, my hands already shaking. "I can't do that if I don't know what I'm up against."

"We'll keep you safe, so don't worry," Riven promises, and I release a half laugh.

"This is something I need to do. If not for myself, then all these girls he's killed before me." For Anna. For Dillon. For Dina and Isabella. I committed their names to memory. They died for nothing, and I won't let their murders go unavenged.

Riven nods. "You sound like Natalia."

The corners of my mouth lift at that. "I told her something similar when she also promised to keep me safe."

Riven grunts but says nothing after that.

I let my eyes drift back to the page the folder fell open on. Dina's smiling face stares back at me, so beautiful and full of life. Her auburn hair falls loose around her shoulders, and she has piercing green eyes that people would write love songs about.

The list of injuries next to that face feels faraway and misplaced. The horror and mutilation she faced was surely nothing this smiling girl ever expected to go through.

I flip the page.

It's worse than anything I could have expected.

My hand flies to my mouth to cover my choking sob. Those green eyes are open wide with terror, her cheeks hollow as if she'd been screaming for hours. Riven had told me the first two victims were killed by suffocation, but Dina's throat had been slit in slow, jagged strokes. Her flesh raises in ridges like a child learned to use scissors by taking them to the skin of her neck. Her nails are bleeding and her fists split.

"She fought back," I whisper. "And he killed her faster for it."

Riven's mouth sets in a hard line. "Yes. The only good thing that came of it is we now know the killer isn't physically strong. If he was, he would have subdued her easier and wouldn't have been so sloppy, but he knew there was a chance she could overpower him."

"So he did something she couldn't come back from."

Riven can only nod, turning his face back to the second file—Isabella, the latest victim. Her body is down the hall. I look over to see those photos too. They're less gruesome than Dina's, and she died the same as the other two. I notice something on her photo that I hadn't seen on the others'.

"What are these eight dots?" I ask, squinting at the dots on Dina's arm—three on top, three in the middle, and two on the bottom.

Riven narrows his gaze. "They look like freckles. Or some minimalist tattoo."

"Did the others have one similar?" I ask hopefully.

Riven shakes his head. "No."

So much for that theory.

"Isn't there any other way we can track this guy?" I

slap the file shut between my palms. "Can't Natalia just use her connections to get access to the police reports and see who's filed a complaint about a stalker recently?"

"In this big of a city? That wouldn't narrow it down any. We already have access to those lists anyway, and they've proven to be less than helpful."

"And now with four dead girls, they still aren't considering helping? Or at least taking the claims seriously?"

"The police have to jump through certain political hoops that we don't have to. It honestly makes it easier for us, but that's beside the point." Riven's face drops into his hands and he glares at the file as if he can burn the killer's name out of it. "Again, it's down to numbers. In a city this large, women with stalkers are killed daily. And while the media is running with it right now, that's only because Dina's roommates contacted the local news station after the police failed to help her. It was smart on their part. It's giving everyone who thinks they could be next a chance to save themselves and be ready."

The logic is sound enough, and I'd be lying if I said that the thought of a few more people at least being aware of the problem doesn't make me feel a little safer.

"I do have a question, though," I finally say, hopping up to sit on the desk.

Riven's grin is mirthless as he replies, "You say that like you ever have anything other than questions."

My leg juts out of its own accord and finds its home in his shin. "Dina's file says she reported having a stalker two weeks before her murder. Isabella reported hers about two weeks prior, as well, but mine showed up months ago. Is there a chance this is someone different?"

"That thought has crossed our minds, too, but the fact

remains that his MO is the same, down to the same first text. We haven't figured out why it's taken him so long to make his move on you, though."

"Maybe he feels deterred because of Natalia? Even if he doesn't know about this whole Mafia thing," I say, gesturing to the gun holstered casually at his hip, "she's also known for Mancini Security. Maybe he knows he's biting off more than he can chew?"

"He would have stopped messaging you then. He also would have taken the bait when you were clearly alone and unguarded at that bar that one time. That was the perfect chance for him to take you, as Ryan demonstrated for us."

The smell of burnt rubber, blood, and asphalt hits me hard enough that I nearly gag.

"Thanks for the reminder."

"Any more questions?"

I purse my lips. "Yes, actually. About you."

"Well, fuck. Those never end well."

Natalia mentioned Riven's family before. I know Marco is his cousin and that he has a few older brothers who want him dead, but what I can't figure out is why. And why they told his mother that he's dead already. All I know of the Mafia is from horrible movies and a panic-fueled internet search once I found out the truth about Natalia, but a common factor is how important family is.

"Your brothers are Mafia, too, yet you choose to run with Natalia, and for some reason, they want you dead. Why?"

Riven's eyes snap up to mine, rage flickering across his hardened face for only a second before it returns to that unflinching swagger he seems to constantly possess. "And if I say that's none of your business?"

"That would be true, but it doesn't mean I don't still want to know."

Riven sighs, throwing his full abdomen into the motion before letting his shoulders slump in resignation. "I can't tell you much, for your safety, but Natalia and I were both born into this life. I assume she told you as much?"

I nod.

"I'm the youngest of three brothers. The Barones deal mainly in narcotics while Nat specializes in weaponry. We ran into each other sometimes, but not often. She deals in politicians and my brothers deal in scum. Being the youngest, I worked as a hitman for whoever my brothers decided needed to be taught a lesson. I hated it, especially when they brought home innocents, but I wasn't in a position to say no. It was either me or the others on that table, and I had to look out for myself.

"Until my father was on his deathbed and declared that it wasn't Malik that would inherit the crown of the Barones, but me. Malik put an immediate green light on my head. That's how Natalia found me, but instead of killing me, she took me in and made me her second. I still don't know why. Maybe to piss Malik off, or make some display of power so that if conflict is to ever arise between the Mancinis and the Barones, they know to back down. Still, she could've made me the muscle, but she gave me a spot in command. She's like a sister to me, and I'd die for her with no hesitation if she asked."

That answer, as heartbreaking as it is, is a lot more

mundane than the fantasies I've concocted in my head—ones that mostly involve gun fights and leather.

"I thought you two were fighting over a girl or something. That shit's a lot sadder."

Riven barks a laugh, leaning back in his chair. "Wouldn't that be simpler."

"Simpler than trying to find this man, at least," I groan. "Or woman. Natalia likes to remind me we could be dealing with a female stalker. Honestly, it would be kind of a girl-boss move."

"You're going to say that in front of the murder files?"

I cringe. "Yeah, that maybe wasn't the most tasteful thing I've said today. I just—"

"Need something else to focus on. I get it." His hand alights upon my shoulder with a reassuring squeeze. "But trust me, Natalia won't let anything happen to you. And neither will I."

"Or Maddy. Have you met Benny the Baseball Bat yet?"

Riven pales. "That thing in the corner of your living room has a name?"

"He usually lives under her bed, but with the stalker, he's graduated to the living room."

Riven swears, and it pulls a laugh from my throat. Despite being in the coroner's office of the city's largest Mafia group, the moment is nice. I haven't had a chance to meet many people since moving to the city. Okay, that's a lie—I *have* had plenty of chances, just haven't taken any of them. I either meet someone decent and my social anxiety clamps an iron fist around my throat or I meet someone crazy who drugs me and stuffs me in the back of his car. Even if Riven is Mafia, he's probably the first friend I've had aside from Maddy that I feel normal around. The anxiety was there at first, sure, but now, things are finally peaceful again. And it's nice. Despite everything going on, I feel at home.

"You and Natalia leave for Italy soon, right?" Riven asks as we exit the coroner's office. We didn't discover anything new or helpful, but I don't think anyone aside from me expected to. This excursion felt more like a trip for me than anything.

"Two days," I say, holding up two fingers.

While things are cooling down here, the temperatures in Rome are still fairly warm during the day yet cool at night. I'm a chronic over-packer, and Natalia must have gone through my suitcase with me no less than five times already. She told me we can take a second bag, but I refuse. The challenge is to fit it all in one bag, and I'm not a quitter.

Natalia might have brought home a bigger suitcase last night, but we aren't going to talk about that.

"Have you been back since everything went down with your brothers?" I ask.

His shoulders stiffen, but he answers once we're seated in his car. "No, I haven't."

"Are you nervous?"

"I'm not sure there's a word for what I'm feeling." He mulls the thought over aloud. "Maybe homesick could describe it."

I understand that feeling well—to long for something that you can never return to, that feeling of wanting something so badly and yet it's the one thing you cannot have.

"I appreciate you coming with and keeping Maddy safe."

Natalia doesn't want to worry about Maddy third-wheeling, or escorting her places, and she sure as hell isn't going to invite Donovan. Riven is the most obvious choice, yet we both know this won't be easy.

"My boss is giving me a fully paid vacation. There's nothing selfless in it."

And there it is again—that wall of charm that he uses to protect himself from what he's really feeling.

I smile for his sake, then look out the window.

I never noticed how blue the sky is before now. I used to complain that the city ruined the sky with its glass towers and metal monstrosities, but now all I can see is Dina's bright eyes that will never see a sunny day again.

The first tear rolls down my cheek like rain on a windowpane as I stare into the sun for her.

CHAPTER 25
ADDIE

Unknown: You can run to the ends of the earth and I will still find you, Addie Collins.

When I think of Rome, I think of the Vatican, the Trevi Fountain, and ancient Roman ruins. Rome is surprisingly modern, with beautiful buildings that weave together the urban with the classic architecture that has filled my Pinterest boards for weeks. Still, I never thought I'd be sitting at a gay bar overlooking the Colosseum.

"People used to fight to the death in there." I shake my head. "And now I'm drinking a martini and looking at it."

"Don't think about it too hard," Natalia replies.

We landed in Rome a few hours ago. Natalia planned for us to rest in the hotel for the night, maybe go somewhere quiet for dinner, before heading to see Riven's mother tomorrow. What she didn't expect was for me to be on a caffeine high from three airport cappuccinos and wanting to see everything immediately. We spotted the bar after wandering for a bit, so we stopped, and Natalia promised we can do the touristy things I want to do *after* we visit Mrs. Barone.

So here we sit, drinks in hand, looking over a bloody history. I've always been fascinated by mythology, which led me to study ancient Greece and Rome. Natalia told me I was a walking stereotype when I had said that. If I went back to school, I think I'd like to be a classics major. Creative writing seems like the obvious choice, but I don't know if studying the art would ruin my love of writing. I took a few classes in high school, and they were all focused on short stories and poetry rather than novels.

"I told Cecile we'll arrive around ten tomorrow morning. It will take about twenty minutes to walk there, so I'd say we should leave around nine so we can stop at a café for breakfast."

"Sounds good," I hum. "Does she know I'm coming too?"

Natalia sighs deeply in a way that makes her look more like an embarrassed teenager than a ruthless Mafia boss. "Yes. She was so excited, I didn't think I'd ever get her off the phone. I've never brought a girl to Italy, let alone to meet her."

"Aw, so I'm special?"

"If you're asking me that, then I haven't been a very good girlfriend."

"You're the best girlfriend I've ever had."

Natalia's eyebrow raises. "Oh, so there have been others?"

"I'm not a prude. I've had my fun." I wink, digging my toe into her shin when she has the gall to laugh.

"And tell me, how do I measure up?"

"Well, I already said you're the best, but if you must know, the last girl I dated might have been the most unhinged. She was about a year before I met you, but she was hot. She had these big blue eyes and light-brown hair."

"Oh?" Natalia's voice drops. "And why did you break up?"

"She thought I sold my soul to the devil because she had a bad dream."

As nice as it is to see Natalia jealous, it's even better to see her eyes widen and jaw drop. She sputters for a moment as if grappling for the right words to say before finally settling on, "Well then."

"Yep," I says, popping the "p."

I don't ask about the one girl she thought she was in love with. I know she didn't do relationships prior to me, but the thought of her with anyone else makes me feel like vomiting. It's only rational that she had other part-ners—we're grown women, for god's sake—but I hate the idea, nonetheless.

"What about me? How do I measure up?" I bite my lip. That came out more insecure than I hoped it would.

Natalia's hand reaches across the table and squeezes mine. "I've already started looking at wedding venues."

"Shut up." I laugh nervously.

She's joking.

She has to be joking.

I was in her suitcase this morning. I stored a few of my things in hers when I ran out of room in mine, despite the larger size. There was no engagement ring in her bag.

"I'm serious," she says softly. "I'm not proposing now, but I will one day, Addie Collins, so you'd better tell me what type of ring you want before I give you the biggest diamond I can find."

Hello, butterflies. Yes, you can live rent free in my stomach.

"I don't need a big rock. You could give me a paper ring and I'd say yes."

Natalia scoffs. "I'm not going to propose with a paper ring."

"It's about the sentiment, you idiot."

"I'm an idiot now? I thought you wanted to marry me."

"Yes!" I throw my hands in the air. "I'll gladly become Mrs. Idiot if you'd stop teasing me and just understand what I'm trying to say."

"I understand." Natalia's smile seeps into her voice. It's deadly, seeing her like this. She wears a casual black top tucked into tan trousers today that highlight the more feminine parts of her figure. I haven't stopped drooling since she came out of our room dressed like that and I just about had a heart attack when she pushed her sunglasses to the top of her head. It's the simple things that light a fire in my ribcage. Nothing needs to be fancy with her, I just need her however she comes.

Which seems hypocritical since we were in Italy on a trip that she paid for.

"What can I expect tomorrow? Obviously don't mention that I know Riven or that he's alive."

"That would be good, yes." Natalia nods. "She said

she's going to make us lunch, so be prepared for not only the best food of your life, but also the largest meal you've ever seen. She gets lonely, having no one to keep her company, so when I do visit, she treats me like the family she wishes she had."

My heart gives a palpable jolt in my chest at that, because she *does* have that family. She just thinks he's dead.

"How did you meet her, anyway? You brought on Riven after everything went down, right?"

"Right. After a few months, he told me about everything and asked if I could check on her. I lied to Cecile and said we'd been friends in the States for a while before his death, and that I came to check on her after I processed what had happened. She was so grateful and treated me so kindly, it just became a normal thing for us. Sometimes Riven texts her from my phone pretending to be me, and I ask all the questions he wishes he could."

My fingers lace through hers, replacing our loose grip on each other with a reassuring hold. "You're a good person, Natalia."

She has to laugh at that. "I think the rest of the world with disagree."

"The rest of the world hasn't had the honor of being loved by you."

Her throat bobs at that, and it's all she can do to kiss my knuckles. It's all she needs to do.

We pay our bill and walk to the hotel across the worn cobblestones, my arm draped over hers to avoid tripping. We've had one incident already where I slipped on the rain-worn stairs leading down outside the Colosseum. I nearly took out my ankle and an elderly woman.

The stars flicker in time with the streetlights as we walk, the breeze a sweet caress on the back of our sweat-damp necks. We throw open the windows in the hotel room in hopes that the breeze will enter our room as well. Rome is beautiful. The lack of air conditioning is not.

Despite the heat, Natalia holds me close while we lay in bed, her bare arm giving me full access to the tattoos weaving up it. I trace circles over one of the roses as she drifts to sleep, her head on my pillow.

Perfect. She's beyond perfect.

I love her. It hits me in every silent moment spent together when the noise of our lives die enough to let me hear it screaming in the back of my mind. I love her, and I have to tell her soon or my heart might stop.

CHAPTER 26
NATALIA

Unknown: The sun touches Italy too, goddess.

Addie's first alarm goes off at seven. Her second goes off at 7:30. By the time eight rolls around, she's turned off all future alarms, as well, mumbling something about "getting up for real this time" in her sleep.

I've been up since dawn again, the light that streams through our open windows waking me. I let her sleep, instead opting to lay everything out for the day and take a shower. When I return, she's still asleep, and the clock blinks 8:12.

Addie lays in the dappled sunlight, looking like she's been pulled from a dream I've never allowed myself to have. The sheets are tangled in between her legs, and her arms reach to the side as if reaching for someone.

I settle in beside her, pulling her prone form half onto my lap. "Good morning, love."

She blinks slowly, those blue eyes still fogged with sleep. My heart melts when she murmurs something that I think is supposed to be, "Good morning."

"You sleep okay?"

"I slept great," she says as she stretches her arms over her head. Her face tilts back to look at mine, and I'm struck again by just how beautiful she is, even while dreamland still has its grasp on her.

My fingers trace over the tiny speckles of hyperpigmentation across her jaw, feeling each divot and curve of her skin. Her cheeks flush crimson and she tries to cover her face, tries to hide from me. I wrap my hand around her wrists and pin them between us, my fingertips continuing to map the planes of her face.

"I was an awful picker as a teen. Still am, honestly." She releases a breathy laugh. "My mom always got onto me about it."

"Your baby battle scars," I murmur against her skin, pressing kisses to every one.

I can feel her laughter against my lips as I dive down to assault her neck, my arms moving around her waist. Her hands press against my chest. I pause only for a moment, propping onto my elbows over her, and just watch. Her hands rise to cup my face, her fingers tracing across the scar over my eyebrow.

With her chestnut curls splayed over the pillow and her blue eyes gleaming, she looks like a fucking goddess. And she's mine. Entirely mine.

"Okay, I'm awake now. What time is it?"

I look at the clock. "8:29."

"Fuck!"

And just like that, she shoots to her feet, staggering

when she stands up too fast, then rushes to the bathroom to get ready.

Watching Addie experience the things I've taken for granted is a new form of joy that I never knew I'd deprived myself of. I let her stumble through her breakfast order, as she requests of me.

"Cornetto con crema," I try to remind her, only to end up with a jab to the ribs.

Then I get to watch the entire walk to Cecile's as she practically moans through each bite. "Our pastries at Tella's aren't half this good, and I'm still hungry afterwards. I feel like I just had a full meal." She smiles and pats her belly, then moves her free hand back to mine, the other holding her cappuccino.

Italy isn't a necessarily homophobic country, but we still catch a few odd stares as we walk together. However, it's no different than living in the city back home, and I'm not concerned. If anyone has something to say, I still know plenty of places to dig an unmarked grave in this city.

"Just wait until you try Cecile's cooking. You'll be waddling home."

"Really?"

"Where do you think I learned to cook?"

Addie's gleeful giggle is well worth the embarrassment I know will be coming when these two women meet. Cecile might not be my mother, but she has enough embarrassing stories of me regardless from my young adult years, which are probably worse.

Cecile's house is a modest yellow building on the outskirts of the city. Her door is weather worn and chipped, but she refuses to let me replace it, or even install a security camera.

"What are you going to do from the States? Watch me get murdered?" she'd said.

I didn't tell her I have people in this city who can reach her, but I did make my displeasure known.

"Oh my god," Addie breathes. "She has flowers in her window!"

White flower boxes hang from the side of the house, sprouting blooms of all colors. It's quaint, and of course, something that Addie would love.

"You can tell her how much you like them in just a moment. She'd love to hear it."

Addie frowns. "Does she speak English? I should have studied my Italian more instead of sleeping on the plane."

"She speaks enough, but just be patient. Besides, I didn't give you much notice."

"Right," she sighs. I can practically see the anxiety building behind her eyes. She knows the rules we set by heart, but it's still risky bringing her here, in all honesty. If she mentions even one word of Riven to his mother, then she'll know he's still alive, and his brothers can come after both of them, and then Addie.

If it comes to that, I'd lay down my life to protect all three of them. I offered as much to Riven, but it was he who told me it's not worth the bloodshed. He misses his mother dearly, but his happiness isn't worth countless lives to him. I begged to differ. Still, it's the one request he's made of me in all the years we've been working together, and I agreed to honor it.

Cecile answers within ten seconds of Addie knocking on the door, as if she'd been waiting on the other side all morning.

"Addie!" She embraces my girlfriend first, squeezing her tightly enough that Addie jumps before hugging her back. "Come inside, come."

"Nice to see you, too, Cecile." I smile and close the door behind us.

The older woman waves her hand at me with a small smile, but nonetheless leaves Addie's side to embrace me as well. "You look skinny." She tuts her tongue.

I hold back my own remarks that she's a thin woman herself, and instead pinch her shoulder. "I'm fit. You should come work out with me."

"And I'm old."

I feel a grin spread across my face and warmth bloom in my chest. This place feels as much like home as anywhere else I've ever known, from the old family photos hung in antique frames to the pottery Cecile made herself.

"I love your flowers," Addie blurts out. "Outside." Embarrassment stains her cheeks pink and she starts to fiddle with the hem of her skirt, but Cecile beams.

"I have more in the back. We can go after lunch."

That seems to soothe Addie's nerves enough for us to make it to the living room. There, we're grilled on everything from how we met—which we make a more family-friendly story—to our flight here.

By the time lunch rolls around, the two might as well have known each other their entire lives. Cecile doesn't have to tell me she adores Addie. I can see it in the way she shows her how to roll the dough for the bundini di riso, and how she frets when Addie nicks her finger learning to cut a vanilla bean. Addie's finger might as well be made of gauze by the time Cecile finishes bandaging it.

Addie says nothing of Riven, even when Cecile tells her stories of the son she lost. Addie's eye's well up as if she's hearing the story for the first time, and I know it pains her all the same. She's an empath with a heart so big, it bleeds out of her.

I love her all the more for it. She hasn't told me she loves me back yet, but I know she does. I see her holding herself back every time the words almost slip out, as if she's afraid of some pain that isn't coming.

I know I hurt her with my secrets. I did more than hurt her—I shattered her heart and trust. I don't blame her for being reserved, and I meant what I said when I told her I would give her whatever she needed, even if all she asked for was time.

Lunch is even better than I thought it would be, and I send the two of them back into the garden while I do the dishes. By the time I'm done and they've returned, Cecile has tears in her eyes and Addie holds her hand.

"Did you tell her?" I mouth, panic flaring in my chest.

Addie shakes her head. "I'll tell you later," she mouths back.

"Thank you for coming." Cecile wraps her thin arms around my neck and squeezes tight. I can smell the lemon shampoo she uses in her gray hair and feel myself melt into her embrace.

"Thank you for having us." Addie dips her chin in respect. She looks like she wants to hug the woman, too, but her arms are too ladened down with leftovers. She tried to argue that the older woman should keep them, that it's too generous, but soon learned that Cecile is impossible to say no to.

"You should come more often." Cecile hugs her as well, then turns to me. "You'd better keep her."

I take the leftovers from Addie so she can hug the woman back. "I fully intend to."

Addie blushes at that. I've decided that her blushing might be my favorite sight. Pride swells in my chest every time—I caused that, she flushed red for me.

Her steps drag as we leave the pretty yellow house and I know what's weighing on her mind before she even says it. Still, I let her come to me first.

It only takes a few more steps before she sighs heavily and relents. "That house is so lonely."

That takes me aback. "What do you mean?"

I've never thought of the house as lonely. Cecile might have been a lonely person at first, but she's always warm when I come to see her.

But Addie shakes her head with a frown. "There's too many chairs at an empty table, most of the furniture hasn't been sat in, and the pictures... it's like she has ghosts framed on her walls."

"Christ."

"I told her about my dad," Addie interrupts, "and my mom. I told her I know what it's like to have lost the one family member that truly loved you and have to live with the one who never comes around anymore. I invited her to come visit us next time. I know I should have asked you first, and that probably complicates things, but she was just so heartbroken... and I couldn't—"

I kiss her then, a single tear sliding down my cheek to where our mouths meet. And then the rain begins.

CHAPTER 27
ADDIE

Unknown: Nymphs run faster than a goddess.

Natalia steps back and I can't understand why.

Then the first droplet hits my face. Then another. And another, until the world blurs in a motion of color and rain. Steam rises from the pavement quickly enough as the short sprinkle turns into a full-blown rainstorm.

Natalia hands me our bags, then holds her jacket over my head, swearing softly under her breath while trying to phone a cab.

I giggle.

Then I step out into the rain, setting my bags down on the sidewalk. I hold my skirt with one hand and an imaginary partner with the other as I step into a slow waltz. The water sprays around me, over me, through me. I'm nothing more than a flash of swirling color in the rain. I'm weightless.

Natalia watches with a bemused expression and something like wonder lining her eyes. "Dancing in the rain? That's a bit cliché for you, Collins."

"Well?"

"Well what?"

"Are you going to make me dance alone?"

I bite my lip as Natalia sighs, then pockets her phone and steps into the rain, a smile growing on her face. I grin too, throwing my arms out as hers encircle my waist, letting me lean back. The rain hits my face, running down my cheek and neck, between my breasts. I'm soaked, utterly soaked. But I'm alive.

Natalia steps easily into the dance with me, spinning me as if music is playing. We are one as we move, my steps admittedly more clumsy and free-spirited than her elegant and trained motions.

"I love the rain," I breathe, letting my head fall back. "I feel so close to the sky."

Lightning streaks the sky behind Natalia, painting her in darkness with a halo of violet around her wet hair. The soaking strands cling to her face and forehead, and she smiles, that beautiful fucking smile. She has to be an angel—a fallen one, at the very least but an angel, nonetheless.

Then her hands grasp my waist and she lifts me. She lifts me above the steam and the asphalt as cars speed by. She lifts me so I can spread my fingers to the sky and see the tiny colorful houses dotting the city.

I am the sky.

I am the heavens and the rain and the lightning that paints her skin golden.

"I love you." She presses the words into my cheek when she finally lowers me.

Natalia has been free in stating as much. She tells me she loves me as often as she can. I haven't found it in me to say it back yet, too scared of what those three words will bring. But I know now I'd rather face the risk of saying it back and opening my heart than lose her. Lose this.

"I love you, too, Natalia Mancini."

And the smile that splits her face in two takes my breath away, leaving me gasping as she plunges her lips to mine. I stand on my tiptoes, trying to reach her with her powerful frame, but she lifts me off my feet, holding me against her.

"I love you," I murmur through every kiss.

I don't care who sees, who hears. I love Natalia, and I need the rest of the world to know it too. The universe needs to know that I've claimed her, from now until the end of all things.

The rest of our time in Rome flies by far too quickly. Natalia makes good on her promise to let me go to all of my tourist traps. We go to the Vatican City first, and I learn that that is somewhere I'm never going again, not with my claustrophobia and their lack of air conditioning. We then stop at the Trevi Fountain and throw coins in. Natalia is less than willing at that point, protesting that she already knows she'll come back to Rome so there's no reason for her to toss a coin in. Still she throws one in at my insistence before we make our way to a rooftop bar nearby. I'm practically crawling to the train station when it's time to leave.

We have to take a train to Naples first, before boarding a ferry to Positano. I'm not a big fan of boats, but Natalia brings us to the front where they have an open window, and the trip is more enjoyable.

I'm ready to fall into bed once we arrive at Natalia's home. Everything on social media warned me that Italy would be a lot of walking, yet I still was under prepared.

"I'll rub your legs out tonight," Natalia laughs, carrying the last of the bags to our room.

"Now I know why you have such great legs."

I throw myself down onto the bed with little ceremony. The comforter is as luxurious as the one she has back in her apartment, but this one is a soft blue rather than the gray and black I've become accustomed to.

Natalia chuckles at that.

I prop myself up on one elbow and watch her unpack our bags, my offers to help falling on deaf ears. I've decided that acts of service is her love language. No matter how much I protest or tell her I can do something myself, she always does it on her own.

"Maddy and Riven arrive tomorrow morning. He just texted that the plane took off."

"Okay," I hum in acknowledgment, far too busy watching her tattoos flex as she opens a drawer.

"I had a few groceries delivered to the house while we were gone so I figured I'd make us dinner tonight."

"Okay."

"And then I was thinking you could strip every time you say, 'Okay,' without actually listening to what I'm saying."

"Sorry, you're very distracting."

Natalia smirks at that and continues to finish unpacking while I lose myself to my thoughts. My stalker has sent a few messages while we've been gone. No more creepy than usual, but the texts have been odd. They aren't his usual threats, and none of them make sense. He keeps making references to nymphs and gods. None of it is specific enough to pull a clue from. *Nymphs run faster than goddesses*, for one example, could refer to any number of Greek myths. The gods couldn't exactly keep it in their pants, and the word no was something they weren't used to hearing. Could the running be a reference to me and the other victims? Am I the nymph who escaped him, and they were the goddesses? It feels significant, yet I can't place my finger on it.

I think it over during dinner and feign fatigue when Natalia questions my sudden silence. We're here on vacation and it's bad enough that I'm worrying about it, but she doesn't need to be stressed over it as well.

Still, guilt gnaws at my stomach when we go to bed, our limbs entwined, and I jump at the sound of a new text.

Unknown: It's nearly time.

CHAPTER 28
ADDIE

Unknown: Five victims. Five souls tied to yours and mine like a wedding band.

A shock of blonde hair catches my eye first. Riven carrying three pink bags catches it second.

I can't stifle the laugh that escapes my lips at Riven's haggard countenance, and even Natalia chuckles before moving to help him. Meanwhile, Maddy all but throws herself at me.

"I missed you!" she squeals. "I need to hear all the details, like yesterday. How was Rome? How are you?"

"I'm good. Rome was amazing. More importantly, how are *you*? I am so sorry I left you alone at the apartment with all this going on."

Mads waves off my comment with a dismissive hand. "Don't even worry about it. Riven was outside my door every night, and as annoying as he is, I felt better having a trained killer on my side."

Maddy has taken the whole Mafia news a lot better than I did. Where I panicked and did a deep dive on the internet, she's held her composure and assured me that Natalia doesn't seem the type to kill someone for rejecting her. "Breakups happen all the time," she said. "It's too much effort to kill someone, anyway."

I'm sure I follow her logic, but I appreciate what she was trying to do, nonetheless. She has always been the forgiving and accepting type, anyway, whereas I am the guarded one who has forgiven too many times and been burned.

I link my arm through my best friend's and show her around the house. I explored it a bit last night and was pleasantly surprised to find that it is the exact opposite of Natalia's apartment back in the city. Where her apartment is minimalist and grayscale, this house is full of color. The wood is a deep brown that contrasts against cream-colored countertops. Colorful art hangs on every inch of the walls, and the furniture is either cream or the same light blue color as the duvet in the master bedroom.

Maddy's room is down the hall from ours, with Riven taking up the room on the first floor.

"This is so nice," she sighs, sprawling herself across the bed. "It's been so boring at home."

"What, Daryl isn't keeping you busy?" I ask. The old man nearly flew into a rage when we told him that both of us would be gone at the same time. He was only placated when we agreed to bring him back a souvenir and work double shifts when we return so he can go visit his family up north.

"Oh no, he was, but you were gone and my parents

don't get back from their cruise until tomorrow morning."

"What about Donovan?"

Maddy stiffens as if on instinct, but brushes it off with a smile that doesn't reach her eyes. "He's working on a case right now. His client is totally guilty, but that's just making his job all the harder. So no boyfriend time for me either."

I lay my palm flat on her shoulder. So much for not feeling guilty this trip.

Before I can say anything Riven knocks at the door. He wears only a pair of red swim trunks and sunglasses that he's pushed to the top of his head. "You two ready?"

"Fuck, I forgot to tell you. We're heading to the beach. I got distracted with the Donovan talk." I turn to Mads, but she's already rummaging through her suitcase for a suit.

I should have brought water shoes. Natalia warned me that the beaches are rock here, but I severely underestimated how much it would hurt to step on rocks with bare feet, no matter how smooth they are, having been rolled by the sea. Maddy, at least, is hobbling with me as we make our way to the water.

All the public beaches were way too crowded, but Natalia and Riven knew a hidden one with barely anyone on it, so we went there. Riven is currently trying to throw Natalia into the water, and she's threatening to emasculate him with one of the blunt rocks.

Riven throws his head back with a sigh before

hanging up on whoever had called him and returning to us.

Natalia's eyes immediately narrow in on his darkened expression. "What is it?"

"There was another murder," Riven says darkly. "Elain Hart. And her body came with a note."

I don't miss the way his eyes trace to me.

"What did it say?" Maddy asks when my words fail.

"'Tell Addie there's only two more,'" he says, his tone grim.

Natalia leads us home, where everything is quickly packed up. I am only vaguely aware of standing, being led to the ferry, and then to the private jet Natalia called to Naples. Maddy has one hand in mine the entire time, only letting go to help load our bags onto the plane.

I hardly hear Maddy asking Riven if it would be safer for me to stay here with him while she and Natalia return home to investigate. He shakes his head and offers some explanation that I can't hear over the rushing in my ears.

Half of me hoped that the other murders weren't connected, despite the multiple pieces of evidence and texts that prove otherwise. I lied to myself for months, saying that my stalker could have just taken credit for the murders to intimidate me, but now...

Now there is a dead body with a note addressed to me.

I can't ignore the evidence any longer. My stalker is the serial killer who haunts the city streets, and he still has two more lives to claim before he comes for me.

CHAPTER 29
ADDIE

Unknown: Sorry to derail your vacation.

The clock on my nightstand blinks back 3:30 a.m. as a sharp rapping sound from Maddy's room fully rouses me from my sleep. Still groggy, I roll onto my side, pressing my face into the cooler side of my pillow.

We landed in the early hours of evening, Natalia and Riven dropping Maddy and I off back at our apartment before heading to the coroner's office to inspect the new body that came in. I offered to come with, but Natalia only shook her head.

"It's one thing to see the pictures a few days or weeks after it happened, but it's a whole 'nother beast when the body is fresh and right in front of you," Riven explained. "You don't need that on your mind."

So we returned to our apartment, the two of them promising to stop by later. Marco was on a mission but promised he was on his way before Natalia and Riven begrudgingly left.

"What are you doing here?" Her voice comes out low and harsh.

Someone is in the house.

Then a scream splits the air.

Maddy's scream.

"It's you!" she sobs as a crash follows. "All along, it was you!"

I can't move fast enough, my legs tangled in the sheets. Marco. Where was Marco?

"Maddy?" I shout, anxiety strangling my voice. Where is Natalia's gun? She left one here a few nights ago, so where...

"Addie, run! Ru—" Her voice is cut off.

The silence that follows is worse than anything I could have imagined.

I don't think, I just run to the sound of that silence.

I barely register the dark figure standing in the middle of my living room. All I see is Maddy's prone figure lying on the ground, a puddle of crimson growing beneath her.

"No!" I gasp. "*No!*"

If it's going to be anyone, it's supposed to be me. He is supposed to kill me, not her. Never her.

I barely register the arms wrapping around my midsection before I'm screaming. The noise that tears itself loose from my throat is raw and animalistic. I've been screaming, so why have none of my neighbors come running yet?

I throw my elbow back just like Riven taught me, hitting my assailant's nose with a sickening crunch. He throws his head back and releases me just for a second, but a second is all I need. I crawl towards the kitchen, towards the knives I know how to use. I have to hold it blade down and handle up, and slash, not stab. If I can just get on the offensive—

I don't notice the smell in time, don't notice how the world begins to spin and my muscles feel like weights tied to my bones. I'm slowing down, but I'm so close. I have to keep moving. I have to...

The last thing I'm aware of is someone grabbing my ankle, then the world goes dark.

CHAPTER 30
NATALIA

Unknown: Checkmate, Mancini.

Our first stop after we landed was dropping Addie and Maddy off at their apartment. I wanted Addie to stay at my place, but she didn't want to leave Maddy alone and I don't have a guest bedroom. She insisted they were fine until I got home. Once we were sure they were locked in safely, we sped for the coroner's.

I sit at the metal table I've become far too acquainted with. The four victims' files are spread out before me. There has to be something we missed that could have prevented this. I have Marco at the victim's house searching for a lead, hence my main reason for being hesitant leaving Addie at her apartment. I have everyone chasing down leads and no one else that I trust enough to protect them.

Riven snaps his phone shut and motions for me to follow him next door.

A pit settles in my stomach at the sight of the white sheet over the table and the outline of the body beneath it. No matter how long I've been in this industry, it never gets easier seeing an innocent death. Even with all the blood on my own hands, it still makes me ill.

"The new body came in. Forensics matched her to a missing persons report. Elain Hart, age twenty-three, reported missing a few nights ago. Autopsy shows the same as the other victims, but I want to show you something." Riven reaches down and pulls back the sheet to reveal the woman's ghastly face. Her eyes are closed, lips split and parted. The body has begun to bloat in areas, the file also noted bruising appearing on her back where the blood has pooled. My gaze drifts lower to her arm that Riven now holds up. On the underside of her forearm are eight dots—three at the top, three in the middle, and two on the bottom.

"It's the same as the last victim," I note, my blood running cold. The bruising was too severe on the previous two victims to note anything on the arms, but what if...

"I want the full autopsy reports on the other five victims. Search for any tattoos, time of abduction, anything minute we could have missed, and then find me the shithead who's in charge and didn't report it to me." I'd grabbed the files before we left the room and now spread them across a clean table, searching for anything at this point.

"Already did, Nat." Riven all but cringes as he runs his scarred hand through his dark hair. "All of them have the same tattoo. All the dots are in the same placement, but the tattoos themselves were in less obvious spots."

Almost like the killer wanted us to find it today.

"And how did we miss this?" I ask, fighting the urge to crumple the files in my fists.

"Coroner was paid off. They found him dead in his apartment this morning with a suspicious amount of cash. Bullet in the back of the head, obviously didn't see this guy coming and thought to get the hell out of dodge. But there's more." He inhales sharply as I thumb through the files, finding all he's said to be true. "The time of abduction was 3:32 a.m. on the dot for all of them. Time of death, 3:32 p.m."

Three dots up top. Three in the middle. Two on the bottom.

The bastard was feeding us clues all along.

I slam the files on the table when a word catches my eye. The latest victim's name was Elain. I pull out the autopsy reports and lay them each beside each other, my gaze narrowing on the line I'm searching for.

Anna Russo.

Dillon Lars.

Dina Saffron.

Isabella Marx.

Elain Hart.

Anna. Dillion. Dina. Isabella. Elain.

Addie.

"What day is it?" I grind out, glancing at the clock. 3:33 a.m.

Riven's eyes track my gaze, then widen as if he realizes the same thing. His lips part as if to argue, as if to proclaim it isn't possible.

I clench my jaw until it cracks.

He fumbles in his pocket, searching for his phone. It clicks open and his face blanches. "It's the second of the month."

Second of the month. The body has been cold for at least three days despite just being found, and it's been nearly three weeks since the last victim.

I'm out the door before Riven can say anything else, my phone in my hand instantly, thumbs flying over the keys as I dial Addie's number.

It rings once.

Then twice.

My name is a distant cry in the background as I hear Addie's voice come over the line. "Hi, you've reached Addison Collins. I'm sorry I can't make it to the phone right now. Please—"

I call again.

And again.

By the fourth time, my keys are in the ignition and Riven's headlights are tailing me as I tear through the streets, driving the path to the place I could find blindfolded.

"Pick up. Goddammit, pick up, Addie!"

The car is barely in park when I throw open the door and leap from the vehicle, taking the steps to her apartment four at a time. I can hear four other sets of footsteps closing in behind me—Riven and backup, presumably. The sounds fade compared to the roaring in my ears as I reach her apartment door. Marco is slumped against the wall, breathing with no signs of external injury but out cold. There's no marks on the door, no signs of a struggle or noise disturbance complaints made by the neighbors

—nothing but a lingering smell that makes my head spin. I pull a mask from my back pocket and Riven does the same, now joining me at the door. He orders our other men to take care of Marco while he follows me.

The wood shatters upon impact as I drive my boot through the door. It wouldn't have been necessary, though, when I find, to my horror, that the lock was never latched. Then I note a few scratches around the key hole that I had failed to see in my panic earlier. The smell is lesser in here, as if it didn't make its way in all the way, or the apartment was an afterthought.

The small apartment is a mess. Their sparse furniture has been overturned, the wooden chair splintered, and blood splattered across their kitchen counter. I rush to her room, already knowing what I'll find. Her bed is a mess, the sheets falling to one side to the floor as if she'd been pulled from her bed while asleep.

I rush to the bathroom.

Nothing.

Then Riven's voice rings out, laced with panic. "Natalia!"

I follow the sound to the living room, where I see my second kneeling on the floor, a familiar blonde woman pulled into his lap.

Fuck.

Maddy's hairline is crusted with rust-colored blood that seeps from a deep wound near her temple and bruising already mottles the rest of her face. Her lip is split and nails torn, bits of tan flesh beneath them. Bruises litter her arms and bare legs, and her breathing is shallow. A bruised rib at best, a few shattered at worst.

"He must have broken in here for Addie but Maddy heard first and tried to save her."

"Why not kill her?" Riven's voice is cold, hollow. The emptiness in his usually warm tone is contrasted only by the rage burning in his eyes.

"Addie probably woke up. Thrashed. Put up a fight. He needed to move her to a secondary location and didn't have time," I say with startling clarity.

I try not to think of how easily the mask slides back on, how quickly I'm able to shut down everything but the calculated killing rage. I point to the spot of the invasion, the evidence, and outline what must have happened for Riven, who remains motionless on the floor, his fingers pressed to the side of the blonde's throat.

My heart strains beneath the fury and rages at the sight before me. Riven has never been able to turn his emotions off like I can. He can mask it for the victims, let them see sympathy and strength instead, but he can never turn off his rage. He can only quiet it as not to startle the untrained eye, but this...

Pure bloodlust lights his face as he rises, Maddy limp in his arms. Her head lolls back, blood driveling down the side of her face, over the curve of her cheekbones. He stares at her, never once lifting his gaze, even as he calls for backup. But time is running thin. This bastard has Addie—*my* Addie—and I have less than twelve hours to find her alive, if that.

"Take her to the hospital. The civilian one, not ours. The fucker must have gassed the whole building, and as soon as they wake up, the public will find out. They'll search for her, and it will look better for us and her if she was found by a concerned friend who brought her to the hospital."

Riven's gaze rises now. "But that will send the police searching for Addie."

And inevitably interfere with our own investigations. At best, it could tie us and the whole organization to the murders. At worst, it will delay us long enough that Addie's body will be found cold.

"I'll find her before the police even hear a whisper of this."

A promise, one as lethal as the gun hanging at my side or the knife on my thigh. I will use my own hands if I have to, but this sick bastard's death will not be slow or kind.

My phone buzzes in my pocket. I ignore it.

Then again.

And again until finally I pick it up to see Addie's name flash across the screen.

Riven goes still, waiting on my every breath before I slide my thumb across the screen and put the call on speaker. There are no cocky phrases, no carefully honed rage when his voice comes through, smooth and low.

"Natalia Mancini. You have two hours and thirty-two minutes to meet my demands."

It's familiar. So fucking familiar.

"Or what?" I breathe.

A gun clicks in the back.

"You know what," he snarls before the call disconnects.

The phone pings.

One new message from Addie.

She's tied to a chair in a dark room, the ropes so tight

that they're soaked with blood as they dig into her skin. Her eyes are unfocused in the light, but they're burning with hatred and rage.

That's my girl.

Then I notice something. There is no shock, even in her concussed state. She knows him.

Most victims know their stalker to some capacity, but her lethal rage runs deeper than the inflicted injuries across her flesh. This is the fury of betrayal. He's someone she knows, who maybe she doesn't like but trusts enough. Just enough to delay her and Maddy a few seconds when he broke into their apartment.

"Run forensics on the skin under Maddy's nails," I bark to Marco.

He nods, quickly collecting the sample under Riven's scrutinizing gaze, then moves to our lab to analyze it.

"Do—" Maddy's voice is a croak that breaks the silence in the room.

Riven jumps, moving to brush the hair from her face, but she shakes him off. Her heavy-lidded eyes find my own and she lifts her hand to her throat as if to force the words from her throat.

"Don—"

"Don what, Maddy?" Riven asks with heartbreaking gentleness. "Who did this to you?"

A shuddering cough wracks her body, and her eyes squeeze shut in pain. Riven's knuckles go white at the whimper that slips through her lips, but Maddy keeps her eyes pinched closed as she whispers,

"Donovan."

CHAPTER 31
ADDIE

Unknown: Two hours.

I'm going to fucking kill him.

The flash of the camera burns my eyes, the sudden light violent in the otherwise dark room. My body aches and I know the blood I see on the floor is mine.

Donovan stands just a foot away, typing a message on his phone. It dings a moment later and he smirks before pocketing the device. He sports a purple bruise across his cheek, curtsey of Maddy, and a crooked nose, courtesy of me.

Yet in the end, my self-defense lessons failed me. Riven and I trained for physical attacks, but hadn't quite breached the gray area of chemical ones yet. He had to have used something on the whole building, and of course, he would have the means to pull off a feat like that.

"Untie me, you bastard," I hiss.

I will kill Donovan, nice and slow, for what he did to Maddy.

"And why would I do that," he smiles, bringing his hand down to trace my jaw, "when I went through all that work to get you here."

I snap my teeth at him, almost catching the skin of his palm, but he's too quick and the ropes around my wrists are too tight. That was the first pain I was aware of when I awoke. Every time I move, the ropes bite deeper into my flesh, the fibers lodged in the wound.

"Are you going to kill me?"

Donovan's gaze bores into me as if I just asked the stupidest question in all of human history. "Again, why would I go through all that just to kill you?"

"Because you're a twisted asshole who gets off on throwing women around?"

"Because I want you alive, not dead."

"Why?" I bite out.

I retrace all the events of the past few months in my mind. It would make sense that he could get into our apartment undetected. He probably has a key or knows where Maddy hides the spare. He would have known where my room is, where I work, when I go out, and when I'm alone. Maddy and I are always together, so she was the perfect well of information.

But why?

Donovan peers over his nose at me, and I bite back bile at the unadulterated lust in his eyes. He's enjoying this, me tied up and fearful before him. God, he wins sicko kink of the year.

"Do you know how we met? Me and Madeline?"

"At one of her galleries. Her photos were on display and you liked a piece so much you came and introduced yourself to her."

"Yes, but did she tell you which photo?"

No, actually she didn't. We were both too excited that someone was interested in her work—and interested in her—that we overlooked the details. I never asked.

Donovan continues when I shake my head. "It was you, in the bathtub, with your knees pulled to your chest. There were flowers in your hair and you were looking up at the camera as if it were your god. The photo was grayscale, but your adoration poured color into it. I knew I needed you the moment I saw it."

So he had used Maddy—my Maddy, who is sunshine personified and loves as freely as she can. Who checks for still-living roadkill, even though it breaks her heart, just in case she can save one who might be alive.

"So what, you used her to get to me?"

And the hell she went through being with him—the manipulation, the snide remarks.

I'm going to kill him.

"I hoped you were a model and I could pose interest and get your number from her, but you had to be her best friend and not interested at all. So yes, I used her." He laughs then, a hollow, chilling sound. "It killed me to be with her, but she was the best I could do to stay close to you. Especially when you eyed me with such disdain, and refused to shed any of that adoring light my way."

Because I like women, asshat.

"You know, I even called out your name in bed once. That was the only moment I think Madeline suspected anything. I never called her Maddy, so it was harder to manipulate her into thinking I'd called her by that name."

Tears drip down my face. "You sick, sick fuck." She didn't deserve that, and I don't deserve this. None of it. Both of us are just pawns to him, things that he can throw around and use however he wants.

"Why didn't you kill her?"

"I'm assuming that's not disappointment in your voice." He smirks, far too close to my face for my liking. "I wanted to. God, she annoys the fuck out of me, but I needed her to get to you. If she died, you would have no reason to speak to me, and you're not exactly the type to come to someone you hate for comfort."

"She's a good person," I spit at him.

"She's too good of a person. No matter how many times I pushed her down, she still smiled at me and thought she deserved it. Not you, though. No, I'd push you and you'd push back. You have the same darkness in you that I do."

"You're wrong."

"It's what drew you to Natalia. You learned the truth about her and didn't care because she was bloodying her hands for you. Well, guess what, goddess?" The laugh that slips between his lips is far from human. "I did this all for you."

"Stop," I plead.

"You're smart. You like a challenge, so I gave you one. I even wrote the hints in a language you could understand."

"But I *don't* understand," I try again. My restraints bite the broken flesh around my wrist, but I'm beyond caring.

I'd rip the ropes from myself even if it meant losing my hands. I'm going to break free and kill him.

Then the chair rocks. One of the legs is loose.

"The eight tattoo dots on the girls, the Orion constellation? You love Greek mythology, so I thought you'd at least figure that hint out, but I guess my friend at the coroner's office did too good of a job hiding most of the tattoos."

He fucking branded them. He did that for *me* because he thought I'd like it.

I'm going to be sick.

"I've been hunting you, this whole time, little goddess, and we are going to go very far away from here the minute your little Mafia friend sends over the money I asked her for."

"How'd you know?" I gasp. If I could lean forward just a bit more, I could break the leg off. I could get free and—

"Jon Michels was good for a few things—including giving me intel on Natalia and planting the first body at her feet. He also gave me the perfect place for you two to meet so you'd have no one to turn to but the one person I gave all of my clues to."

My heart thuds to a stop in my chest.

He wanted me to meet Natalia? As some part of his sick game?

"Speaking of," he says so casually, as if he were referring to a change in the weather, "I'm expecting a call from her."

"I won't go with you." I thrash, if only to give me an excuse to loosen that chair leg. "I love her, and I could never love you. If you want me to go with you, you'll have to kill me and just drag my body."

Donovan runs a hand through his greasy hair with a sigh. "You know, I thought you'd say that. That's why we're having this little phone call."

He moves faster than I thought possible, closing the distance between us with a gun now in his hand. One arm drapes lazily around my shoulder and he holds the phone in front of our faces as he dials Natalia's number, the other holding the gun to my temple.

Then Natalia's face comes on the screen.

CHAPTER 32
NATALIA

Unknown: Tick tock, Natalia.

Donovan makes perfect sense, and I'm a fool for not seeing it sooner. He has the means, the manipulative charm, and the gall to pull this off. Not to mention, he has access to Addie through Maddy.

Riven returns to my office after Maddy goes into surgery to repair her internal bleeding. He called her parents, who are on their way. Ever since he returned, he's been cold, calculating, and all too much like the hitman I found years ago.

"The dots on the victims!" I snap my fingers as I call to Riven. "They match the constellation of Orion."

"Who?"

"The hunter who fell in love with Artemis. She's the virgin goddess of the hunt," I explain. I make a mental note to thank Addie for her Greek mythology knowledge when I see her again.

"So she's unattainable, like Addie."

"In some myths, she loves him back. I don't know if that part matters. What *does* matter is that he sees himself as a hunter, and he's been hunting her all along. If he's that committed to getting her and proving that he can best me, he won't kill her right away."

"Not unless she refuses him, which she will. He has an ego that bruises easily. You saw Dina's file too."

All I see is Addie's flesh torn. Him pinning her down as he drags that knife across her throat for refusing to submit to him.

I push the thought from my mind. I can't be distracted, not now. Not while her life hangs in the balance.

"Is there anything else from the myth that could lead us to him?"

My hands pull at my hair. He was a hunter. Artemis was the goddess of the moon. He was placed in the stars.

Then my phone buzzes. A text from Addie's phone.

Addie: My demands are simple. The little goddess refuses to submit because she believes she is in love with you. You will call her and tell her that you never loved her and that you just used her to find me. After that, you will let us leave this country with no resistance, or I will kill her.

Fuck.

I show Riven the text.

His face pales. "You need to stall until the end of the two hours. If we can't find her by then, you can call and stall them. If you call now, he'll just take her out of the country sooner. How much time do we have left?"

I glance at my watch. Less than an hour.

"Not enough." I feel raw anxiety crawling its way up my throat. "Think. He's a lawyer. Has he taken any cases with any hunting companies lately? Any companies in related fields—astrology, mythology?"

Riven types something on his computer and swears lowly. "He took on a defamation suit against the owner of the old conservatory earlier this year."

"Send someone to the conservatory."

My second shakes his head. "It was torn down three months ago."

A low growl slips from the back of my throat when Riven's eyes widen.

"Wait," he says. "There are plans to build a new conservatory. The property they bought is half an hour from here. It's close to the private airport strip too."

I'm already halfway out the door. One glance at my watch tells me we won't make it in time. There's only twenty minutes left until he kills her. I'll have to make the call soon.

Fifteen minutes later, Donovan makes that choice for me when he video-calls me from her phone. The first thing I see is a gun pressed to the side of Addie's head, Donovan's finger on the trigger.

"I hope you can talk fast because you're running out of time," Donovan says. "Unless you'd rather I kill her."

"I'd rather you kill me," Addie spits, fighting against her restraints.

"Do *not*," I growl.

This catches Addie's attention and she looks at the screen. A light seems to go off in her mind as I tilt the camera slightly to let her see the motion outside the car window. We're coming for her, she just has to stall him.

"Addie—"

"Don't," she breathes. "Don't do this. Don't talk like you're about to say goodbye."

"I can't let him kill you," I plead. "If he takes you, then I can find you. I will rip this world apart for you. I can't bring you back from the dead."

"I won't go with him."

I swallow the bile rising in my throat. "You have to."

Addie's voice does not waver, even with the gun pressed to her temple. "I'd rather spend the last minute of my life loving you than spend the remaining years without you."

"And what if I don't love you?"

"You don't mean that."

"Donovan challenged me when he started killing girls right under my nose. I needed someone I knew he wanted to have, then you walked right into my office and you were perfect. If I could get close to you, then I could use you to find him."

I can't bear to look at her, and yet, I can't tear my eyes away, knowing that if I fail, this might be the last time I ever see her.

I want to vomit when I say, "You called it yourself on our first date. Ulterior motives, remember?"

I watch the light drain from her eyes the moment the words pass my lips, and even though I know it's all fake, the sight nearly kills me. I know when this is over, she will be in my arms and this will all be behind us, but god, right now, it takes all my effort not to keel over.

Those rosy lips part, swollen and split, but before she can say anything, the call is disconnected. The last I see is her red-rimmed eyes burning with a broken rage and sorrow.

"Damnit!"

We're only a few minutes away," Riven says as he speeds down a dirt road. The GPS says we're only five minutes away, but too much can happen in five minutes. Backup is on its way, but they're too far. We'll get there first and even then, we might be too late.

Then another text comes through.

It's a voice memo. I know from the first few words that he sent it on accident. Donovan is swearing, then there's the sound of splintering wood. Addie tells him to eat shit.

Then Addie's voice is near breaking over a scream, then the sounds of thrashing, before a gunshot.

Silence.

CHAPTER 33
ADDIE

"**Y**ou can eat shit," I choke out to the man holding the gun to my head.

Natalia didn't mean any of what she said, I know it in my soul. She loves me, and whatever she said must have come from Donovan and his threats. Still, I fight the tears that burn my face as they fall.

She wanted me to stall, I can feel it. There was something in her gaze that told me to fight, that she's coming even as she broke my heart. Even if Natalia wasn't lying, I know her too well. She wouldn't leave me to die.

I need to get out of here. If Natalia truly sent Donovan money, then he will try to move me to another location, probably an airstrip where we can leave the country. He has bags packed in the corner of the room and the means to hire a private jet that won't ask questions. I probably have a few minutes at best, a few seconds at worst, to make my move.

Donovan, too busy gloating his victory to notice my

plotting, pockets his phone and drops the gun a fraction of an inch.

Now. It has to be now.

Seeing my chance, I throw my head back into his jaw, letting the chair fall with it. The gun goes off and I scream despite myself, even as it just grazes my collarbone. The chair shatters upon impact, freeing my arms.

Donovan careens to the side, clutching his jaw. "You bitch!"

"How original," I gasp, even as I try to get to my knees.

My head is spinning and I can't hear out of my right ear. The gun was too close when it went off, so all that remains of my eardrum is a hollow ringing sound. Still, I crawl forward, the arms of the chair I was tied to sliding free of the ropes. I nearly sob with relief as the bonds fall free as well, finally giving my skin reprieve.

Donovan stumbles blindly, his eyes lit with fury. His gun skittered across the room, forgotten as he lunged for me, but I'm up and waiting for him. My self-defense training with Riven comes back to me in the form of muscle memory that somehow manages to override my panic. I wait until his hands reach for my throat to grab his arms with one of mine while the other drives my elbow into the side of his face. The blow sends me staggering just as much as it does him.

I fight the urge to vomit as I fall to my knees again. The wood of the splintered chair bites into my knees as I gag. Damnit. Whatever gas he used on my apartment complex is still in my system and fighting to regain its hold on my consciousness. I can't afford to lose it now. I have to get out of here.

I crawl maybe a step before a heavy foot stomps down

on my back and I cry out, stars swimming in my vision. Donovan is there, his hands fisting in my curls and yanking my head back to the point of pain.

"All you had to do was stay down," he seethes in my ear. "Was that so hard?"

"Get off of me!" I don't know why I bother screaming at him. Anyone who murdered five women as a gift is beyond reason. He's insane—and he has me pinned on my stomach, any number of weapons on his person.

"Why?"

Tears prick at the corners of my eye when he flips me onto my back, his knees spreading mine apart, effectively pinning me to the cement. Panic flares in my ribs. He wouldn't... would he?

Of course he would. I can't make any assumptions on his morals at this point.

"No."

"Why?" he asks again. "Why don't you love me?"

Love.

He asks me of love?

Love is Natalia, playing twenty questions with me in her car on a stakeout. Love is bringing me into her world with pride. Love is her smile, her laugh, the feeling of her skin on mine.

Laughing in Donovan's face is not the right move, I know that, but it's all I can do. My hot tears stream down my face freely, dripping onto his hands where they're wrapped around my neck.

"Who..." I grit my teeth. "Who could love you?"

Donovan's face is one I've seen most days for the past few years, yet I can't find any trace of him in the face I look at now. The distinction has nothing to do with his bruised jaw or broken, bloody nose. It's his eyes, so soulless and full of hatred, yet his mouth screams that he loves me.

"If that's how it is…" He sounds heartbroken as his grip tightens around my throat and I gasp. He's going to kill me, actually kill me this time.

My hand scratches at his as they continue to cut off my air. Red tinges the corners of my vision and my fingers splay before they wrap around what I'm searching for.

Donovan lurches, his grip loosening enough that I can get a breath in. His gaze drifts down to where I've run the broken chair leg into his stomach. Blood dribbles from his mouth and he laughs, blood spraying across my face.

"We die together then." He grits his teeth.

The last thing I see is a bloody hole appear in his forehead before the world goes black.

CHAPTER 34

NATALIA

I thought I knew terror in my life before, but I realize I was wrong the moment I opens the doors to the warehouse where Donovan is keeping Addie. Whatever I thought was true fear pales in comparison to the ice that flows through my veins when I see them there, him pinning her to the ground by her throat, her eyes rolling back. I barely register her stabbing him with something before I fire my gun.

He slumps forward right as her head hits the ground, and he falls over her.

I can hear Riven calling my name, but I don't stop.

My knees slam into the cement ground, tearing the fabric of my pants and staining them red with my blood. I hardly notice as I push Donovan's body aside and press my ear to Addie's mouth. Her breath is a death rattle, but she opens her eyes only for a moment before closing them again.

"Don't do this to me, love."

I fight to get air in my lungs. I can't breathe, can't do anything as she lays dying in my arms.

I swore I'd protect her. I swore to her.

I cradle her head close to my chest, brushing back her hair and scanning for less obvious injuries. "You're safe. You're safe." I repeat it like a chanting promise, more for myself than her. "Where are you hurt?"

Her eyelids flutter as she drifts in and out of consciousness, and I grip her tighter. Addie raises a trembling finger to her head, then drifts down her arms, her abdomen, then legs. Everything, her whimpering breaths, seem to say. Everything hurts.

"Help is coming, okay? I'm going to get you up now."

No response.

My muscles bark in response as I force them to move, will my legs to stand without buckling. The sirens close in outside and Riven is there holding the door open. The paramedics rush in, and he barks orders to them.

"I didn't mean it, not a word of it," I whisper against her cooling cheek. Because now that she is in my arms and help is drawing near, it seems the most important thing to say, the only thing that makes sense as the world seems to burn around me. The only pillar of heaven left untouched by the flames, until now.

"I love you," I say again, even as her eyes roll back.

"I love you." I say it into her face, her hair, her hands.

As the paramedics take her from me.

I love you.

A tiny shred of salvation for a sinner like me, cut off by slamming white doors and sirens.

I love you.

Riven says nothing on the drive to the hospital. He knows I'll probably rip his throat out if he tries.

By the time we arrive, the doctors have taken her back for inspection. A nurse tells me I can wait in the waiting room until they stabilize her.

"What did he do to her?" I growl. I know she was drugged and those wrists were probably infected. God-knows-what else he did before I got there.

"I'm sorry, I can only tell immediate family."

"I'm her fiancée." The lie slips out before I realize it, and I fish the ring box of my pocket.

The nurse doesn't ask why the ring is still in the box, or why Addie isn't wearing it. It's probably the least convincing lie I've ever told, yet he fixes me with a soft glance and guides me to a chair. "The majority of her wounds were superficial. There are signs of strangulation, so we're putting her on oxygen and monitoring her for now. I'll come find you when she's been moved to a room. In the meantime, the police might have some questions for you."

Fine. Addie is going to be fine.

It's the only thought that keeps me going through police questioning. In the end, they give me a business card and tell me someone will be in contact, and I pocket it, not bothering to look. I can worry about that later. Right now, all that matters is Addie.

Riven settles in the seat next to me, the plastic crunching under his jeans. "Maddy just got out of surgery. They stopped the internal bleeding and have her resting in a private room. She's concussed and shattered three ribs, but aside from superficial bruises, that was all."

"That was all" doesn't seem like an adequate way to describe what Maddy has been through, but I see his hands shaking and decide to say nothing of it.

Hours pass before the nurse from earlier finds me again. "We've put her in a private room on the second floor. She's resting, but the doctors said you can see her."

My throat clogs with emotion. "Thank you."

The nurse nods and leads the way. The hallways are too white, too sterile. The room Addie is being kept in is even worse, all white walls and paper sheets. It does nothing but emphasize the paleness of her skin, the crimson of her blood on her lip, and the purple ring of bruises around her throat.

The nurse clears his throat. "I'll give you two a moment. Press the pager if you need anything."

I don't bother thanking him, even though I know I should. All I can see is Addie, so pale and wounded. I should have protected her. I should have seen this coming.

Slowly, I slip the ring from its box and onto her finger. I bought the ring the day after Addie forgave me. I knew then it's her or no one for me. There will never be anyone else that can hold a light to her, not even a flicker.

"You did so good, baby," I breathe, running my hand over her hair. "What you did with the chair leg was smart. You gave me time to find you. You saved yourself, love. I'm so proud of you."

Her eyes remain shut as I speak to her throughout the night. I tell her how her mythology ramblings led to us finding the killer, and how the families of his other victims will have closure now. I tell her again how much I love her, and that I'll be here when she wakes up.

I'll be here forever. My heart only beats for her, and I wat no part of this life if she isn't there to walk through it with me.

So I sit beside her bed, her hand in mine, and wait.

CHAPTER 35
ADDIE

Me: Rot in hell.

The first thing I notice when I come to is the thin paper gown I wear and the draft that drifts over my arms. I shiver, and someone pulls something warm over me. It smells of leather and cinnamon, and pulls me back under.

The second time I wake up, I dare to open my eyes, only to close them again. The world is too bright, too white, and too harsh.

"Addie?"

That voice sounds nice, like someone who should narrate audiobooks.

"Addie, baby, can you hear me?"

Addie. *I'm* Addie.

And I'm dying.

My eyes shoot open and I dart up with a gasp. Donovan has his hands around my wrists and that damn gun is too far away to reach. I'm dying. I'm running out of air. I'm—

"Addie!"

I'm being held by Natalia.

Natalia is here.

The room stops closing in on me and the scent of blood is replaced with something more sterile. I look down to see Natalia's hands covering mine from where I'm trying to scratch Donovan and remove the ropes. Only Donovan isn't here, and I'm actually trying to pull out my IVs.

"What happened?" I croak.

"Baby steps," Natalia says, and settles me back against the pillow. "You've been out for two days."

Two days? God, Maddy must be worried sick. The last thing I remember is Donovan trying to kill me and—

Maddy.

Everything comes back in fragments, but one memory screams at me from the back of my mind. Maddy bleeding out on our rug. Maddy screaming at me to run while she tried to fight him off. Maddy being used for months. Maddy dying.

"Where is she?" I throw off my blankets and the weight, which was apparently Natalia's jacket.

"Whoa, sit down. Maddy's fine, Maddy's fine." Natalia's eyes go wide in panic. "She's recovering next door. She just left right before you woke up. The doctors won't let her stay for long because she needs to be resting. We can go see her in a bit."

"What's wrong with her?"

Natalia chooses her next words carefully. I can see her mulling them over in her mind, as if whatever she says next might make me leap from my bed. "Three broken ribs, internal bleeding, and a concussion. *But*," she says when she sees me trying to stand again, "she's going to be fine. The doctors repaired the bleeding. Only time and rest will heal everything else."

"Did someone call Daryl?"

"Marco went by yesterday and explained. Daryl stopped by earlier and left that basket over there."

My gaze drifts to the basket Natalia nods towards. He stuffed it full of pastries—fresh ones, by the smell—and flowers.

"Did someone call Maddy's parents? What if—"

"*Addie*." Natalia's voice breaks. "You almost died. Please, love, focus on yourself for a moment and not everyone else."

Maybe it's the way her voice cracked on the word "died," or the fact that I did almost die that makes me pause. Suddenly, I'm too aware of the paper sheets against my skin, the throbbing of my wrists under layers of gauze bandages, and the stitches across my collarbone.

Yet no panic attack comes. My breathing remains even as I takes Natalia's hand. "But I lived, Natalia," I whisper.

Then I notice the ring on my finger.

Natalia sees where my gaze went moments after my heart begins to race. The ring is perfect, exactly what I would have chosen for myself, and has Natalia written all over it.

My girlfriend, however, pales until she's lighter than the sheets I'm under. "The nurses wouldn't let me stay unless I was related to you, and I can't really threaten the people saving your life, so I said you're my fiancée. I was holding on to the ring anyway, but you can take it off if you'd like," she says, her fingers already reaching for the band.

I snatch my hand away, holding it to my chest. "No," I say, my throat burning." I want to keep it on. Ask me."

Natalia's voice breaks. "You want to marry me?"

"Not like that. Do it properly."

She laughs, already on her knees. "Addie Collins, will you marry me?"

"Yes!" I beam despite my pain. "Yes, I will, Natalia Mancini."

My head spins when Natalia kisses me, this time, slow and sweet. She takes her time exploring my mouth, and I savor the curve of her smile on mine. She brings her free hand up to cradle my jaw, angling my head upwards to deepen her kiss. I'm drowning in her. Her scent, her touch.

And I get to for the rest of my life.

Natalia pulls back for a breath, and only then do I look at her, fully look at her. She's tired, so tired, and the first tear rolls down her cheek.

"I'm sorry. I'm so sorry," she sobs.

"No, baby, no." My arms reach for her as if on reflex. "Why are you sorry?"

"I promised I would protect you, and I failed. The signs were right in front of us the whole time. I should have been there with you and I wasn't. He almost—"

"But he *didn't*," I finish firmly. "Because you found me. None of us saw this coming, but what matters is that you saved me."

"You saved yourself."

I smile at that. "We both saved me, then. See? We make a good team."

Natalia's dark eyes are bloodshot as she stares up at me like I hung the goddamn moon. The devil would weep if he saw her this way, too stricken with grief that someone like me stole his most beautiful demon.

Mine.

Natalia is mine for the rest of our lives, and I swear I will spend every day of it making sure she never weeps like this again.

EPILOGUE

You have blocked unknown caller.

Two weeks pass by in a blink. I get out of the hospital after a few days, and, to be honest, I never want to set foot in another hospital ever again. Maddy is discharged a few days after me. She stays with her parents while I stay with Natalia—Natalia, refuses to leave my side, even for a second. I try to go to the bathroom by myself one night and she threatens to kick the door in.

After that, we make a rule that if I go somewhere, I have to tell her, and if I want to go to the bathroom, she is not allowed to destroy my doors.

The physical recovery is the easy part. There are nights I still wake up in a cold sweat thinking I can hear Donovan's voice in my room, my phone buzzing with texts from him.

Even now, it feels surreal knowing that it was him

behind those messages the whole time. I went through and reread them while I was stuck in a hospital bed, and tried to place the words to his voice. It got harder as he descended into madness, and Natalia held my hair back as I vomited at the thought of the five girls before me who received the same texts. Their faces haunt me more than his.

Dina's parents come to visit me one day. They bring flowers and thank me for finding their daughter's murderer. I don't know what to say to that. "You're welcome," doesn't seem to suffice. All I can see was Dina's green eyes in her father's face, and her hair on her mother's head. I can't tell them that I'm the reason she's dead, that I don't deserve their thanks.

I start seeing a therapist after that, and things slowly get better. She's nice enough and doesn't try to tell me that she understands what I went through. It comes as a shock to no one when she tells me I'm showing signs of PTSD. Still, I'm one of the ones who got to live through that ordeal. The memories that haunt me are just that—memories, no matter how real they seem.

Donovan's funeral is on a Monday. I try to tell Maddy not to go, but she insists. It's only been a few weeks since he tried to kill us both, and she's still in a wheelchair, so I wheel her through the ceremony. We sit in the back, my hand wrapped in hers as they begin to shake. We leave when the preacher tells the congregation we'll see him all in heaven again someday.

It's Sunday now, and I sit on Natalia's new couch while she, Marco, and Riven move boxes into our house. We spent the week packing up our respective apartments and preparing for the move. Natalia bought the house while we were in Italy. It had just come onto the market and was too perfect for us to pass up, she justified.

In exchange for buying the house without my approval, I get to decorate every inch of it on Natalia's budget, which is practically unlimited. The walls finally dried yesterday, and we could move all the furniture in now—and by we, I mean Natalia and her crew.

"A little to the left, boys!"

"How about a little up your ass, Collins?" Riven hollers back.

I can only snicker as Natalia tells him all the ways she'll kill him if he makes another threat.

Riven's wink tells me he knows she's bluffing just as well as I do.

Poor Marco, on the other hand, is ghastly pale, which is truly a feat, given how tan the man is.

By noon, all the furniture has been moved in and everyone is gathered around our new kitchen table which reminds me of the one Cecile has in her kitchen in that lonely yellow house in Rome.

"What do you want put up next, boss?" Riven asks, draping his arm over my shoulder. He holds it at a weird angle to avoid my still-healing neck, I notice.

I lean into the touch with a smile. "Pictures next, and the artwork."

There are pictures of me and Maddy during our first year in the city, some of us at Tella's, and then random selfies we've taken through the years. Then there are photos we took in Positano, the four of us smiling as if we have no care in the world, not knowing our lives would be turned upside down less than twenty-four hours later.

My favorites, however, are the photos that Maddy

took. There are some from galleries, that Natalia bought for me. There is one of Natalia kissing my palm at her anniversary gala, and Mads managed to capture my blush in high quality. Another is of me working on my manuscript, hunched over our kitchen island with nothing but the glow of the laptop screen to illuminate my face. Natalia bought that one without telling me, and promptly hung it in the library.

Oh, yeah.

Natalia bought a house with a library.

Swoon.

"When are we filling the library with books?" I ask her with a smile. "The shelves look so lonely."

She grins back. "When you're healed enough to help me carry them all."

"As long as you get some smut. No stalker romances," Maddy calls from the doorway. Marco lets her use him as a crutch as she walks, determined to be wheelchair-free after nearly three weeks of sitting in it.

"Maddy, have you finally come to help?"

"Just here to offer my skills," she responds to Riven.

"Managing us?"

"Hey, I'm not managing. I'm *micro*managing—don't forget the first half. It's part of my niche."

Riven mumbles something that sounds like, "I'll show you a niche," and Marco only sighs.

My heart swells at the sight of the four of them, even as they squabble with each other. I never thought I'd have a group of friends who love me as much as I love them, let alone ones who would be willing to lay their life down for mine.

Too lost in my gratitude, I almost miss when Maddy

settles next to me on the couch and pulls out her laptop. "So I made a few invitation mockups. You'll have to tell me which one you prefer so I can get them sent out."

With all the chaos of moving, I've nearly forgotten I asked Maddy to put together the wedding invites for me. As soon as I was released from the hospital, Natalia and I had started wedding planning. Neither of us has many people we want there, so putting it together should have been easy enough.

Or so we thought.

So far, the best decision I've made about this wedding is having Maddy as my maid of honor. The second best decision was asking Daryl to be the flower girl, if only to see his face before he turned down the offer.

While the others finish hanging the artwork and unwrapping our furniture, Maddy and I pour over every detail of the wedding until our eyes became blurry and our necks go numb from craning them.

I laugh while she swears at a detail we missed and my heart swells. Somewhere in the house Riven drops something and Natalia barks out orders. I can practically see Marco's wide grin in my mind while Riven gets bitched out.

Somehow, between cheating death and falling in love, we all found each other. The thought comforts me, that all the pain we've been through in the past few months will be worth it when I finally get to walk down the aisle to my newfound family.

Everyone departs after dinner, leaving Natalia and I alone for the first time in our new home.

I try not to stare at her neck as she lets her head fall back, and releases a throaty groan. "God, I'm exhausted." The look of her being so unkempt should not be as attractive as it is. But can I really be blamed for that?

We haven't had sex since Italy, which feels like a lifetime ago now. The doctors banned all physical activity for at least two weeks after the hell my body went through. My therapist warned me that I might experience some anxiety the first time again, as well, given how Donovan chose to pin me down. Natalia assured me I could sit on her face and suffocate her at any point that I felt panicky. As if that does anything to help my never-ending lust for the woman.

"It's late," I agree. "We should probably get to bed. We have to go tour venues early in the morning."

"Or..." she says in a seductive tone that sends goosebumps across my skin, "we take advantage of the fact that your two-week waiting period is over and I can show you how excited I am to marry you."

"Have I told you lately how much I love you?" I ask, unable to keep the smile out of my voice.

In an instant, Natalia has her arms hooked under my legs and is carrying me upstairs, towards our new bedroom. "No, but you can show me all night when I fuck you against all this furniture we just moved in."

The grin that splits across her face is infectious, and I find myself throwing my head back to laugh.

I always dreamed of a love like the ones I read in my romance novels—a love so epic that it can defeat even death, a love that is better than any one I could write.

Before Natalia, that love seemed like just that—a dream —but now I know that isn't true. Love is waiting in the form of my darkest fantasies, and she looks to me for the light.

"What are you giggling about?" she asks as she lays me back on our bed.

My hands reach up to trace her face, and she kisses my palm. "I'll tell you tomorrow."

Tomorrow, and the day after, and every day for the rest of our lives.

ACKNOWLEDGMENTS

Burning Heaven was a "fuck it, let's do it" kind of idea that I never thought I'd actually get to write. I am so grateful for the journey Addie and Natalia have taken me on, and being at a place in my life where I can write something like this.

To my best friend Kennedy, thank you for always supporting me. Whether I'm writing fantasy or a sapphic mafia romance, you've always read everything and picked me up when imposter syndrome kicked me down.

To my editor Jess. I cannot imagine handing this story over to anyone else. You have shown so much love to these characters and truly went above and beyond to make sure the story I was telling was its best version. I am so grateful for all the work you've done on my books, but especially with this one.

To my friends Megan, Madelyn, Laura, and Phae. Thank you for taking me to my first Pride event and listening to me ramble about this story at our kitchen table. By the way Madelyn, it's your turn for the squeaky chair.

To my cousin Emily. You are one of the best people I know and the first person I came out to. Thank you for all the love you've shown me and giving my high school self a safe space to exist. I will always be grateful to you, for many things, but especially that. I love you.

To my cousin Madison, who not only answered all my baby author questions during The King's Queen, but always is one of my biggest supporters for any of my books. Thank you for being my built in support system. I love you so much!

Finally, to all the readers who have searched for characters that they can relate to and finally found them in these pages. I am so proud of you and grateful that you've given this story a chance to be loved.

ABOUT THE AUTHOR

Haydn Hubbard is a North Carolina native who spends most of her time daydreaming of worlds filled with love, magic, and occasionally dragons. The King's Queen is her debut fantasy series and the first of many to come. When Haydn is not writing she can be found competing with her horses, in any local coffee shop, or anywhere where there is a dog.

For more information visit her website at https://hhubbardauthor.com

ALSO BY HAYDN HUBBARD

The King's Queen Series

The King's Queen

Oracle of Ruin

Smoke and Ice Duology

Burning Heaven

www.ingramcontent.com/pod-product-compliance
Lightning Source LLC
Chambersburg PA
CBHW022105310726
48972CB00007B/1887